This book is dedicated to my family: my wife, Nora, our four children, their spouses, and our seven grandchildren.

UNWAVERING LOVE

BY

PHILIP LEHPAMER

(1) Parker Discovers the First Murder

Parker Spooner got lucky and found an empty parking space for his car on the street in front of the apartment building where Dave Curtis lived. Parker was an actuary who ran his own insurance consulting company, but today he was acting as a private investigator looking for a missing woman. Dave had been dating Nicole Elkhart, and Parker decided to start his search for the missing woman by talking to her boyfriend. That's why Parker drove to Dave's apartment in the New Town section of Chicago on a Monday morning in late September 1970.

The three-story brownstone was old but in good condition. Parker climbed the stairs to the third floor where Dave lived and rang the doorbell. There was no answer. He turned the knob, and the door opened. It stood ajar. A telltale stench told him there was ugly news inside. Parker called to the darkened interior, "Dave Curtis? Nicole Elkhart?" No response. The foul odor of death filled his nose as Parker pushed the door wide open and entered the unlit apartment. *It's not possible to describe the ugly smell of death*, thought Parker. Some police officers had told him even lighting a cigar and circulating the smoke wouldn't help. That wasn't relevant to Parker because he didn't smoke and didn't have a cigar to light.

Parker found the cord that raised the window shade in the living room and

pulled it. Sunlight streamed in, illuminating dust particles in the air. The

body of a tall, blond man, his shirt caked in blood, and his face contorted

with fear, lay dead on the floor. He'd been repeatedly stabbed. Parker

thought the man was Dave Curtis, and that he'd been dead for about thirty-

six hours, which would place the murder late on the prior Saturday night.

Parker walked around the apartment, but no one else was around. No

murder weapon, a knife or switchblade, was in sight and likely remained

with the killer. A lamp had fallen to the floor and was next to the body, but

otherwise everything else was in order. The apartment hadn't been

ransacked or turned over. Two empty highball glasses, one with lipstick

on the rim, were perched on top of a coffee table. A sleeping bag stretched

across the floor next to the far wall—men's socks and underwear were on

top of it. Parker had been given a photo of Nicole, and an identical photo

of this beautiful woman stood upright on a desk next to a photograph of

Dave, the tall, blond man who was dead on the floor. The front closet

contained clothing for a man and a woman. The kitchen was empty except

for dirty dishes in the sink. The bedroom was neat except the bed was

unmade. The top of the dresser contained a hairbrush, combs, and bottles

of perfume. One of the dresser drawers contained bras and panties. It was clear Nicole was using the bedroom, and Dave had taken the sleeping bag in the living room.

There was a nightstand in the bedroom with a lamp, a book, and a pamphlet on top. The book was Protter and Morrey's *College Calculus with Analytic Geometry*, and the pamphlet was from the Society of Actuaries, giving their Requirements for Admission and Syllabus of Examinations. Nicole Elkhart's signature was scrawled on the cover of the pamphlet. *Wow, Nicole is studying to become a life insurance actuary* thought Parker, and he immediately felt a strong connection to her. Actuaries are the mathematicians who set insurance rates. The Syllabus of Examinations booklet brought back memories for Parker to a time when he'd finished all the society's examinations and became a Fellow of the Society of Actuaries. That was nearly two decades ago, when he'd been married for over a year and his eldest child had just been born. The entire examination process to qualify actuaries was long and grueling, requiring years of study and weeks of solving practice problems to pass all of the exams. Apparently, Nicole was not only easy on the eyes but also had an analytical mind, and Parker, who had an eye and mind for physical and intellectual beauty, felt immediately that this missing woman was going to be a test for him.

(2) Parker Is Hired by Frank

Parker's mind went back to earlier in the day, when he opened his office door, snapped on the light, placed his briefcase on the desk, and turned on the window air conditioner. Chicago was in a late summer heat wave, and Parker smiled as the cool air touched his face. Suddenly, a man appeared at the office door. Parker immediately recognized his face, and seconds later recalled his name, Frank Lawson, assistant professor of physics at the University of Chicago. A month earlier Parker had heard Frank speak at a lecture open to the public on the subatomic world and its many surprises. Afterwards, at a reception, the two men exchanged social pleasantries, and Parker, always trying to attract business to provide for his wife and four children, gave Frank his calling card, which read, in part, *Parker Spooner, licensed private investigator*. Frank's eyes opened wide as he read the card, but he said nothing as he placed it in his shirt pocket.

Thus, Parker was surprised to see him at his office at the start of a new work week and asked Frank to take a seat in the chair next to his desk. An upright Catholic calendar graced Parker's desk and showed that, for today, Monday, September 21, 1970, Parker didn't have any appointments. In the liturgical calendar of the Church, September 21 was designated as a feast day for St. Matthew, apostle and evangelist. The Gospel according to St. Matthew was Parker's favorite gospel because it contained multiple references to currency, debts, business transactions, and financial matters, along with its description of the Beatitudes and the Sermon on the Mount. Parker transferred his briefcase from the desk to the floor, removed his suit coat and hung it on the back of his chair, sat down, and slightly loosened his tie. He always wore a suit and tie when he was in the office. In contrast, Frank Lawson was dressed casually, wearing tan pants and a light blue short-sleeved shirt that sported a pen clipped in its front pocket. Parker noted Frank looked to be in his mid-thirties and had a pale, aesthetic face, horn-rimmed glasses, and dark brown hair that matched his eyes.

Frank was looking at the two photographs on the desk and the two paintings on the wall behind Parker's desk. The first photograph showed a young Parker and his bride, Rosemary Boyle, on their wedding day. The second photograph was recent and showed their four children. The first painting on the wall behind Parker's desk was George Washington taking the oath of office as President of the United States of America while the second painting was of Jesus as the Good Shepherd.

Parker smiled and asked, "What brings you here, Professor Lawson? Why do you need a private investigator?"

Frank quickly responded and kept talking, "Please call me Frank. It's a friend of mine—she's disappeared. She took my physics course a couple of years ago when she was in college. After her graduation we kept in touch and went out together a couple of times on dates; however, I haven't seen or heard from her in weeks. Mutual friends also haven't seen her and have no idea where she is. I even went to see her parents at their Chicago home, though they weren't close to her, and came up empty. Nicole wouldn't suddenly go away without letting someone know where she could be reached. Her roommate, Denise, seems to have also disappeared. I'm w-worried about Nicole, perhaps something bad has happened to her. I just want her found." His voice had become husky with emotion by the end.

"What's your friend's full name?" Parker asked.

"Nicole Elkhart. She just celebrated her twenty-second birthday. Here, I have a photograph of her." Frank dug into his wallet and produced a colored snapshot. "You can keep this photo of Nicole if it helps you locate her." The girl was drop-dead gorgeous, with intelligent blue eyes and attractive dark hair, but a sensitive mouth that suggested a certain look of sorrow. Nicole was tall, and the full-length photograph showed her wearing a white blouse with a yellow miniskirt that displayed chorus girl legs that ended in bare feet and flat sandals. Parker would see another copy of that exact photo later in the day after he entered Dave's apartment and found him murdered.

"You mentioned her parents. Are you acting on behalf of them?"

"No, I'm acting on my own. Her parents don't care what happens to her. I'm . . . I'm in l-love with Miss Elkhart." Frank hung his head, and his shoulders drooped. Parker didn't ask if Miss Elkhart was in love with him. He'd seen the look of one-sided love before.

"Why do you think Nicole's parents don't care what happens to her?"

Lawson sighed. "That's obvious once you talk with them. George and Martha Elkhart are elderly, and he's retired. The Elkhart's raised four other children and saw them marry and move on. Only Nicole is—was— left at home. She feels her parents rejected her, and she's probably correct. After all, she's at least seven years younger than her brothers and sisters and barely knows them. It's likely her parents didn't want another child in the first place. In any case, her home situation was difficult for Nicole. Her father is an alcoholic, and her mother considers her a tramp."

Parker gave him a puzzled look.

"She gives that impression to many people, but Nicole isn't a tramp," insisted Lawson, his voice rising and becoming loud. "Her mother doesn't understand short skirts or rock music or the entire youth culture that has emerged since the 1960s. She thinks Nicole is sleeping with every man. I know personally that isn't the case." Frank Lawson stopped talking and hung his head again.

"So, you want me to find Nicole?" Parker asked softly.

"Yes."

"What do you want me to do when I locate her?"

"Let me know where she is and what her situation is. You can tell her I hired you. Here's a list of names and addresses of some of her friends." He handed Parker a sheet of paper. "I've asked many of them about Nicole's sudden disappearance but have not received any answers. Perhaps you, as a private licensed detective, will have more success."

Parker noted that, in Frank's speech, Parker had become a detective rather than an investigator. A detective is usually a police officer. Parker, as a private investigator, didn't have police powers and operated with a license under the powers of an ordinary citizen to conduct investigations. Also, Parker never carried a firearm. Saying nothing about these distinctions, Parker instead pored over the names on the list, immediately spotting a Denise Walters. The note next to her name said she was Nicole's roommate.

"You mentioned Denise is also missing," said Parker. "Summer is ending—isn't possible the two roommates just took off together for a late vacation?"

Frank shook his head no, "They might have gone somewhere for a couple of days, perhaps a weekend, but certainly not for this length of time. Denise is an actress and is always busy. She works at Second City. I have a playbill from one of her recent performances that also contains information about her. I'm going to give it to you because it may help you locate Denise and, through her, Nicole."

Parker opened the Playbill booklet, and a large full-length colored photograph of Denise stared back at him. She was petite—about 5 feet 2 inches tall—with a pleasant open face, low cheekbones, a brunette with short, fair hair, light brown eyes, and fair skin. Apparently, she was a very versatile actress and had played a variety of roles, all with excellent reviews. Using make-up, wigs, and costumes, she'd played parts that ranged in age from a teenager to a grandmother. She appeared accomplished and experienced, and she was still young, only in her early forties.

Frank continued talking, "The way I understand it, Nicole and Denise never spent much time together because of their twenty-year age difference. Denise had her heavy acting schedule, and Nicole had moved on to other . . ." Frank's voice drifted, and he didn't complete his thought. Parker shifted his weight in his chair. Lawson hadn't told him everything. Frank said he was in love with Nicole and showed concern for her safety, but, apparently, he had a reason to worry, and he hadn't yet stated that reason. "Do you think Nicole has run away with another man?" Parker ventured.

Lawson's face flushed a gentle pink. "Yes, I-I think that's possible," he stammered. "She has been dating this guy, Dave Curtis, the last few months. Curtis was also a student of mine a few years ago, and I have his name on that list I gave to you. He lives near New Town, and I've been up to his apartment a couple of times in the past week, but no one answers the door, and no one has seen him."

"When was the last time you saw Nicole? And did anything unusual happen at that time?"

"It was July 18, over two months ago. We bumped into each other at a Grant Park concert that Saturday night, and I said I'd be interested in seeing her again. She told me no, go away. She said she was bothered by a dark secret and needed time to work it out alone."

"And you agreed?"

"Not at first. She looked very troubled after she mentioned her dark secret, and I got worried. I told her I was fond of her and wanted to help her if I could. When I verbally pressed her, she became upset and started crying. She said I was getting too serious with her and that she wasn't ready to confide in me. I told her to take her time and figure out whatever was troubling her. But now it's been two months, and that's too long. It worries me nobody seems to know where she is. I just want to know she's okay."

"If Nicole and Dave did go away together, do you have any idea where they might have gone?"

"No, I've reached a dead end. I've been up and down the city and haven't found a clue. I even drove up to Fox Lake. Nicole's parents have a cottage there, and I'd been there earlier this summer to see her. This time I didn't have any luck. The place was vacant." Lawson hung his head in desperation and then looked at Parker. "Will you be able to help me and find out what's happened to Nicole?"

Parker thought Frank might be immature when it came to women, but he told him he'd locate Nicole. Lawson quickly responded with his first smile, "If you talk to Mr. Elkhart, Nicole's father, be careful with him. He has quite a temper. He threw me out of his house on Saturday."

"Why did he do that?" asked Parker.

"I told him it was possible Nicole and Dave Curtis had run away together. He became angry, and I thought he might hit me. I got out of there quickly."

Parker nodded. They then discussed his fee. Lawson took the pen and a folded blank check from his shirt pocket and wrote out a retainer. He methodically fastened the pen to his shirt pocket, stood up, and shook hands with Parker, giving him a second smile, "By the way, there's a second lecture coming up tomorrow evening. It features my twin brother, Thomas, who's an assistant professor of philosophy and theology. He's developed a geometric model of eternity and relates it to the Big Bang theory. Do you think you'll be going?"

Parker wasn't aware Frank had a twin brother but recalled an announcement of the upcoming lecture at the conclusion of the last one. He was struck by its title, "Boethius and the Big Bang Theory," and responded to Frank, "My other profession is actuarial consulting, and so I'm interested in subjects that use mathematics, especially physics, which is a difficult, albeit fascinating, subject. I also like philosophy and theology, two other difficult subjects that your brother has mastered, given his degrees. I'm definitely looking forward to his upcoming lecture."

Following those concluding words from Parker, Frank went to meet his morning class. He was pleased Parker would attend the lecture and was surprised the private investigator had a mathematical background as an actuary. Frank would also have been surprised as to how Parker's interest in religion and theology came about. Growing up, Parker and his sister went to public schools, and their parents weren't active church goers. At the same time, they weren't hostile to religion and had their two children baptized as Roman Catholics. They taught their children to be honest and straightforward. In high school, Parker realized mathematics required intelligence and that the world, along with the universe, ran according to mathematical principles, which implied a Divine Mind. Then he discovered the Gospels, and the words of Jesus startled him. It seemed obvious Jesus was neither crazy nor evil, and consequently Parker accepted the view that He was and is God.

All of this led Parker to Sunday mass at the local Catholic church one block from his home. His mother encouraged him, buying a missal that had the words of the mass in Latin on the left side of the page and an English translation on the right side. When he went off to the University of Chicago to study mathematics, chemistry, and physics, he approached the Calvert House on campus, where Roman Catholics gathered, and it was there that Parker subsequently received the sacraments of penance, communion, and then confirmation. It was a time in history after World War II, when many individuals in the United States found organized religion compelling and moved toward it. Parker never questioned his decision, made during his early university years, to come into full communion with the Church. He found a certain coherence in

Catholicism, and in fact his understanding and faith had grown with his marriage to Rosemary and the births of their four children. Now, more than twenty years after his UC college experience, he had an investigation handed to him by a UC physics teacher.

Parker sat at his desk and reviewed Frank's list, making notes and a copy of all the pertinent names, addresses, and telephone numbers, including the location of the Fox Lake cottage that the Elkhart family owned, and then he mentally reviewed what he'd just learned from Frank. He thought about different approaches to locating the missing Nicole. Finally, he decided he'd try to locate Curtis first since Dave was currently dating Nicole, and based on Frank's comments, Nicole may have run away with Dave, leaving Denise her roommate in name only.

Thus, Parker left his office that Monday morning in his green 1966 Oldsmobile Cutlass and drove to the North Side, toward Dave Curtis's apartment. Traffic snarled on the Kennedy Expressway—*one of these days*, thought Parker, *someone will figure out a way to quickly update drivers about upcoming road delays ahead of them*. He got off at Fullerton Avenue and drove east and then wound his way north on side streets toward the apartment. His mind meandered. Autumn was two days away, but Chicago remained hot. The temperature was forecast to hit 90 degrees before thunderstorms would usher in cooler air. Delivery trucks clogged the streets. Young kids, playing hooky from school, tossed a softball on a side street, and nearby an elevated train screeched.

Parker found a parking space and then Dave, a dead man, on the floor.

(3) Nicole and Frank

The Elkhart cottage is just one of the many houses that border Fox Lake, Illinois, northwest of Chicago. The driveway to the house was off a road that followed the lake. Along the side of the driveway was a lawn that led to a large outside porch and the entrance to the house. There were similar cottages on either side of the Elkhart house. One summer afternoon in late June, Frank sat on the outside porch next to a table. Nicole sat on the porch railing, wearing yellow hot pants and dangling her long legs in front of Frank.

"Frank, do you prefer me to wear these hot pants or my miniskirt?"

"I think you look good in either one, Nicole."

"No preference then?"

"Not really. Why do you ask?"

"I thought you'd have said a miniskirt because it has easier access."

Frank blushed as a laughing Nicole stood up and became serious. "But you're correct—it doesn't matter which one I wear because you're not getting anything. I don't know why you keep following me up here to the summer house. This is becoming awkward for me."

Nicole had been one of Frank's smartest students; however, she wasn't interested in physics and preferred mathematics that supported financial institutions, such as actuarial science, and now she was telling Frank she wasn't interested in being Frank's girlfriend either. He didn't know what to say and quickly got up to leave the cottage.

(4) Nicole and Denise

One evening, Denise Walters and Nicole Elkhart were in their apartment, talking, "Nicole," started Denise, "I'm going to be away for a couple of weeks, rehearsing for an important gig that's going to pay me big time. I'm going to leave my car here and take a set of keys. You can have my other set and drive the car in my absence."

"Thanks, Denise, I'll use the car but probably only on weekends. If you're going away, I think I'll move in with Dave temporarily because I don't want to be alone in the apartment for two weeks. His place is also an easier commute for me into work downtown, and I'll be able to see him every day."

"Whatever you want is fine with me. I have your work phone number, and I'll be in touch when I'm ready to come back. Have fun at Dave's place."

"Thanks," replied Nicole. "I think moving in with Dave—even temporarily—will be a real test of my relationship with him, and I believe this is the time to find out."

The two women looked at each other knowingly. Denise said, "You've been seeing him for some time, and you're probably at the point where you're going to have to decide about your future. Either way, I wish you the best."

A faraway look entered Nicole's eyes. She was troubled by her relationship with Dave. He was a kind person, but she loved mathematics, and he wasn't an analytical person. She enjoyed studying for the actuarial examinations but found there were time conflicts between her studying and being with Dave, who was becoming more demanding. Perhaps sharing his apartment would lessen the problem. Regardless, Nicole knew she had to decide about Dave, and she was determined to resolve the issues she had with him and settle them, one way or another.

(5) Nicole Is Missing

Parker left Dave's third floor apartment, leaving the dead body untouched on the floor. Frank had asked him to find Nicole—she'd been living in Dave's apartment, but she was still missing. Frank Lawson told Parker he was in "love" with Nicole Elkhart, but Parker wondered what a thirty-five-year-old male physics teacher teaching college kids in Chicago circa 1970 meant by the word "love" when he applied it to a twenty-two-year-old attractive female who'd been his former student. The English language was rich in words and can distinguish subtleties in meaning; however, that wasn't true with the word *love*. A man will say he loves his pets, his friends, his children, and his wife, along with loving steak, beer, baseball, his car, and his country; but there are nuances in all these loves that remain unstated. Parker knew the word love needed qualifying adjectives to accurately reflect its meaning. The classical Greeks and Romans had many different words to distinguish differences in love among people. Parker thought *eros* or *pragma* might be two classical words that could apply to Frank's love for Nicole. *Eros* is erotic, romantic, passionate love that wishes to express itself sexually, whereas *pragma* is a committed, companionate love that lasts. Pragma is genuine, binding lovers together, and likely to last, whereas eros tends to be more fleeting and perhaps not genuine and thus not permanent. Apparently, Nicole was not interested in either of these loves from Frank. Parker thought that had to be tough on Frank's ego—and equally tough on Nicole in her attempts to avoid her former teacher.

Parker walked down to the first floor where the mailbox read, "Mrs. Sarah Meyer." A gray-haired woman in her sixties answered when he rang the doorbell.

"Good morning. Are you Mrs. Meyer, the landlady of this building?"

"Yes." She had a round, open face accented by silver-rimmed glasses that matched her hair color. Her neat housedress, well-groomed hair, and pleasant smile harmonized perfectly.

Parker showed her his private investigator credentials saying, "I'd like to ask you some questions about your third-floor tenant, Dave Curtis."

She looked at him carefully and then replied, "Please come in and have a seat."

He entered the living room, which was decorated in an early American style. Bookcases covered two walls. Encyclopedias, the great books, and the classics graced the shelves. The Great Books brought back Parker's undergraduate days at the University of Chicago in the 1940s. These books and the classics were the hallmarks of his education, leaving indelible influences on his mind and thoughts. Before embarking on his actuarial career, he'd majored in mathematics with a minor in physics, and his overall general education was solid, as he had an interest in practical knowledge and its applications in many disciplines. Now as Parker reclined into a large and comfortable chair in Mrs. Meyer's living room, he caught his reflection on a polished end table. An air conditioner hummed softly in a side window, keeping this clean and airy room cool. The contrasts between Mrs. Meyer's room and the horrible death two floors above were stark.

Three oil portraits dominated the back wall. The first showed a young man, the second was that of a dignified man near age sixty, and the third showed a much older man. "My son, my late husband, and my father," said Mrs. Meyer, following Parker's eyes. "My father is still alive and will be ninety next month." Parker smiled and thought about how some men live to be ninety while others die in their twenties. The world at times appeared to be uncaring, but that was not the case in Mrs. Sarah Meyer's apartment, where all was well.

24

She peered at Parker over her bifocals, "Is Dave in some kind of trouble?"

Parker ignored her question and asked his own, "Could you please describe Dave for me?"

"He's very tall—about 6 feet 2 or more. He has blond hair and blue eyes." Parker nodded. Her description matched the dead man upstairs. Mrs. Meyers was perceptive, and she caught his nod. "Something's wrong. Isn't that so? Has Dave been hurt?"

Parker replied in a quiet voice, "I'm sorry to tell you Dave has been murdered."

Mrs. Meyers groaned, clutching her face with both hands. Tiny sobs echoed from within her.

"I found his body upstairs in his apartment. There's no one else up there. There was no sign of a robbery, and he's been dead for some time. I'll have to telephone the police." She pointed to the phone in the kitchen, and Parker got up to make the call. Parker decided to call the Homicide Unit of Area Six directly, rather than going through the Nineteenth District police station on Halsted Street. Detective Sergeant Michael Boyle handled homicides in this area of Chicago and was Parker's father-in-law. The sergeant picked up his phone and was surprised to hear his son-in-law's voice.

"I'm on a case, looking for a missing woman, and I've found her boyfriend dead in his apartment, stabbed several times in the back. I thought I'd save some time and call you directly rather than going through the Nineteenth District police, who'd likely come here first to view the body, ask questions, and then call for a homicide detective." Parker gave him the address and told him he was with the landlady owner of the house on the first floor, while the body was in the third-floor walkup. Sergeant Boyle said he'd get Town Hall police officers and himself over to the house immediately. Town Hall was the name of Chicago's Nineteenth District police precinct. Parker hung up the telephone and returned to the living room.

Mrs. Meyer sat on her couch. Tears were in her eyes, and Parker wanted to reach out to console her by holding her, but he stopped himself. Instead, he merely sat next to her and waited. "Do you have any idea who killed that young man?" Mrs. Meyer finally asked.

"No, but perhaps you could give me some clues."

"I'll help in whatever way I'm able." She had a hanky and dabbed her eyes.

"Do you know his friend, Nicole Elkhart? She's disappeared. That's why I'm here in the first place. I hoped to locate her through Dave."

"Yes, I know Nicole. Dave introduced us several months ago. We had many long talks, but she hasn't disappeared! I spoke to her and Dave in this very room on Saturday around six o'clock just before I left for my son's home."

Parker gave her a surprised look.

Mrs. Meyer continued, "I spend Sundays with my son's family. They have a lovely home in Skokie, and they pick me up every Saturday to visit them. This past Saturday before my son arrived, Nicole and Dave stopped in for a drink. They were on their way to dinner, and we had some wine. Both were happy. That was the last I saw of them. Why did you think Nicole had disappeared?"

"One of her former teachers was worried about her. He hasn't heard from her in weeks and hired me to find her."

"That would be Mr. Lawson."

"Yes. Do you know him?"

"He spoke to me last week—Thursday morning, I believe—after knocking and not getting an answer upstairs. He's the scholarly type but a bit too serious as far as I'm concerned. Nicole asked me not to say anything to him about her or Dave if he came around. I got rid of him."

"Do you know why Nicole didn't want to see him?"

"Nicole told me Mr. Lawson was trying to date her. She wasn't interested, and, apparently, he wouldn't take no for an answer. Anyway, she wanted to avoid him."

"Does Nicole have a job—is she working?"

"Yes, she has an incredibly good job. She's terrific with numbers and is working as an actuarial assistant downtown at Continental Assurance. She's already passed the first couple of actuarial examinations and is studying for another one that's coming up in a few weeks. Actuaries must take these difficult and competitive examinations to get their credentials, and her company gives study time from work. She was lucky to get the position at Continental. My other tenant, Mr. Richard Blackburn, who lives above me on the second floor, also works at Continental but in a different department. He works in claims but was the one who told Nicole about the job opening in actuarial when Dave first introduced Nicole to him a few months ago. I believe Richard and Nicole are both at work right now."

Parker wondered about both being at work but decided not to pursue it with Mrs. Meyer, changing the topic with the hope of getting more information about Dave and Nicole. "When did Nicole start to share Dave's apartment?" he asked.

Mrs. Meyer gave him a measured look. "Don't get the wrong idea about that. Nicole's a good girl, and Dave always treated her with respect. She moved in recently but wasn't sleeping with him. He slept on the floor in a sleeping bag and gave her his bed. You see, Nicole's regular roommate, Denise, is off working somewhere, and Nicole didn't want to be alone, so she came over here temporarily to be with Dave. Besides, her apartment with Denise is out in Berwyn, a western suburb, and this is a more convenient commute into downtown for her."

"Did Dave pal around with someone else? Do you know if he had any siblings or a best friend I might be able to talk to?"

Mrs. Meyer nodded. "I don't know anything about Dave's immediate family, but he was friendly with Rick Henderson, a young guy his age who works in a family grocery store a couple blocks up the street. You can't miss Henderson's with its big green awning."

"Thank you for that information, Mrs. Meyer. I have one more question. I'm wondering whether you noticed anything else that might have some bearing on his death. Do you know if Dave has any enemies or people who dislike him?"

"Oh no, not really . . . I can't think that was a factor . . ." Mrs. Meyer hesitated.

Parker gave her a smile and an encouraging nod to continue.

"Okay, well, when Dave first moved in a couple of years ago, Richard, my other tenant, was dating a younger woman, and then that stopped because she and Dave had become friendly, and they started seeing each other. Richard and Dave got into an argument over the lady, not a physical fight, just angry words, and they didn't talk to each other for some time. Dave then broke up with that woman; this was before Nicole appeared, and slowly Dave and Richard made peace because they started saying hello to each other. I certainly don't think Richard holds a grudge or would do anything to harm Dave, and I probably shouldn't have mentioned their past argument."

At that moment, the doorbell rang. Mrs. Meyer looked relieved she didn't have to talk about her two tenants any longer. She excused herself to open the door. She had given Parker information about Dave and Richard's argument over a lady, yet she wasn't a gossip. Parker had a way about him that allowed people to confide in him.

Mrs. Meyer opened the door on Detective Sergeant Boyle of homicide and two police officers who worked out of the Nineteenth District station. Parker had married Michael Boyle's daughter, Rosemary, twenty years ago and started a family, and now they had four children, two boys and two girls. Michael, in turn, trained Parker to be a private investigator, and now Parker had two occupations, consulting actuary and licensed private investigator, and two different calling cards to match each profession. His actuarial consulting job usually consisted of establishing or certifying life insurance reserves for small companies and studying their mortality experience, whereas the private investigator work ranged from missing persons, many of them teenagers, to unfaithful spouses, to blackmail, and occasionally murder.

When police matters brought the two together on a particular case, Sergeant Boyle and Parker treated each other professionally, somewhat formally, and not as family. Thus, Parker explained to him that Frank Lawson hired him to find a friend, Nicole Elkhart, which led Parker to Dave Curtis. Parker gave the sergeant Frank's list of names and filled him in on the details of the case that he'd learned from Mrs. Meyer, and then they walked up to the third floor, along with the two uniformed policemen. The sergeant entered the apartment with the police officers and looked around, shaking his head. He asked Parker, "You haven't changed or removed anything? This is exactly the way you found it?"

"That is correct, except for opening the living room blinds and turning on the lights. The place was dark."

Sergeant Boyle continued his walk through the apartment, looking at everything and saying nothing. He stopped twice to write notes in his black book, returning it to his vest pocket when he'd finished. "I don't see the weapon that killed him anywhere. We'll have to check the trash bags and the surrounding area, but probably the murderer took the weapon." He sighed deeply that this piece of evidence was not immediately available and then laughed at his thought because he knew his job was seldom easy.

"How long do you think the kid's been dead?" Parker asked.

"I would estimate thirty-six hours. The murder likely occurred late Saturday night," replied Boyle. Parker smiled at this confirmation of his guess and excused himself, leaving the sergeant to his task of gathering evidence in a murder investigation. The Society of Actuaries pamphlet with Nicole's signature on the nightstand, along with her clothes in the closets, would establish her presence in the apartment. One of the empty highball glasses on the coffee table next to the dead body would likely, through fingerprint and lipstick analysis, place Nicole at the scene of the murder. Parker speculated that one of these days forensic analysis would come up with additional ways of identifying other people who were present at a crime scene, but as of now it looked like it was all Nicole.

On his way out the door, Sergeant Boyle reminded Parker to file an official police report about finding the dead body. He then whispered to him, "No insights or ESP flashes thus far for you on this murder?" Parker shook his head. Many police detectives develop "hunches" or premonitions about their investigations, based on prior experience and what they're currently observing. They then spend time following up to validate or discredit their initial thoughts. Parker would get sudden thoughts that were involved but specific about a particular case. These thoughts were instantaneous and came like sparks. He recalled the first time he discussed these insights with Rosemary. They were walking, holding hands in Grant Park, on a beautiful spring day a few weeks before their wedding, and she asked, "These insights—do they happen suddenly and unexpectedly, or do they develop over time?"

"They develop very suddenly—I have an unexpected thought—it's like a spark or a flash, and, just like that, I know something new, and I'm left wondering, where did that thought come from?"

"And is this thought about some event that will happen? Or one that has already occurred?" asked Rosemary.

"It's an insight into the past that turns out to be basically correct. When I get my flash, I know something specific has happened and that certain things or people are connected."

"Wow, that's funny—I've never heard of a man who has flashes!" replied a laughing Rosemary.

Parker joined her in laughter. This was one of the many reasons why he loved her. She had a sense of humor and was smart, with a good understanding of people. "For clarity, Rosemary, I guess we should name them ESP flashes, or perhaps just refer to them as insights."

Parker knew these sudden thoughts were never one hundred percent correct, but they were always very close to the truth and the reality of what had happened. Thus, Sergeant Boyle and the other police officers who worked with Parker always wanted to know what he *knew* after the sudden thought or flash. Today, father-in-law Michael was disappointed Parker hadn't had at least one small flash of insight on the murder he'd discovered while looking for the missing woman, Nicole Elkhart. Parker would soon experience one of his flashes or insights, but it would be on another case—and foreshadow a second murder.

(6) Parker Gathers Evidence

There were two police cars double-parked in front of Mrs. Meyer's brownstone building as Parker walked out. The police hadn't blocked his car, and Parker saw he had enough space to pull out from the curb into the street. But, first, he looked north for Henderson's grocery store as Mrs. Meyer had instructed and started walking toward their green awning two streets up on the corner. Henderson's grocery was a large store with huge plate glass windows and green awnings on each side of the cross streets, with an entrance in the middle facing the intersection. Inside, a female clerk was ringing up grocery items for a customer while another customer with her shopping cart loaded waited. Parker thought, *One of these days, a business will figure out an efficient way of bringing groceries and goods directly to a house.* Scanning the aisles, he noticed a young guy wearing a tie and holding a clipboard while looking at the shelves. Parker walked up to him. "Excuse me; I'm looking for Rick Henderson."

"That's me. What I can I do for you, sir?" Rick was 5 foot 10, with a friendly face, brown hair, and brown eyes. Parker introduced himself, showing his private investigator credentials, and then, thinking that being upfront with Rick was the best way to get information, quietly gave him the bad news that his friend, Dave Curtis, had been murdered. After the initial shock had been absorbed, but before Rick could become emotional, Parker asked if he knew Nicole Elkhart, and Rick quickly responded, "She's his girlfriend. You know, my girlfriend, Susan Clark, and I have been double dating with Dave and Nicole for a couple of months—going to movies and bowling." Rick slowly and sadly shook his head, recognizing those days were over.

"I'm trying to find Nicole," asked Parker. "She likely doesn't know about Dave. Do you have any idea where she might be?"

"She should be at work. You know she works as an actuarial assistant at Continental?" asked Rick, who had a distinct, somewhat repetitive, speech pattern using the words "you know" to convey his thoughts.

Parker was happy with that answer because it told him Rick was knowledgeable about Nicole—namely, that he knew her job, where she worked, and was willing to share that information. Parker continued, "I believe she may have temporarily moved in with Dave since her regular roommate, Denise, isn't around; however, Nicole hasn't been in Dave's place for the last two nights. Does she have girlfriends, other than Denise, she could have gone to for a visit?"

"I don't think so. You know Nicole has a lot of friends, but most of them are guys." He paused for a moment to think before continuing, "I don't believe there's another special female friend. Even though Denise is her roommate, they have different interests, and there's an age difference. They don't spend much time together. As far as girlfriends, you know, Nicole is really good-looking, tall, and stately, and she likes to flirt with men and does it easily, and, you know, other women might be a little jealous of her."

Parker thought again about the different words the classical languages had to distinguish differences in love among people. With Rick's last statement, the Latin word *ludus* or game came to his mind. For some folks, flirting with the opposite sex was their way of loving. They were playful and carefree, as if love were a game, but they ran away from *pragma,* love that became committed, or *agape,* empathetic love that was universal or always there. Parker wondered if this was a glimmer into Nicole's inner life when it came to love. He asked, "You said Nicole liked to flirt with men—didn't that make Dave jealous?"

Henderson took a step back, "Yes—you know it did a little bit. As a matter of fact, when Dave first introduced me to her, she started flirting with me. When I got him alone, I mentioned that to him. Why was he going out with Nicole? You know she appeared to be a party girl and not someone you could have a lasting relationship with. Dave looked worried but brushed it off. He told me Nicole wasn't that way; that she sometimes conveyed the wrong message; that if I tried to get serious with her in the wrong way, she would back off and drop me. He said in time I'd come to appreciate her playful manner."

"And did you?"

"Well, you know, yes, sort of . . ." Rick equivocated. "I talked it out with my girlfriend, Susan, and we kept going out on double dates with them, and, you know, we really enjoyed bowling together, but Susan and I thought deep down Nicole was bothered by something, you know, dark. However, she never mentioned anything, and, you know, we never discussed it. I know she didn't get along with her father. She referred to him by his first name, George, and I always thought that was weird."

Parker noted Rick used the word "dark" to describe a trouble that Nicole had, which was the identical word Nicole had used with Frank, when she told him she had a secret.

Henderson's head and shoulders now drooped, and he let out a little sob. The weight of Dave's death was starting to take hold of him. They were close friends, and now Dave was dead. *Classical* philia *love, authentic friendship between men, was evident in Rick*, thought Parker, who decided to get one more question in before he left. "Rick, did Dave have any enemies or someone who really dislikes him?"

Rick got a faraway look in his eyes and didn't immediately answer. His mind went back to an incident when Nicole, Dave, Susan, and he were bowling, and Carlos Able and his girlfriend, Tiffany, were in the lane next to them. Carlos had just gotten a spare by knocking down a ten pin, and Dave had an identical shot in his lane and wound up throwing a gutter ball. Carlos laughed at Dave, who got angry, and the two men started to argue and moved toward one another. Tiffany grabbed Carlos to hold him back, as did Nicole with Dave. She pleaded with him, "Dave, don't. Just ignore him. It's not worth it. We're having a good time. Don't let him ruin it." Cooler heads prevailed, and the men backed off, sitting next to their dates in different lanes.

Parker brought Rick back to present-day reality and out of his inner world by repeating his question in a louder voice, "Rick, did Dave have any enemies or someone who really dislikes him?"

"Just Carlos Able; he lives over by the El, near the gas station. They're blood enemies going way back. I think it started in grammar school. You know they really hate each other." Then Rick looked at Parker and appeared to recognize he'd gone too far with what he just said and quickly added, "Of course, you know, that was years ago—I don't think they've seen much of each other recently."

Parker thanked Rick for his time, expressed his condolences to this young man at the loss of his friend, and walked out of the grocery store, returning to his parked car. A police ambulance was now double-parked behind the police cars near Mrs. Meyer's apartment building; however, Parker still had plenty of room to move his car. He thought his father-in-law was probably finishing his interview with Mrs. Meyer. Sergeant Boyle and his detectives would then work their way down the list of names Frank Lawson had given Parker and that Parker, in turn, had shared with him. The police would be moving Dave's body to the morgue, and then they'd clean the third-floor apartment, trying to remove the odor of death.

Parker returned to the Kennedy Expressway and headed downtown, parking in a garage near the Continental building that overlooked Michigan Avenue and Grant Park. Mrs. Meyer said she expected both Nicole and her tenant, Richard Blackburn, to be at work; however, Nicole being at work didn't make any sense to Parker. If Nicole and Dave went out Saturday and returned to the apartment that night, then where was Nicole when Dave was murdered? Did she return to the apartment with Dave on Saturday night or not? If she did, then she witnessed the murder or murdered him herself—unless she left the apartment before the murder. If she didn't return with Dave or left early that night, then where was she Saturday and Sunday nights? Perhaps she went back to her roommate's apartment. In any case, Parker had been hired to locate Nicole, and it was now Monday, half past noon, and she was still missing as he walked into the Continental building.

A receptionist in the lobby called Nicole's work number and came back with the message that she wasn't in the office today. However, Richard Blackburn was, and he agreed to meet Parker in the lobby since he was on his way to lunch. Parker took a seat in the lobby and thumbed through a year-old copy of *Time* magazine. Within a few minutes, a stout man with broad shoulders, thinning hair, and an expanding waist came out of the elevator bank. The receptionist pointed to Parker. Blackburn walked over and sat next to him, "I understand you're a private dick and wanna talk to me. What gives?"

Parker met his gaze evenly, "This morning I found your neighbor, Dave Curtis, murdered in his apartment. He was probably killed sometime late Saturday night." Looking shocked, Blackburn whistled through his teeth. He said nothing, but if he was faking surprise then he was a very good actor. Parker continued, "The police are at the scene right now, and I think they'll want to talk to you later. Right now, I'd appreciate your help."

Blackburn shuffled in his chair, and, for a moment, Parker thought he was going to jump up and leave, but he settled back, "I don't know how I can help you. I don't know much about the guy other than that he lives above me on the third floor. He's quite a bit younger than me, and we seldom talk—usually hello or good morning. I certainly don't know any reason why anyone would kill the kid. Was it a robbery that went wrong?"

"No, there's no evidence of robbery; however, a young woman, Nicole Elkhart, was staying with him, and now she seems to be missing."

Blackburn went pale and then got excited, "Nicole's missing? She didn't come to work today?"

Two back-to-back questions, and Parker answered them in order, offering

an explanation to the second, "Yes, she's missing. No, she didn't come in

to work today. I had the receptionist call her company phone number and

found out she didn't show up this morning."

Blackburn now looked worried, "Did you say Curtis was murdered

Saturday night?"

"Yes."

"She was there. Nicole was with him Saturday night. I heard her."

"What time was that?"

"I got back from the pub before midnight, and the house was dark. Only a

small light in the foyer and a third-floor rear light, either from the kitchen

or bedroom, was on, so I figure Dave is home. I know my landlady, Mrs.

Meyers, visits her son every weekend and isn't around. When I got inside

my place, I was beat but took a shower and then hit the sack. Suddenly I

hear a woman scream—and then some sort of shouting and arguing

upstairs. A few seconds later a door slams, and Nicole, sobbing

hysterically like a little kid, is running down the stairs."

"Did you get up to investigate?"

"Nope. None of my business. Besides, after Nicole ran away, everything became quiet. In a few minutes I drifted off, and, once I fall asleep, nothing disturbs me."

"Could you hear anything they were arguing about?"

"No, the words were a jumble, but they were loud. When Nicole ran down the stairs, she was yelling something, perhaps about her father, but I really couldn't make out much of what she was saying because of her crying."

"Are you sure it was Nicole?"

"Absolutely. I recognized her hysterical crying. It was the second time I'd heard it."

"When was the first time?"

Blackburn, suddenly annoyed, stood up. "I'm not saying. I've already said too damn much. I gotta eat lunch and get back to work. I'm busy." And with that, he quickly walked away from Parker, who sat there for a few minutes, assimilating what Richard had said to him. The case was growing ugly for Nicole. She apparently ran out of the apartment right around the time Dave was murdered, and there was a commotion and argument. With a good prosecutor, Blackburn's testimony in court could be fatal to Nicole.

However, Blackburn didn't say he heard anything like a lamp, or a body, hitting the floor above his ceiling. Parker wondered if he was in the shower or already asleep when that happened.

(7) Parker Balances Home and Work

Parker's stomach growled, reminding him it was time for lunch, but first he needed to call home to see if anyone had contacted him this morning. Fortunately, there were a couple of phone booths at the far end of the Continental lobby. He dropped in the coins and dialed the number. Rosemary answered, and he heard Anna, the youngest, age four, crying in the background. "She's kicking up a fuss," said Rosemary. "She doesn't want Nana to put suntan lotion on her."

"She has your fair Irish skin, Rosemary, and like you she doesn't like the sun. She knows it's too hot outside today. She probably prefers to stay in the air conditioning."

"Your mother is just the opposite. She's been in the cold air conditioning the entire morning and wants to get out, but she did say she'd walk on the shady side of the street."

Parker smiled and thought his mother didn't mind the sun so much because of her Slavic skin. Parker's father was English, and his mother traced her roots to what in 1970 was called Czechoslovakia, but both his parents had been born in the United States. His father had died young, and his mother now lived with his older sister and her family, who also resided in the Hyde Park area of Chicago. "We're lucky to have Nana to help. You're holding up, okay?" he asked Rosemary.

"Oh, yeah, all is good," Rosemary responded. Parker could mentally see the twinkle in her beautiful clear blue eyes. Parker remembered the first time he saw her. It was at a parish dance, and she was seated at a table with one of her sisters. She was drop-dead gorgeous, with beautiful red hair, and he couldn't take his eyes off her. He introduced himself, and they talked the entire evening. She was finishing college at De Paul University, majoring in history and literature, and was younger than Parker, who'd already graduated from Chicago and was well on the way to finishing his actuarial examinations. He was impressed with her intelligence and asked for her telephone number, thinking he may have finally found a woman who might be more than a friend. Rosemary was more prescient, telling her sister that very evening as they went home that she'd met her future husband. Now more than twenty years later, she remained an intelligent woman, being a voracious reader, a full-time mother to four precocious children, and very much in love with Parker.

"You had two calls," said Rosemary to Parker. "First, Manan and Son called. They finished the reserves using your latest formula and need you

48

to review them and sign off with the certification. They'd like you to come in sometime this week and suggested Wednesday afternoon."

"All right. I'll let them know. Wednesday afternoon should be fine. I got a new case this morning that had an unexpected development. Fortunately, I don't have to deal with that development because it's a police matter. Your dad's guys will handle it. I just need to find a missing woman and notify my client as to where she is. I hope to be able to locate her quickly."

"Find a missing woman. That sounds like it could be exciting for you— should I be nervous?" said Rosemary in her usual joking manner.

"Perhaps you should. Her photograph shows she's young and gorgeous, but fortunately for us she doesn't have red hair, so I don't think I'm going to be tempted." This was a standard joke between Rosemary and Parker, given her beautiful red hair and his attraction to women who were natural redheads.

Rosemary laughed, "Speaking of red hair, your second call was from Natasha Pillsbury's secretary. Natasha, the red-headed dragoness, would like to see you this afternoon, if possible, in her office, any time before five p.m." Natasha, a former Parker client, had red hair, but her personality canceled any physical attraction Parker might have had for her.

"Good grief. I thought we were done with her problem months ago," Parker replied.

"Apparently not—will you be able to make it? You should call her if you're not going to be there."

"Yes, call her if I'm *not* coming—thus, that way, she expects me, and if I call to cancel, she can yell at me directly. However, going there this afternoon does work for me because I'm downtown now, which is only a mile away from her office. It's convenient for me to fit her into my schedule today. Take care, my love. Oh, and I don't hear Anna crying anymore."

"She just went out the door with Nana, who promised to buy her ice cream. Be careful, my darling." Parker laughed that Anna's tears had produced the promise of ice cream. *Kids*, he thought, *learn quickly*.

Parker wanted to bring Frank Lawson up to date, and because he had more change in his pocket and had possession of a phone booth, he called him. Frank was in his office and picked up the telephone quickly, "Have you found Nicole? Where is she—is she okay?" he asked in his usual rapid succession, as soon as Parker had identified himself.

"No, Nicole's still missing. However, Dave Curtis has been murdered in his apartment. I have talked to the landlady, Mrs. Meyer, and Richard Blackburn, the other tenant in the building. There's evidence Nicole was with Dave right before the murder. The police will be looking for her as a possible witness or suspect. Hello—are you all right?"

Parker thought Frank might have fainted because he heard a loud gasp, but Frank's choked voice responded, "How can these things be?"

That was a strange question for a physicist, thought Parker. Physics studies the world and objectively attempts to explain how things are. Understanding the reality of being is what they do. He answered Frank, "The police will contact you. I'm the one who found the body, so I had to give them your name to explain why I was there. By the way, remind me, when was the last time you were at Dave's apartment looking for Nicole?"

"Last Saturday night."

"What time Saturday night?"

"It must have been around seven-thirty. The sun had already set, and all the apartments were dark. No one was around. Yes, about half past seven because afterwards I went to see Nicole's parents, and I remember their clock striking eight."

"Is that the time you mentioned Dave Curtis to them, and Mr. Elkhart threw you out?"

"Yes."

Frank's statement about Mrs. Meyer was consistent with what Parker had been told—by that time in the evening, Mrs. Meyer was visiting her son at his house up in Skokie, Blackburn was at a local pub, and Dave and Nicole were out to dinner. So when Frank was there early Saturday night, the apartment building was vacant. But Frank had also visited the Elkharts later that night. Parker thanked Lawson and thought a visit to the Elkharts might be worthwhile.

He still had enough change in his pocket to make another call. He was struck by a thought, *one of these days, some inventor would come up with a phone that you could carry around with you, eliminating the worry of finding a phone booth and having the correct amount of change.* From Frank's list, Parker found Denise's and Nicole's apartment phone number, picked up the phone booth's receiver, deposited the coins, and dialed their number. The phone rang for about two minutes, unanswered, before he hung up. It didn't look like Nicole went back to her roommate's apartment after she ran down the stairs crying late on Saturday. It would be a long shot, but Nicole may have gone to her parents, and thus that would be another reason to visit them.

However, his stomach kept reminding him it was lunch time, and a hamburger was waiting. Parker thought about the things he had to do. First, there was Natasha Pillsbury's phone call to his house requesting Parker visit her office. Second, there was Sergeant Boyle's request to file a police report about Dave Curtis's murder. Third, there was a visit to Nicole's parents' house. His stomach reminded him eating a hamburger was the priority.

Parker was only a block away from the Loop and knew of a Wimpy's Grill next to the Shubert Theater. Wimpy's was his favorite hamburger, even though the chain was in decline, losing business to McDonald's golden arches and its clown mascot while White Castle continued to stay in business, selling small square hamburgers. Parker walked under the El as a train passed over Wabash Avenue and bought the *Chicago Tribune* and the *Chicago Sun Times* to read the news that seldom made the TV or radio. One of the newspaper's gossip columnists wrote that Natasha Pillsbury's doppelganger had apparently returned, and Chicagoland should be aware of this and watch out for scams pulled by the double. Perhaps that was why Mrs. Pillsbury wanted to talk to Parker in her office today.

Perhaps she was going to give him a second case. It was impossible to

determine what this mercurial woman might do, and Parker's mind went

back in time to late last year when he first met Natasha Pillsbury.

(8) Past Investigation

Natasha first called him nearly a year ago. They set up a meeting at her office—his first time there. The office was part of the magnificent mile that stretched north up Michigan Avenue from the Chicago River thirteen blocks to Oak Street. Nestled among the known landmarks, such as the historic Chicago Water Tower, the Tribune Tower, the Wrigley Building, and the John Hancock Center, was a relatively modest building with an arcade of shops and offices that housed Regular Solids Investments, the firm that had Mrs. Natasha Pillsbury as its president. Parker walked through its large, golden colored lobby and found the Regular Solids office. Their glass front doors had the company's name engraved in gold on them, and their clear glass front windows had large golden engraved images of the first two Platonic solids on them, with a cube on the left side of the door and a pyramid as a regular tetrahedron on the right side. Inside, their well-illuminated reception room had white side walls with splashes of golden glitter and a rich oaken back wall that had three doors. A tall brunette woman around thirty-five years old, wearing a gray business suit, sat behind the front desk. As Parker approached, he thought she had an air about her that said she liked men—and they, in turn, her. She was protected by a golden railing in front of the desk, along with a name plate that identified her as Miss Paula Dean.

Parker introduced himself, saying Mrs. Pillsbury had arranged an appointment for him. Miss Dean gave him a warm smile, handed him some reading material, and motioned for him to sit in a white-colored sofa on his right, saying, "Mrs. Pillsbury has someone in her office and will be with you shortly."

Taking this seat, Parker had a full view of the left wall, where two very young-looking female clerks were working at their separate desks; one was a pert blonde while the other had curly black hair. Each of them had a typewriter, a Friden calculating machine, and a telephone in front of them. They were opening letters, removing checks, and recording information. Periodically, each of their eyes would furtively look across the room to check Parker out. The office door in line with the clerks was labeled "Miles Clayton, Chief Financial Officer," and the inside was dark. The door behind Miss Dean was labeled "Mrs. Natasha Pillsbury, President," and its room was illuminated. Finally, another door labeled "Conference Room" was dark.

Parker started to read the material given to him. It was information about

Regular Solids Investments and included an introduction to two of the five

Platonic or regular solids from early Greek mathematics. There are exactly

five Platonic or regular solids. The two most familiar solids are the cube

and regular tetrahedron; the former being six congruent squares coming

together as a solid cube, whereas the latter is a pyramid of four congruent

equilateral triangles. These two regular solids, outlined with gold edges,

were the advertising symbols of Regular Solids Investments, sending the

message that this company was stable and solid, and by investing with

them customers were going to become rich. The advertising material then

showed a photograph of Founder and Chairman of the Board William

Pillsbury, when he was a young man. It described the growth of the

company over the years and their investment strategies that were "always

structured to meet and exceed the objectives and goals of the customer."

The company's advertising material, however, was silent about recent

developments in the running of the company—namely, Natasha Pillsbury.

Natasha had been an independent young woman from a Chicago family

and several years ago married William Pillsbury, a man thirty years her

senior. He had by the time of the marriage earned serious money from

opening and operating investment and financial counselling firms under the Regular Solids Investments brand throughout the Midwest, using the Chicago office as their headquarters. The rich Pilsburys made quite a couple in the city's social circle and never missed the opportunity for a photograph. They had even hired Joseph Johnson, a well-known Black photographer as their personal photographer. He had media connections and followed them around the city, taking photographs. Most of these photographs have William, now clearly a senior citizen, smiling proudly next to his vibrant young wife.

Three years ago, he had a stroke, leaving him bedridden with minor difficulties speaking. He turned some of his daily business responsibilities over to his wife, giving her the title of president. To give her some ongoing exposure in the daily operations of the company, he promoted his business manager, Miles Clayton, and gave him the title of chief financial and operating officer, moving his office physically next to Natasha's in the executive suite. Miles was to take care of all the internal workings of the company while Natasha would handle external matters. William would still oversee running the entire company as chairman of the board, albeit from his bedroom, and the Regular Solids firm would remain private, with the intention of eventually going public.

Since receiving the title of president of Regular Solids, Natasha had been in the news almost weekly with the help of Joe Johnson and his photographs. Natasha, barely forty, petite, only 5 feet 2 inches tall with a pleasant, open face, low cheekbones, flashing blue eyes, fair skin, red hair, and an outgoing highly emotional personality that attracted celebrities, became an upper-class social magnet throughout city, despite her known temper. She was always at the theater or running an event at one of the museums, attracting a crowd and the press that followed her. Little was written about Natasha's business acumen, either positive or negative, or the relationship among the bed-ridden founder, promoted business manager Miles Clayton, and Natasha. It remained murky as to who was running the privately owned company; however, the scuttlebutt was that William Pillsbury's handpicked board of directors were upset at Natasha's constant need for public attention and looking to Miles to take the reins at Regular Solids once William fully retired.

The door behind Miss Dean opened, and a very tall, strapping hulk of a man, fashionably dressed in a dark blue suit, emerged from Natasha's office. He nodded to Paula, closed the door, and walked across the room and out into the arcade. He had a handsome face, black hair, blue eyes, and was in his mid-forties. His tall legs moved like he was marching in front of a parade. As he passed, the clerks opposite Parker stopped their work; the eyes of the blonde opened wide, as did her mouth. Curly black hair fanned her face with her hand, showing that this guy was simply too hot for her. After this excitement, several duller minutes of clerical work passed before a buzzer sounded on Miss Dean's desk, and she told Parker Mrs. Pillsbury was ready to see him.

The inside of her office continued the pattern of the outer room, with white walls with splashes of gold glitter and an oak wood back wall. On the right side stood a bookcase with a globe on the top shelf, and the lower shelves were loaded with books about investing. On the left side, there were two tables with various sizes of models of the five Platonic solids, not only the cube and tetrahedron but the other three: the dodecahedron, icosahedron, and octahedron. A rather small desk was in the middle of the room, and Mrs. Pillsbury sat in a stuffed chair behind it. She was a petite woman, only a couple of inches over 5 feet in height, and the smaller desk harmonized well with her physical size. The desk was also elevated, resting on a platform about a foot above the floor, and, thus, when Parker went to the front of the desk to shake her hand, she was a couple of inches above him. When he sat in the chair in front of Mrs. Pillsbury, he was looking up to her, and she was looking down on him.

"I've asked you here, Mr. Spooner, because you come highly recommended, and I need you to do an investigation for me and keep it confidential, and that includes keeping it from the rest of my staff."

"Who recommended me to you?"

"Do you know the man who just walked out of my office?"

"No, I've never seen him before."

"His name is Jeremy Wilson, and he's a partner in the independent company that audits our books. It was his boss, the man who started that auditing firm, Benjamin Q. Damon, who recommended you."

"Yes, I know Mr. Damon; however, I never had any dealings with a Jeremy Wilson, and the work I did for Damon Auditing was as a consulting actuary looking at reserves, not as a private investigator."

"He told me you're a consulting actuary, but he also mentioned you did surveillance work and that you were competent and able to keep things strictly confidential. That's what's important for me. I must have your assurance no one at Regular Solids will know about your investigation on my behalf, not my secretary nor my husband and certainly not Miles Clayton. Whatever you find, you must bring it only to me. If I hire you,

you'll be working for me directly, not the company, and I, as your boss, will be paying you. Do you have any problem with that?"

"What is it you want me to investigate, Mrs. Pillsbury?"

Her ice-cold blue eyes flashed annoyance, and she became testy, "You didn't answer my question. Do you have any problem with being confidential and bringing whatever you discover *only* to me?"

"As a licensed private investigator, I'm bound to bring all discovered crimes to the appropriate civil authorities."

She smiled, "If you discovered a real crime with your investigation, especially if it involved Miles Clayton, I'd be delighted and would provide you with all the help you needed to contact the proper authorities."

"That's good, so I think we agree. So what is it you want me to investigate?"

"I want a complete dossier on my business partner, Miles Clayton. I want to know everything about him, from his birth up to now, especially any infractions or missteps he may have taken in the past before his employment at Regular Solids—and since his employment here some twenty years ago. I also want to know what he does in his spare time. For example, he's not in the office today, and he's not married. He lives alone, as far as I know. I wonder where he is today and what he does on his days off."

In essence, Natasha wanted some dirt on Miles Clayton, and Parker knew as a private investigator he'd be doing the digging. Parker decided to probe a little more, "I can start an investigation on his current activities; however, that requires surveillance. I would need to hire at least two men to follow him around for a month to see what we came up with. It would help if we had some hints as to where and how this might take place. What do you suspect he may have done or is currently doing?"

Natasha became blunt, "I don't like Miles, and I don't trust him, but I have nothing tangible on him. I thought he might be cooking our books, but Jeremy my auditor told me again that our financials are clean. Thus, I leave it to you to find something else to support my lack of trust in Miles. I have a copy of Miles's personnel file for you, which you can take and look through. To a trained investigator, there may be some hints buried in those records. I will authorize payments for you to hire surveillance, but I expect weekly reports, and we'll stop it quickly if it doesn't seem to be going anywhere. Moreover, I want this kept quiet—no talking to his neighbors or friends—you understand I want secrecy and no leaks that Miles is being investigated?" asked Natasha in a fierce voice.

Parker understood she wanted him to investigate, but not talking to neighbors or friends would make it a challenge to find hidden secrets. Despite his reservations, Parker nodded yes to her orders. "Now let's talk about surveillance money—exactly how is it going to work, and what are your fees?" continued Natasha in a slightly friendlier voice. They started talking about expenses and spent a good hour hammering out the details. Natasha was someone who had to be in charge of every situation. Parker realized that, if he couldn't find anything bad in Miles's past, that Natasha might begin pressing him to invent something, and that would be a parting of ways for him. As he walked out of Natasha's office, he started to say good afternoon to Paula, and then just nodded goodbye to her when he noticed she had earphones on and was probably listening to dictation. As Parker passed the desks of the two hardworking clerks, he said good afternoon to them, recognizing they were undoubtedly disappointed he was no male fantasy replacement for the good-looking and very tall auditor, Jeremy Wilson, who had previously passed.

Back in his office, Parker called two friends, Jim Rowdy and Ray Ulster, who'd helped him in the past with surveillance, and, thus, within a couple of days, Miles Clayton was covered from the time he woke up to the time he turned off the lights and went to bed at night. His personnel file contained information about his formal education and prior places he'd resided, which helped Parker start the long and tedious searches of public documents. Parker hoped one of these days someone would figure out a way to gather and collect information quickly. He communicated at least weekly with Natasha by telephone, keeping her up to date on his work. She didn't want him coming into the office because that might arouse suspicions that his involvement with the company was something other than that of an investor.

Besides digging into Miles's private life, Parker also directed his attention toward the company, Regular Solids Investments, itself. Many stock investors thought the company might go public soon. He talked to brokers, and they told him going public wasn't likely before the leadership issue was resolved at the company. The chairman, William Pillsbury, was bedridden, with twenty-four-hour care, living with Natasha in a five-bedroom penthouse apartment near Chicago's Gold Coast. Board meetings were held in his bedroom, with both Natasha and Miles present. Miles, as the chief financial and operating officer, understood the business and worked behind the scenes, leaving President Natasha to generate publicity for the firm through her strong personality, media contacts, and the captivating photographs of Joseph Johnson. Insiders thought Miles would be one day running the place when William decided to fully retire; however, Natasha acted as if she expected to run the company when the time came. Miles might have the business experience, but Natasha was William's wife, and she saw him every night, not only at board meetings. Moreover, her title as president further confused the situation because, in many corporations, the president was the executive in charge, even though the title chief executive officer was starting to become popular. The tension between Miles and Natasha at board meetings was palpable, according to the board members, who talked with brokers about making Regular Solids a publicly traded stock company.

Parker's investigation wasn't finding anything untoward about Miles, and, thus, Natasha kept offering suggestions as to what to do—and giving him grief. She found it difficult to accept the fact Miles didn't have a current love life, and perhaps never did. Parker's operative, Ray, was also surprised Miles didn't have a girlfriend because, as a teen and into his early twenties, school yearbooks and old newspapers showed he did date.

After a month of futile searches and surveillance, it became clear Miles didn't have many friends or family, and he spent most of his time at work or doing company work, such as visiting their auditors—Jeremy Wilson in particular. In his spare moments and on weekends, he watched Chicago sports teams on his television. Parker told Natasha that, to make progress, he'd have to start interviewing neighbors and contacts to find out if there was something hidden in his life. With that, Natasha stopped the investigation, thanking Parker for his work. She muttered something about how she had underestimated Miles but had figured out a way to get things under control. She also said she went to the Regular Solid's board of directors and told them she had investigated Miles, and that now the investigation was over. Parker didn't completely understand all her rambling remarks; however, he was happy she'd given up and the investigation was over.

During the investigation, Parker never saw Miles in person, but the personnel file had recent photographs that showed him to be a middle-aged, slightly balding man with a goatee, wearing glasses that had almost invisible clear rims. One of the photos in his file was that of a much younger Miles, without the goatee and glasses but a full head of hair, standing next to the founder, William Pillsbury, and receiving the company's Employee of the Year Award. The corresponding article implied Pillsbury was mentoring the young man for more rewards and noted Miles had a cube tattoo on his left arm and a tetrahedron tattoo on his right arm. Clearly, it appeared Miles Clayton was a committed Regular Solids employee, and Parker wondered if he had the other three Platonic solids on other parts of his body, not visible in the photograph.

Several weeks after this investigation concluded, newspapers reported another woman who looked like Natasha had donned a red wig and started to pass for her. This doppelganger had fooled some people into thinking they were talking to Natasha. When Natasha found out, she exposed the double, who then disappeared, and the story faded. But now, on this hot day at the end of summer, the same day Parker had discovered a murdered body, the newspapers were reporting the doppelganger had returned, and Natasha had called Parker's house and wanted to talk in her office. Thus, Parker, after finishing his Wimpy's hamburger, hailed a cab to go up the magnificent mile to the Regular Solids office, rather than walking in the heat. His mind was more on the murder of Dave Curtis and the missing Nicole than on the events from months ago, when Miles Clayton was investigated, and nothing out of the ordinary was discovered. Parker couldn't know this trip to the Regular Solids office was about to be as eventful as his discovery of Dave's murder, and that it would lead to his involvement in a second murder. It would just take some additional time for that murder to actualize into reality. Moreover, although he was not aware of this, he was two hours away from one of his insights, not about Dave's murder but about his prior investigation into Miles Clayton.

(9) A Conversation with Natasha

The Regular Solids office hadn't changed significantly since Parker's last visit. The two women clerks on the left side of the office were busy at their desks. Both briefly glanced at Parker and then returned their gazes to the work in front of them. The executive secretary, Paula Dean, alluring as before in her gray suit, was at her desk behind the golden railing. Miss Dean said the same thing to Parker as last time, "Mrs. Pillsbury has someone in her office and will be with you shortly," but this time she didn't hand him any marketing information about the company. Instead, she slyly added, "You're looking good, Mr. Spooner. Keeping out of trouble, I hope?"

"Yes, Miss Dean, but now that I'm here, we shall see if that continues."

"I would never be any trouble to you, Mr. Spooner," said Miss Dean in a sultry voice.

Parker merely smiled, saying nothing more, content to observe the outer office. Changes from his prior visit were that Miles Clayton's door and the conference room's door were both open. By sitting on the white-colored sofa available to guests and turning his head slightly to the right, Parker was able to obtain a clear view of the interior of the conference room, consisting of four chairs and a table loaded with folders and papers surrounded by bookcases. About this time, Miles came out of his office, and Parker recognized him immediately from his photographs. His goatee was trimmed neatly, and the tattoos on his upper arms were partially visible because he wore a short, white, sleeved shirt. He was looking intently at a piece of paper in his right hand as he walked in front of Paula's desk and past Parker on the sofa, without glancing at either, focused completely on the contents of the piece of paper as he entered the conference room and sat on a chair, leaving the door open. He then took a book that was on the table in his left hand and started comparing a page of its contents with the contents on the paper in his right hand.

As Parker watched him, he thought of all the details he knew about his life, and a feeling close to guilt touched Parker's soul. Miles had lived his entire life in the same house in Oak Park and had graduated from the local high school with high honors. He then went to Loyola University in Chicago as a business major, graduating in time to serve in the Army during World War II. He served stateside and, after his honorable discharge, went to the University of Chicago for an MBA about the same time Parker attended their undergraduate college. Soon thereafter Miles landed a job at Regular Solids. He had a younger sister, who went to New

York City after War World II and was now married with two children. They remained in touch with each other, especially after the death of their parents, both of whom had passed within a year of each other. Parker wondered about the ethics of a total stranger like him investigating Miles because his boss didn't like or trust him and hoped to find something bad about him by paying Parker to investigate him.

At this moment, the door to Natasha's office opened, and a young couple stepped out, with Natasha behind them. She shook their hands, wished them well, and said with a broad smile that they'd made a super smart investment. She then spotted Parker and waved, "Mr. Spooner, I'm glad you were able to make it this afternoon. That's wonderful. Come in now." Parker got up from the sofa and noticed Miles was moving out of his chair in the conference room, his concentration apparently disturbed by the talking. Their eyes met for a few brief seconds, and Miles's eyes flashed recognition of Parker, even though they'd never met face to face. Parker realized Miles knew of him, just as Parker knew of Miles. Miles's clear, framed glasses had Parker in full view as he closed the conference room door, and Parker entered Natasha's office.

"So, Mr. Spooner, how have you been? It's been quite a while since we last saw each other," said Natasha, climbing the platform that elevated her desk and chair.

"All is well with me, Mrs. Pillsbury, thank you for asking." He took the seat in front of her desk and gazed up to look at her face, which remained attractive and young looking, free of any wrinkles and highlighted by very cold blue eyes and flaming red hair. There was a new photograph of her on her desk, angled so Parker could view it. She noticed his gaze and remarked, "That's another photograph taken by Joe Johnson. He's a brilliant photographer, able to capture light and shading in creative ways." Parker had to agree that, in this colored photograph, Mr. Johnson had caught Natasha's physical beauty, her blue eyes and red hair—and the underlying toughness that showed on her face. Natasha continued talking, "Joe is also immensely helpful, a real gofer. Besides photos, I can ask him to do small things for me or the firm, and they get done quickly and efficiently. I wish everyone were that way."

"That's an outstanding photograph of you. He's talented. You also look well in person, Mrs. Pillsbury," remarked Parker, "and I hope the same is true for the Regular Solids firm."

"Yes, all is going well with the firm. The investigation you did for me was helpful. It changed my mind about Miles Clayton, and I've developed a new approach to him. I believe it will be worked out in a satisfactory manner, but that's not why I asked you to come in today. Another potential problem has arisen, and I need your advice as to how to proceed."

"Please continue, and I'll let you know if I might be of assistance."

"Some person has been impersonating me. This started several months ago, and when I got wind of it, I was able to stop her by calling the affected people, and the imposter woman went away. The surprising fact is that some of my friends thought the woman both *looked* and *sounded* like me. 'You must have a double or an identical twin out there' was something I was told by the many different people who were approached by this doppelganger."

"That *is* a strange story. Had you ever been told before you looked or sounded like someone else?"

"No, never, but now that woman is back and trying the same nonsense. The thought that there is a double of me out there really bothers me, and, thus, this time I called the police to report that someone was causing

trouble by impersonating me."

"What happened?"

"No report was filed. The officer explained that, thus far, no crime had

been committed. He said it's not the pretense but the purpose and result of

the deception that makes it a crime. Impersonation for the purpose of fraud

is a crime, but it's not illegal to play a hoax on someone. That kind of

made sense to me, but I have two questions for you: First, if I recall

correctly, your father-in-law is a police officer, and of course you have

some expertise in these matters. Thus, do you think it's correct that there's

no basis thus far to file a police report on this impersonator?"

"Yes, I'd agree with that assessment."

"Second, I'm notifying my friends about this imposter and hope that

publicity stops her. However, if this double continues to bother me, would

you consider starting an investigation and helping me find out who she is

and why she's doing this?"

"Of course, that's why I'm in business. I'm a private investigator and help

my clients."

"Thank you—that's a big relief to me to know I have support if needed," replied Natasha, standing up and shaking Parker's hand. He was surprised the discussion had ended that abruptly and wondered what Natasha's purpose was in contacting him besides what she'd just stated.

Exiting her office and closing the door, Parker nodded goodbye to the secretary, Paula Dean, who was seated at her desk and wearing earphones. At that moment, a sudden, unexpected thought flashed through Parker's mind: Paula was eavesdropping on Natasha's conversations with those earphones and not listening to the dictation! Parker's mind immediately told him she'd also been eavesdropping the first time he was in Natasha's office, and, afterwards, she told Miles about Natasha hiring him and the investigation. That's why the prior investigation came up empty and didn't discover anything—Miles knew he was being watched! It also explained why Miles recognized Parker earlier, when their eyes briefly met. With this insight, Parker knew something else was happening at Regular Solids, and his involvement with Natasha wasn't over. He had just experienced one of his insights, which connected the eavesdropping of Paula with the behavior of Miles.

Parker retrieved his car from the downtown garage, drove to the Nineteenth District, and filed an official report regarding his discovery of Dave Curtis's murdered body. By that time, the afternoon was nearly over; rain and thunderstorms had moved into the Chicago area, bringing much needed cooler air and breaking the heat. Parker drove his car home. By now, the three older kids were back from school, and his mother had left for the day. Parker's eldest, John, age seventeen, was a senior in high school, planning for college with the idea of majoring in either mathematics or chemistry. He was taking calculus and physics his senior year and doing his math homework when his father stopped by his room. "Dad, if you're not busy, maybe we can talk tonight about physics. I'm getting very confused about the introduction to quantum mechanics."

Parker's next child, Grace, age fifteen, was a junior in high school, and her favorite subjects were history, literature, and religion. "Dad, if you're not busy, maybe we can talk tonight about Padre Pio. I'm getting very confused about the nature of miracles."

Next was Peter, age ten, sitting on the floor and reading a Hardy Boys mystery. He didn't say a word. He just waved to his dad. Parker gave

Rosemary, who was cooking supper in the kitchen, a kiss, and then picked Anna up. "It was hot, and Nana bought me ice cream," she said, smiling.

"I heard that, sweetheart. You're a lucky girl," Parker replied, kissing and returning her to the floor and watching her run away. "Now, go wash your hands. We're going to be eating."

After supper Parker called Nicole's telephone number, and once again there was no answer. It was clear to Parker it was more important as a father to talk to his teenagers about their questions than to run around Chicago as a private investigator on a Monday night, looking for the missing Nicole. Nevertheless, before starting with his kids, he made one further call to his friend, Ray Ulster, "You remember the surveillance you did on Miles Clayton a few months ago?" Parker asked.

"Of course, really boring. The guy did nothing after work but routine stuff."

"He may have known about our investigation and modified his behavior. I'd like you to return a few more nights this week and certainly this weekend to see if anything has changed with him."

"Okay, I'm free tomorrow, Tuesday night, and certainly Friday night and this weekend."

"Thank you and call me if anything has changed."

With that out of the way, Parker's mind was clear to talk to his teenagers. They had questions that involved issues such as physics, philosophy, and religion—basic mysteries of reality that dwarfed his investigations.

(10) Quantum Physics and Religion

"So, John, what's happening with your physics course?" Parker asked, walking into his son's room and taking a seat next to his desk.

"The teacher gave us this handout that makes no sense," replied John, waving a paper in front of him. "It's labeled a thought experiment and titled 'Schrodinger's Cat.'"

Parker smiled. He knew of Edwin Schrodinger, a world famous physicist who in 1926 developed an equation that gave the energy and position of an electron in space and time. His work was part of the scientific upheaval that changed our understanding of how the subatomic world worked.

"Let me read to you this thought experiment," said John. "A cat is in a locked steel box with a radioactive atom with a fifty-percent chance of decaying within an hour. If it decays, it triggers a Geiger counter that releases poison and kills the cat. Whether it decays or not is governed by the laws of quantum mechanics, which says the radioactive atom is both in the decayed state and the nondecayed state simultaneously. This simultaneous effect is called superposition of states and has been verified experimentally at the subatomic level. Thus, after an hour, the cat is in a combined state, half alive and half dead. It is only when we open the box that a single definite state is known. Before the observation is made, we don't know if the atom has decayed or not. The result, whether the cat is alive or dead, is only known when the box is opened."

"Okay," the father replies, "that's the standard way of explaining this thought experiment, which was first devised by Schrodinger—and thus how this imaginary experiment and cat received his name. What's your question about Schrodinger and his cat?"

"The statement that the cat is in a combined state, half alive and half dead, is crazy," said John. "The cat cannot be both dead and alive at the same time. What's the point of the thought experiment? What's going on here?"

"Very good, John. I think that's exactly what Schrodinger was getting at. It's ridiculous to think of the cat as both alive and dead at the same time. However, the subatomic world is very different from the world we experience. The electron is not thought of as a single particle but also as a wave, and it exists in two locations or states simultaneously. If the atom is a decay state, the cat is dead, but if the atom hasn't decayed, the cat is alive. Observers don't know the cat's status in the box and only know it when the box is opened. However, reality is determined when the atom decays or doesn't decay. The terminology used is that the atom collapses from its superposition of combined states of decayed/not decayed to being decayed or not decayed. If the atom decayed, the cat is dead, and if the atom didn't decay, the cat is alive."

"That makes sense," replied John with a look of relief.

"Here's the difficulty, John, in this century, mankind has discovered that the subatomic world is vastly different from the world we know through our lived experiences. We interfere with this micro-world when we attempt to analyze it, and uncertainty becomes part of the mix. In physics, there's something called the Copenhagen interpretation, which states a system of elementary particles doesn't occupy a definite state or location until it's measured. Before then the system is just a blur of overlapping possibilities, like Schrodinger's thought experiment, and we must deal with uncertainty, the simultaneous effect of superposition of states and probabilities. When the system is measured, the terminology used by physicists is that the simultaneous effect, the superposition, collapses, and they now know the system's state or location."

"And this was just discovered? It wasn't an issue for physics in the past?" inquired John.

"That's correct—much of it came to the forefront in the 1920s and 1930s—in my lifetime. Physics is rapidly developing. Why it's just been in the last decade that, in another area of physics known as cosmology, the Big Bang theory has replaced the steady state theory. I'll be going to a lecture on that topic tomorrow night."

Parker then noticed, out of the corner of his eye, that Grace had appeared in John's doorway. "Excuse me, Dad, but I heard you and John talking about a cat that was either dead or alive, and today I heard a similar story about a little bird and Padre Pio."

"Padre Pio and a little bird, really? Grace, come in and tell us." Parker knew Padre Pio was an Italian priest who died in 1968. He was known throughout the world for bearing the stigmata and for his holiness and was expected to be canonized a saint by the Roman Catholic Church someday.

"Here's the story," said Grace. "Two boys were walking. In the hand of one of the boys was a very tiny baby bird that had fallen out of a nest and couldn't fly or feed itself. The boy without the bird noticed that, in the distance, Padre Pio was walking toward them. He said to his friend that Padre Pio was approaching, and that he heard this priest could read people's minds. The boy with the bird in his hand expressed doubt, saying that was impossible, and that he'd test Padre Pio as he passed. He put his free second hand over his first and completely covered the bird. He intended to tell Padre Pio he had a bird in his hands and then ask the priest if the bird was alive or dead. If the priest said dead, then the boy would open his hands and reveal the bird was alive; however, if the priest said the bird was alive, then the boy would squeeze his hands together and show a dead bird. Either way, Padre Pio wouldn't be able to read his mind! And thus the boy stopped the priest and showed his folded hands, asking whether the bird was alive or dead. Padre Pio looked carefully at the boy, and, after a few seconds said, 'The answer to your question is in your hands' and continued to walk. Dad, isn't that a beautiful story?"

"Oh, yes, Grace, that's delightful and a counterpoint to the cat story because it shows that, in our world, we have the freedom to decide—many things are in our hands and not subjected to impersonal probabilities that aren't fully understood. One of Padre Pio's prayers is 'Lord, what would you have me do?' When that question is answered and actualized, the person is at peace because the Will of God has been accomplished."

"But, Dad, I don't understand miracles. Sister Helen mentioned things about Padre Pio that don't make any sense. He seems to contradict the natural order, the way God created things. Do miracles contradict reality?"

"I don't think so, Grace. A miracle is simply supernatural intervention in the natural order. This intervention doesn't violate natural law because natural laws are based on observations, not assumptions. There's no logical contradiction. Any intervention merely adds another observation to our understanding of what's possible. I think the miracles mentioned in the Scripture or those documented by the Church should be of significant interest to everyone. For example, your brother John is starting to learn about developments in physics. There, the subatomic world is showing us observations that seem impossible. Walking through walls is physically impossible in our world; however, quantum tunneling shows it's possible in the micro-world. Superposition of states or bilocation is discussed in the quantum world all the time and is thus part of physical reality. It doesn't happen in the macro-world in which we live, but, if it unexpectedly did, we would refer to it, and perhaps aptly call it supernatural."

"You're wonderful, Dad" said Parker's oldest daughter, who gave him a kiss on the cheek and ran back to her room.

That evening Parker climbed into bed and waited for Rosemary to finish her evening prayers. Always devout, she finished them by blessing herself and then smiled at him, knowing he wanted to talk. He told her about his conversations with John and Grace, and that he was impressed with how they handled their schoolwork and that questions about religion and metaphysical truth were important. He added that Rosemary did an exceptionally good job raising four children. "Thank you for the compliment but don't think for a second that flattery is going to get me excited tonight," she joked. "It was a long, hot, and humid day, and I'm exhausted. I'm glad this rain will bring in cooler temperatures." She paused. "How did your visit with Natasha go? Did she ask you for another investigation?"

"No, she didn't. It was a strange visit. She's been bothered by a double who's tricking her friends into believing they're talking to Natasha. She hopes to stop the person by making it known a double is out there. If she can't stop the woman, she'll hire me to find out who her imposter is. I don't understand why she invited me in to tell me all that. It doesn't make any sense. At the same time, I think there might be some trouble at Regular Solids because I had an insight, or one of my flashes, as you call it, just as I left her office. The secretary, Paula, had earphones on, and I don't think she was listening to dictation but rather eavesdropping on Natasha's conversation with me. Moreover, I suspect she may have done that months ago and interfered with our investigation of Miles back then."

"Really, that's terrible. What are you going to do about it?"

"I asked Ray to start watching Miles again, and we'll see if anything develops this time."

There was another pause and then Rosemary asked, "Did you find the missing woman?"

"No, she remains missing. Your father and his police are also looking for her since her boyfriend was murdered. I found his body this morning."

"Murder—you didn't tell me that when you called earlier."

"It was ugly. I didn't want to talk about it."

"I should have realized it was murder. You said my dad was involved, and he's the homicide sergeant in Area Six, so of course it was murder. How silly of me to miss that. How are you doing after discovering this murder? Did you have any insights there?"

Parker sadly shook his head no, saying nothing, and then Rosemary reached over, grabbed the top of his pajamas, and pulled him over to her.

"You've had a rough day, my darling husband, and fortunately for us I'm not that exhausted," she said with a twinkle in her blue eyes and began kissing him. He returned the kisses, thinking what a wonderful wife she was. She was tired after a hot, humid Chicago day, but Rosemary was thinking of him and his terrible day.

The classic Greek word for love in a family is *Storge.* It refers to a natural or instinctual affection such as love of parents toward their offspring and the corresponding love that parents receive from their children. This love is wonderful, and Parker was blessed to have his family where family love was displayed every day of the year. At the same time, it was also good for those parents to experience *Eros*, as Parker and Rosemary did that Monday night on the day when he discovered the body of a murdered man and began searching for a missing woman.

(11) Parker's First Dream

That night Parker had a dream not about love or its many variations but about quantum physics. The dream started with two electrons in superposition, and then this simultaneous effect of electrons in superposition grew quickly to many electrons and then entire atoms, followed by molecules. As the molecules grew larger and more complex, he began to wonder how large the superposition could become before it collapsed.

In Parker's dream, it didn't collapse, and suddenly the molecules morphed into life, and then there were two cats in superposition, and both were alive. He recognized that this was a variation of a Schrodinger cat, with both being alive, but the cat was in two locations at the same time—or perhaps, to avoid a contradiction in human terms, the universe had split into two, and there were actually two distinct and separate universes and cats. Regardless of what was happening, Parker became excited because he was seeing something alive and the size of a cat in a state of superposition. The dream continued as the superpositions became larger and more complex and finally ended dramatically when Padre Pio turned out to be in superposition or bilocated!

Parker woke up and sat straight up in bed. He was relieved Rosemary was asleep next to him and that he had returned to a familiar world. He started laughing to himself. His discussions with his two teenagers had probably triggered this bizarre dream.

Of course he'd always had the desire to understand physical reality, and that a searching mind would always speculate and attempt to understand it. Indeed, the search for truth was the first philosophical transcendental that separated humans from the other known species on earth. The desire to know truth was how discoveries were made. Indeed, his work as a private investigator was about finding facts, putting them together, and coming to the truth. Parker believed this would happen in the world of physics, and eventually an understanding of the micro-world and its impact and relationship on the macro-world would become clearer.

With that thought, Parker became happy about his dream. He was happy because he knew, if something rare occurred, even if it happened only once, then it could happen again. For him the notion of the resurrection of the body was an example of that idea. Jesus died and had been resurrected. That happened once to human nature, and therefore it could happen again. His skeptic friends merely shook their heads because they didn't believe the resurrection of Jesus was a true story. According to them, it never happened in reality. However, looking at evidence, Parker knew the Gospels were based on historical facts—they described real people and real places in time. He even thought his own birth in one sense could be thought of as a resurrection. Certainly, before his birth, he was dead to the universe, but, somehow, he'd come to life. His birth was a resurrection for him, and, if it happened once, then it could happen again.

Thus, that night he was happy knowing that, if superposition of states was a reality in the micro-world, then it should not be immediately dismissed in our macro-world. He thought that, one of these days, someone would figure out how to place giant molecules and even bigger objects in quantum superposition. Then the notion of bilocation for someone like Padre Pio might move from the completely impossible category to the very unlikely but theoretically possible category.

Parker loved the Scripture passage, 1 Thessalonians 5:21, which read, "Test everything; retain what is good." He wondered how supposition of states for large objects could be maintained before they collapsed. In his dream-like state, he thought *there might be a way for this to happen in the future*, and, with that thought, Parker was happy and returned to a sound sleep.

(12) Nicole's Parents

The next morning, Parker was up at the usual time and took the three older children to school. The temperature and humidity had dropped, and the summer heat was gone. The forecast called for rain. He tried again to reach either Nicole or Denise by dialing their telephone numbers but only got endless ringing. He decided to renew his search for Nicole by visiting her parents, George and Martha Elkhart.

The Elkharts lived on the South Side in a neighborhood that was changing from Eastern European to Mexican. Mrs. Elkhart answered the doorbell. She was a plain woman with a thin face, gray hair, and a wrinkled brow. She looked her senior citizen age. Her brown eyes were fearful, as if she'd known trouble and expected more. Parker sat on a dusty couch. The curtains were drawn across the windows, and the room looked drab. Photographs of the Elkharts' family were on the far wall, where a round clock ticked off the seconds. One of the photographs was of Martha when she was in her early forties. At that time, she was attractive; her brown eyes were bright with hope, her face was full, and her brown hair carefully groomed—the last couple of decades had been hard on her. Another recent photograph showed her five children standing in a row. Nicole stood out, not only because she was the youngest but also because of her height. She was also the only one with dark—almost black—hair.

A large trophy case dominated the living room, loaded not only with trophies but also with rifles, bow and arrow sets, and hunting knives. The trophy case was 6 feet long, 3 feet deep, and stood on four sturdy legs about 2 feet above the floor, going up 7 feet high, with three sides of glass and the back closed, all illuminated by lights at the top of the case. Three hunting bows and four rifles hung on the back wall of the case, and there were four trophies, each for killing the largest deer in different years—and with George Elkhart's name engraved on each. Several arrows and hunting knives of various sizes were on the floor of the trophy case. Parker eyeballed the contents of the trophy case and looked at Martha.

She acknowledged his observations, "My husband hunted when he was a younger man. He slept late this morning, but he's now awake and will be out here in a few minutes." She then added, "I'm afraid he hasn't been feeling well."

"I'm sorry to hear that. Nothing serious, I hope?"

"No. He's just been terribly upset lately. Your card says you're a private investigator. The police were here yesterday afternoon. You're not here to upset him some more, are you?"

"No, that's not my intent; I just want to ask a few questions and talk."

"But why would you, a private detective, be visiting us? Is it about Nicole? The police were asking us about her." Mrs. Elkhart sat very straight, bracing her back against the chair, waiting for something bad to happen as the clock loudly clicked away the passing seconds.

"Have you seen or heard from your daughter Nicole in the last two days?"

"I don't have a daughter named Nicole any longer!" It was a harsh statement, and Mrs. Elkhart said it harshly. "George and I raised four children successfully, and then Nicole came along. The girl failed her father and me completely."

"In what way?" Parker inquired.

"In an especially important way, Mr. Spooner. It wasn't pleasant to see Nicole grow into a tramp."

"Perhaps you're being too severe on her, Mrs. Elkhart."

"I watched her. Every weekend she had a different date. She would encourage the fellow to paw her in front of George and me. If they were hugging in front of us, just imagine what they did in private." A shudder rippled across Mrs. Elkhart's body. "She moved out of our house years ago when she first went off to college. She took her clothes, her belongings, and moved into a dormitory and then into an apartment. Good riddance! She's no daughter of mine, acting like that with men."

"How does your husband feel about the situation?"

"The same way I do. He doesn't say much, but he's hurt and angry. Nikki—we used to call her Nikki when she was a child—Nikki and George got along wonderful as daughter and father." A faraway look of lost days flashed across Mrs. Elkhart's eyes. "Then she grew up and discovered men. From that time on, she's been impossible to control. George tried and couldn't do it. After we raised four wonderful children, it was quite a blow to him—to both of us."

Mrs. Elkhart had not answered Parker's original question, and thus he repeated it with a slight change in wording, avoiding the daughter word, "Have you heard anything from Nicole recently?"

"No," she responded. "Is she in trouble with the law? The police were very evasive."

"It's possible." Parker kept his voice noncommittal. Martha Elkhart didn't seem to know Dave Curtis had been murdered. Apparently, the police had merely inquired about Nicole's whereabouts, and Parker decided to remain quiet about the murder.

A loud voice shouted, "Martha, who is that man?" George Elkhart came staggering out of the bedroom and stood before Parker.

"This is a private investigator," she said quietly. "He wants to speak to us about Nikki." George Elkhart didn't seem fully awake and ran two nicotine-stained fingers through a shock of his gray-yellow hair. "More people looking for Nikki? Let me throw some water on my face," he growled as he disappeared into a bathroom.

"Be careful how you mention Nicole to him," whispered Mrs. Elkhart. "Last Saturday he became upset when one of Nikki's teachers tried to question him. He threw the man out of the house. Then he went out himself and got very drunk." Martha was nearly in tears. Parker nodded to her, and she continued, "George has been drinking too much the past few years and is a completely different man. He cannot accept Nikki's carrying on with boys—it upsets him so much, and yesterday the police were here asking about her."

George came out of the bathroom and stood next to his wife, who remained seated. He was a pudgy man with a florid face and a large double chin. He looked tired and somewhat exhausted and appeared to be laboring under duress. Martha took one of his hands and held it.

They both stared at Parker, who carefully launched into his brief speech, "I was hired by a client who wishes to locate Nicole. My client is worried about her because he hasn't seen her recently. I'm hoping you can help me find her. Perhaps give me a clue as to where she may be."

Martha Elkhart said emotionally, "If she's not at her apartment with Denise, then we don't know where she is."

George Elkhart showed no emotion at all. He glared at Parker like a stout Buddha. He started speaking, normal at first, and then his voice grew quite loud, "My wife and I haven't seen Nicole in weeks. She's been on her own for some time, and we have nothing to do with her anymore. Last week one of her teachers was here. Yesterday the police were here asking the same thing, and today it's you." Now he thundered and stepped forward, "We're tired of these questions. We don't know where she is, and we don't have to talk to any private eye, so you damn well better clear out of here and don't come back."

Parker was dismissed. They'd answered. They didn't know where Nicole was, and, of course, George was correct. Parker couldn't make them discuss Nicole since they didn't want to talk. Martha stood up and led Parker to the front door while George, his arms folded in determination, watched him go. One of the photographs on the wall caught Parker's attention, and he paused to look at it. A young Nicole Elkhart—the first signs of womanhood evident—stood smiling on a porch. The inscription read, "To Daddy on Father's Day. Love, Nikki. XXX." It was dated eight years ago.

Mrs. Elkhart, seeing Parker's gaze, remarked, "Wasn't she a beautiful girl. That photograph was taken at our summer house. That was the summer when we started to have trouble with Nikki. Up to that time, she'd been a good daughter."

"Martha, be quiet!" George Elkhart took another hostile step in Parker's direction. "Mister, I told you to go." The look on his face was now brutal. Parker went, quickly, thinking he wouldn't want to get too close to this angry man, but future events would transpire that would bring him face to face with George Elkhart one more time.

(13) Nicole Elkhart

Parker decided to drive to Fox Lake, where the Elkharts had their summer cottage. The village is a good one-hour drive northwest of the city, and he stopped for lunch in the town before finding the lake road that led to their house, which had a long driveway. This portion of Fox Lake had single family houses on 60-foot lots separated by fences or bushes. The backs of the houses had direct access to the lake. Small piers were put up every spring so boats could go out on the lake, and the piers were taken down in the autumn and stored in backyard sheds to avoid being destroyed during winter freezes. The Elkharts' was one of the few houses that didn't have a pier in the water this past summer. The rain had now stopped, but it remained overcast, with temperatures around 70 degrees, considerably cooler from the prior heat wave.

As Parker pulled into the driveway, he saw a light blue two-door 1966 Ford Falcon parked, and he placed his dark green two-door 1966 Oldsmobile Cutlass behind it. The cottage had a front porch, and Nicole with a pencil and a book in her hands was sitting next to a table with papers on it. Parker recognized her, and again he was immediately struck by her natural beauty; the photographs certainly hadn't lied. No one else was in sight, and the house appeared deserted. Nicole stood up. She looked warily at this middle-aged man she didn't know.

He got out of his car and said, "My name's Parker Spooner, and I'm a private investigator. I believe you're Nicole Elkhart?" She stood tall at 5 feet 10 inches and wore a yellow miniskirt, which enhanced her long, chorus girl legs. Tan sandals and a loose-fitting white blouse completed her wardrobe. Parker noted her dark hair, which came down to her shoulders and highlighted her blue eyes. *Yes*, he thought, *a perfect match to the photograph Frank had given him and the photograph in Dave's apartment.* But now she was very real, standing before him.

"Yes, I'm Nicole. What do you want?"

Parker walked slowly to the porch stairs. She was beautiful, and beauty anywhere aroused a desire in Parker. There were only four steps to the top where Nicole now stood, and Parker recognized the book she held, *the Theory of Interest* by Stephen Kellison, a textbook for individuals studying for Part Three of the actuarial examinations.

That's fortunate, thought Parker. It allowed an easy segue into further introducing himself to her, and he quickly said, "I'm sorry to interrupt your studying—I know your examination is coming up in about six weeks.

I also happen to be a Fellow of the Society of Actuaries, and I recognize the importance of studying and solving many problems before the test to have any chance of passing it. The society grades on their curve and limits the number of students who pass the exam."

Nicole smiled for the first time, "Yes, they really make it tough. I'm fortunate my company gives me study time and allows me to take it in days and not go into the office. I've been studying like crazy the past three days and solving many problems involving interest calculations. I have to be back at work tomorrow." Parker had rested his left hand on the stair railing, and Nicole noticed he wore a wedding ring. This eased her anxiety because married men with wedding rings generally didn't bother her. It was only when the ring came off that she knew that she was about to have a problem.

"I remember those study days," replied Parker. "I used to work at Bankers Life, but I had to take the study time in their office, and the company gave only half-days of study, not full days."

"Wait," she said with some amazement in her voice, "you are an FSA, a fellow, a real actuary, and a private investigator? You have two jobs?"

"Yes, I'm a consulting actuary—I run my own firm, and I'm also a licensed private investigator. People hire me to find folks who are missing. That's why I'm here—my client said you were missing and hired me to find you. He said that, once I locate you, to let him know, and I could go back to doing my actuarial work."

"Wait, who thought I was missing? I haven't been anywhere. Who would hire . . . oh, of course, Frank—it has to be Frank Lawson. I told everyone to ignore him, to say they hadn't seen me, so he goes and finds a private detective. Isn't that correct? It was Frank Lawson who hired you to find me?"

"That's correct. He said he was worried about you. Are you okay?"

"Yes, I'm fine, thank you, but I wish he'd leave me alone."

Parker gave her an inquiring look, and she elaborated, "I'm not interested in him. Can you give him that message when you talk to him? I would appreciate it." She looked directly at Parker and waited for his response and wasn't disappointed with his answer when he said he'd convey her message to Frank.

"Unfortunately," Parker then added, "I also have some bad news to convey that doesn't concern Frank. May I come up on the porch and sit with you for a few minutes to talk about it?"

She looked surprised and perhaps a little frightened, but she motioned for Parker to come up and take a seat on the porch. "What's your bad news?" she asked, sitting next to him at the table. Her sky-blue eyes looked directly at Parker, and he was struck again by her because it seemed her very presence and natural beauty brightened what was an overcast day.

Suddenly, a voice from the neighboring house behind Parker yelled, "Nicole, is everything all right over there?" Nicole waved to the neighbor and yelled back, "Yes, Mrs. Novak, everything is good." Nicole then leaned in close to Parker, winked, and whispered, "Mrs. Novak and her husband are nice and always watch over me."

Parker was pleased with this temporary interruption from the neighbor, Mrs. Novak, because it allowed him to ignore Nicole's question about bad news and ask one of his own, "First, would you please tell me when you arrived here at Fox Lake for your visit?" At that moment, Parker realized Nicole, who'd moved closer to him to whisper, was still very close to him and carefully examining his face and eyes. In fact, their faces remained within inches of each other because she hadn't moved back. Parker thought her lips were inviting, and he quickly retreated back into his chair.

Nicole smiled as she answered his question. She knew her action of moving close to him had caused Parker to move back, and she enjoyed that she had that effect. "It was late Saturday night; wait, more likely early Sunday morning by the time I got here. I drove up from the city."

"That's your car in the driveway?" Parker asked pointing to the Ford.

"No, I don't have a car. The Ford belongs to my roommate, who's been away for the past week. I borrowed it in her absence."

"That's good, and I understand from Mrs. Meyer that you were temporarily staying with Dave Curtis while Denise was away."

Parker's mentioning these names caused Nicole to blink and sit up straight, "Yes, that's true. I see you know the names of my friends, but wait, what's going on with your questions? You said you had bad news. Tell me, what's happened?"

Parker thought it best to level with her. "I found Dave dead in his apartment yesterday morning. Apparently, he died sometime early Sunday morning when you were arriving here."

Nicole muffled a scream and started to cry. Parker gave her a clean handkerchief that he carried in his pocket. She repeated, "Dave dead? Oh, no," two times, wiping flowing tears from her eyes. Then the questions he expected came, "He was young—was it a heart attack? How did he die?"

"No heart attack. He was murdered." She screamed again, this time loudly. Her head went down almost to the table, which she started pounding with her fists. Parker expected Mrs. Novak to reappear, but she apparently had gone deep into her house and didn't hear this outburst. When Nicole raised her head, her face was flushed and her blue eyes were blocked by tears, but she still managed to convey anger. When Parker saw her clenched fists, he thought she was going to hit him and quickly said, "I know you were close to Dave, and I have sorrow for you in your loss. I'm sad I have to be the person to bring this to you."

She wiped both her eyes, regained composure, and in a second her entire mood had changed, "It's not your fault. Dave and I had an argument late Saturday night, and I broke up with him. I packed some things into my bag and ran away from him. Now I'll have to live with the fact my last memory of him will be our fight. He was sweet in many ways, but I could never express my feelings the right way." She paused and then said out loud, "Why am I so confused and messed up when it comes to affection?" She started crying again. Startled by this message and changes in mood, Parker sat there for a few seconds and then reached out with his right arm along the tabletop, offering his palm. She grabbed his hand and squeezed it hard. They sat in that position for a long time, looking into each other's eyes before she relaxed and let go of Parker's hand. Nicole sat back in her chair and asked him, "What happens now?"

"The Chicago police are looking to question you. They know about this house, so they'll have the Fox Lake police come here for you to discuss the murder investigation."

Nicole understood where he was going, "Wait, the police suspect me of killing Dave? That's crazy. How could they possibly think that?"

"The thought that you had something to do with the murder will certainly have crossed their minds since you were in Dave's apartment that night and are the last known person to have seen him alive. However, right now my guess is they're following many other leads."

"I would hope so—to think it's me is ridiculous. Dave certainly had a couple of people he didn't get along with, and they may have been upset enough to kill him."

"Can you give me some names and details about these people?"

"There is this guy, Carlos Able. A couple of months ago, Dave and I were out bowling with some friends, and Carlos and his girlfriend were bowling in the lane next to us. Dave and Carlos nearly got into a fist fight over something they'd been arguing about for years. If his girlfriend hadn't pulled Carlos away, there would have been real trouble because I think he had a switchblade in his pants pocket."

Parker didn't say anything; however, this latest information confirmed what Rick Henderson had told him about the bad blood between Dave and Carlos. He also noted Carlos likely had a switchblade. Nicole then brought up Mrs. Meyer's other tenant, "Dave got angry at Richard Blackburn. I shouldn't have told Dave that Richard made a pass at me, but I did. I had to calm Dave down, saying Richard really didn't mean anything by it, and that he was harmless and never touched me. Fortunately, Richard wasn't around that day, and Dave backed off. The two seldom see each other, so I believe the incident passed without further trouble."

This was confirmation that there was women trouble between the two men. First, Dave had taken Richard's girlfriend, and then Richard tried to do the same to Dave. Parker asked, "When did Richard make a move on you?"

"About four months ago, shortly after I started working at Continental," she responded. "He mentioned the job opening to me and then took my thank you the wrong way."

Parker noted Nicole had been quick in mentioning two other possible suspects besides herself, thus taking focus away from her involvement in the murder of Dave Curtis. Nicole then took a deep breath before asking him, "You mentioned the police would be coming here to question me. What do you think I should do?"

"Before the Fox Lake police get here, I'd gather your belongings, jump into Denise's Ford, and go to the Area Six police station in Chicago and talk to the homicide detectives this afternoon. Tell them the truth; tell them you heard from me the police were looking for you, and that you want to tell them what happened Saturday night. They're in no position to hold you or to book you. If you're innocent, then they'll not find any evidence you did it. If they find something that implicates you, they'll want to interrogate you, and they'll read you your Miranda rights. At that point you'd better get a lawyer."

"Wait, you said *if* I'm innocent. But I am. Do you think I killed Dave and that my tears were just an act?"

"It really doesn't matter what I think. The evidence the police are gathering will determine what they conclude happened to Dave. You have the chance to freely give them your evidence this afternoon."

"The truth will set me free?" Nicole said in perhaps a mocking or questioning manner.

"Yes, it will. Don't have any doubts," Parker firmly replied.

She thought for a few moments. She liked this man. She believed he was an actuary and in what he'd told her. She felt she could trust his advice and thus asked for the location of the Area Six police station. Parker told her she could follow his car. He was headed back to Chicago and would lead her directly to the police station. She liked that idea and ran into the house to get some of her clothes. There was a large purse up against the side of the cottage near the table. While she was inside, Parker took the liberty of looking inside her purse. He was looking for a knife. The murder weapon was missing, and if Nicole had killed Dave, then she may have taken it with her when she ran out of the apartment. But there was no knife in her purse, only a wallet, feminine cosmetics, a mirror, a pen, and another notebook. The table was loaded with papers, where Nicole had solved dozens of theory of interest problems. Parker could see this was a determined woman—solving actuarial math problems next to a lake instead of sunning herself or swimming—especially during the last couple of days, when it had been hot outside.

Nicole came out of the house, stuffed some clothes and all her actuarial study materials into the purse, locked the cottage door, and said, "Let's go." A few minutes later, with Nicole in her blue Ford Falcon following Parker in his green Oldsmobile Cutlass, they were on the road, US Highway 12 south, to Chicago. One of these days, thought Parker, an automobile manufacturer will figure out a way to give explicit driving instructions to a driver of a car to navigate to a specific location, but, on this day, he was the navigator.

About an hour and half later, they pulled into a parking garage near the Area Six station on Damen Avenue, and the two of them entered the three-story building. It had a tall front door entrance with the words "Police Station" above it in exceptionally large letters. Officer Chester Wojcik, a young rookie policeman, was inside, directing people who walked in. He greeted Parker, and his eyes went up and down twice at the stately Nicole and her legs. Parker smiled and said, "Officer, this is Nicole Elkhart. If Sergeant Boyle is available, you can inform him Nicole and I are here." A few minutes later, Officer Wojcik told Parker they could walk up to the third-floor rear, where the Homicide unit worked. Nicole and Parker climbed the creaking staircase. She remarked that the building seemed somewhat dilapidated and could hardly believe police detectives worked in such a place. Parker nodded at her correct observation. Sergeant Boyle met them at the top of the stairs, and they followed him to his desk and sat next to him.

Parker quickly filled him in, "I went out to the Elkharts' summer cottage in Fox Lake, and there I found Nicole reading. She drove up there late Saturday night after leaving Dave's apartment. I informed her I'd found Dave's body yesterday morning, and, after a discussion, she agreed to come in and talk to you. I have a lecture to go to this evening, and it's time for me to be going so the two of you can talk."

Sergeant Boyle was pleased, "You must have just missed the Fox Lake police. They went to the cottage at my request to investigate and called me back around four to report the place was deserted. I was wondering what my next move was going to be to find you, Miss Elkhart, and then just like that you walk in—thank you. Once Mr. Spooner leaves, I'm going to get another police officer, Detective Brendan, who's been assigned to this case, to join us."

Nicole gave Parker a worried glance, and he reassured her, "It's okay; remember to tell the truth and help the police put the case together. That's why you're here. I'm going to give you my calling cards, both the investigator and FSA cards. You can call me if you have any questions." With that, Parker handed her his two calling cards.

Nicole, wide eyed and with a smile, jumped out of her chair, flung her arms around him, and aggressively kissed Parker on his cheek, very close to his lips. "That's so sweet. Thank you!"

Sergeant Boyle's eyebrows shot straight up, and Parker, smiling, said to Nicole, "Sergeant Boyle is my father-in-law, and you may be giving him the wrong impression."

"Oh, wait; I don't know what's wrong with me. I'm so screwed up. I'm sorry—I didn't mean anything by that kiss. I know you're married because of your wedding ring. I'm just grateful you're helping me at this time."

"Married with four kids," replied Parker, "and an innocent kiss of thanks is okay. There's no problem—all is good," Parker said, trying to ease her mind. In his mind, he was pleased she'd kissed him. He waved to her and the sergeant as he exited his father-in-law's cubical space. Detective Brendan was waiting outside. His last name was difficult to pronounce, a hyphenated African-Irish Gaelic combination name that no one could say and that everyone simplified by using his first name, which Detective Brendan loved. He was tall, 6 feet 3 inches, and muscular, with a black, pockmarked face that instinctively you wouldn't want to mess with, but he had the proverbial heart of gold if he thought you were honest. Parker and the detective exchanged quick pleasantries before Brendan disappeared into Boyle's space.

Parker walked down the stairs, and, on his way out of the Area Six station, Officer Wojcik winked at him and said, "I think I'm going to become a private investigator like you, if that's what it takes to attract beautiful women. What a pair of legs on her." Chester Wojcik was a young, rookie police officer who'd just finished his bachelor's degree in engineering at Northwestern University. He was a good-looking man, 6 feet tall, with brown eyes and hair and a clean, open face.

"Chet, you're a young guy and not married. Have you ever met a girl you recognized as special in some way, other than being physically attractive?"

"Why, yes of course. What are you getting at?"

"Well then try to forget about passing infatuations and sexual attractions and ask yourself if the lady is emotionally or intellectually attractive. I'm sure you've met women who are attractive in one of those special ways."

"Yes, of course. I can think of a couple."

"Have you asked them out on a date?"

"No."

"Well, why not? Perhaps you should. For many guys, there are only a few special women, and you don't want to have them drift away if you discern something special. Remember there's physical beauty, but women also have intellectual beauty and emotional beauty. Indeed, beauty is one of the five transcendentals in philosophy. We all recognize beauty in a person's appearance, but we also see beauty in nature, music, art, and literature. Beauty excites us and evokes inspiration, pleasure, and love."

Chet gave him an amazed look, "Okay, Parker, you're making good points. I guess I experience beauty all around me, but I don't think about it. Definitely, and perhaps unfortunately, when I look at a woman, I'm only thinking about physical beauty, which can be fleeting."

"Yes, and as you imply, most folks are never satisfied with the beauty they experience. People are always taking pictures of sunsets from different angles, seeking perfection, and looking for more and more beauty."

Chet nodded, "Yes, you're correct, and I need to think about the intellectual and emotional beauty I experience in people and reality. I certainly wouldn't want to lose a special lady."

Parker went home for supper and called Frank Lawson to give him the good news that he'd located Nicole and that she was fine. He then gave Frank her message that she'd "disappeared" because he was bothering her, and that she wanted him to back off. Frank didn't take that very well and was in denial that she felt that way. Parker told him in no uncertain terms: do not immediately contact Nicole. Frank protested. Parker then explained Nicole was holding up well, but she was part of a police investigation involving the murder of her boyfriend. Frank absolutely had to allow things to settle down for a few days, and he and Parker could talk later, perhaps next Monday, to discuss a plan as to how he should proceed with her. Finally, Frank reluctantly agreed to stay away from Nicole for at least a week. Parker hung up the phone, and Rosemary, who'd heard the conversation from the kitchen said, "Apparently you found the missing woman."

"Yes," replied Parker, "and she's going to be a handful."

"Why do you say that, my love?"

"Because she's both physically and intellectually beautiful."

Rosemary immediately understood and nodded to her husband.

(14) Thomas Explains Boethius

That evening, Parker drove to Hyde Park and the university auditorium, where the lecture, "Boethius and the Big Bang Theory," was being held. He was greeted by a student who handed him the evening's program. Parker saw the main speaker was Thomas Lawson, and there were two panelists, John Applegate from the Philosophy Department and Frank Lawson from the Physics Department.

Parker entered the auditorium, which was large and sloped downward. It was designed so you entered at the top and walked down either the left or right aisles to where the stage was. A podium was on the left side of the stage, with a screen in the middle, and on the right side there was a table with two microphones and two chairs. As Parker walked down the stairs, he saw three men talking among themselves on the stage near the podium. He recognized Frank Lawson, who was dressed casually, and then his twin brother, who was in a suit and tie—as was the third man, Applegate, who sported a white beard. The twin brothers were obviously related, being the same height and weight and having similar posture, both with brown hair and eyes, but they were not identical in the way they dressed or in their faces. Frank, with his horned rimmed glasses, was pale and somewhat gaunt, whereas Thomas had a ruddy fuller face and no glasses. Applegate walked to the other side of the stage, and the two brothers came down the stairs from the stage so Frank could introduce his brother to Parker. Thomas and Parker shook hands and started talking. Frank kept looking at Parker, who sensed Frank was anxious to discuss Parker's earlier admonitions about Nicole. This wasn't an appropriate time or place to do so, and Parker, after finishing his conversation with Thomas, quickly moved away from the stage, smiling, and saying goodbye to Frank, "As discussed earlier, all is well, and we'll talk next week."

As the brothers went up the stairs to take their places on the stage, Parker looked for a seat in the auditorium. There was a good-sized crowd, perhaps two hundred people, and over half looked like college-aged students. Parker slipped into an empty seat in the middle section next to the aisle, a few rows from the stage. The front rows were completely full. Parker spotted a very tall man in the center of the first row, wearing an impeccable dark blue suit. He could only see his face from the side, but Parker recognized he was the man who caused fantasy excitement for the Real Solids clerks—namely, the auditor, Jeremy Wilson. Jeremy had a yellow legal-size pad of paper on his lap, a pencil in his hand, and he was ready to take notes, looking eagerly at the stage as Thomas Lawson moved to the podium and welcomed everyone.

Thomas began his talk by explaining who Anicius Boethius was. Boethius was born around 480 A.D. into a great Roman family during the time when the Roman Empire fell apart and non-Romans became rulers over Italy. His father died when Boethius was just a young boy, and he was raised by another Roman family, receiving an excellent classical education and becoming thoroughly familiar with Greek philosophy, including detailed knowledge of its many diverse subjects. Theodoric the Great, king of the Ostrogoths, ruled over a kingdom of Romans and Goths in 493–526, and Boethius served his ruler, rising quickly to the post of chief minister; however, he wasn't politically astute and became ensnared in a treason controversy and sentenced to death. In prison, he wrote his magnum opus, *Consolation of Philosophy,* a book that had a far-reaching impact well into the Middle Ages and beyond. Subsequent theologians drew on his immense knowledge of philosophy and synthesis of classical and Christian civilizations. Here, using the overhead projector, Lawson showed the audience a sketch of how Boethius may have looked.

Thomas then told his audience he would concentrate on the final part of the *Consolation*, where Boethius discussed eternity, and link that understanding to a simplified model of the Big Bang theory. For Boethius, eternity was not time stretched out infinitely into the future or infinitely back into the past. Eternity was not perpetuity. Boethius defined eternity as "the whole and perfect possession of unlimited life at once," said Thomas, slowly. He then repeated the definition and explained that, for Boethius, eternity is outside of time, and when we say God is eternal, that means we cannot think of God within time, for that creates difficulties. Considering God outside time solves the problem of free will because what mankind perceives successively, as happening in time, God perceives simultaneously. There's no foreknowledge on the part of God because God abides forever in the eternal, a state of existence not dependent on time. This, Thomas conceded, isn't easy to understand because we all live in time and pass from the present to the future, and there's nothing familiar to us in time that can "embrace simultaneously the whole extent of life." Here Lawson paused to drink some water from a glass that was resting on a shelf affixed to the podium.

Parker looked around the audience, and they were engaged in the talk, intently paying attention, and following the presentation closely.

Certainly, Jeremy Wilson in the front row was busy writing on his legal pad. At this point, Thomas moved into a summary of the Big Bang theory, which had our universe beginning from a small, hot, dense point, quickly expanding and cooling over time. He then discussed the mounting evidence for this model and showed a mathematical x and y axis on the screen behind him with several geometrical figures. He explained this diagram would illustrate how Boethius's concept of eternity could be related to a highly simplified two-dimensional model of the Big Bang.

The audience looked at the diagram and then at Thomas, who held a small flashlight in his hand that pointed a large red dot at the diagram to reference what he was saying. As Thomas lectured, Parker noticed Jeremy was furiously sketching the mathematical diagram onto his legal pad.

When Thomas thought enough of the audience understood his thoughts, he shifted the red dot to the left side of the diagram, where there was a narrow rectangle that vertically extended the screen. There Thomas spoke as to how the rectangle shifting to the left becomes a line off the graph and is outside time with all the physical matter in the universe there. "This is the vision of Boethius, updated to twentieth century cosmology," said Thomas Lawson, bringing his talk to a conclusion. He'd talked for nearly an hour and had explained how all the events that happen sequentially in the expanding universe happen simultaneously outside of time.

There was a smattering of applause that grew quickly to a loud ovation. The two panelists leaned forward, anxious to participate, and there soon followed a lengthy discussion. Applegate stated Plato and Aristotle thought of eternity as perpetuity. An eternal present that Boethius presented was distinctly Christian because Aristotle could only think of God as a first cause or prime mover. The idea of a personal or loving God was alien to the Greek philosophers. Boethius, a Christian, broke away from the ancient philosophy through his idea of an eternal present. Boethius noted God's perception of present actions doesn't impose any condition on actions or affect human freedom because God perceives all events simultaneously, and free will isn't restricted. There is freedom, and there is providence, and neither compromises the other. Thomas's brother, Frank, said understanding the mathematics of the singularity at the Big Bang would take years and involve integrating quantum theory and general relativity. He finished saying the next decade should be exciting. The audience made comments, and there was Jeremy Wilson in the front row, raising a yellow piece of paper above his head, the Big Bang diagram he'd drawn on it clearly visible. He was checking his sketched version held in his hand against Thomas Lawson's diagram, still showing on the screen in front of the audience. Convinced he'd drawn the diagram correctly, Jeremy folded the piece of paper, and Parker observed he placed it inside his yellow legal pad.

The panel then noted implications of this concept of eternity for the current day world. Modern societies think about "progress" as being time-bound. We think the future is worthwhile for its own sake and often don't have goals that lie outside of time. Often goals are all about what we're going to do tomorrow and not about what we are. We're not aware of the medieval concept of a goal; namely, life is worth living for the goal's own sake.

The session ended around 9:00 p.m., and everyone was invited for light refreshments and reminded about next month's lecture. Parker stopped for a glass of water and left quickly, deciding against staying and talking to Frank, who he felt might ask too many questions about Nicole that Parker was in no position to answer. Once outside, there were dozens of people milling around, and several cars and cabs. The sidewalk and street were wet from the rain, and there was a light drizzle in the air. Parker was surprised to see Jeremy Wilson get into the back seat of a large, black, chauffeur-driven Cadillac, holding his yellow legal-size pad of paper and lingering with a long kiss on Natasha Pillsbury's eager lips. He then sat next to her and placed his yellow legal pad in the pocket slot provided by the back of the front seat ahead of him. The limousine pulled away from the curb, and Natasha jumped onto Jeremy's lap, pushing her body into his. Her two hands grabbed each side of his face, and she began kissing his mouth as the Cadillac slowly drove away.

(15) Building a Case

The next morning, Ray Ulster called Parker at his office to report on his renewed surveillance of Miles. His news was that Miles Clayton spent a rainy Tuesday evening in Paula Dean's apartment. "He got to her place before eight o'clock and went home after ten. He went to work this morning, but his evening behavior last night was not the behavior we saw when we investigated him months ago." So Miles and Paula apparently were more than coworkers in Natasha's office. Parker told Ray to continue his surveillance of Miles and explained that Paula had been eavesdropping on his first conversation with Natasha months ago, when he was first hired to investigate Miles. Thus, Miles changed his daily routines because he knew he was being watched. The thought of being outfoxed back then was annoying but eavesdropping by Paula and likely collusion with Miles revealed internal intrigue at the Regular Solids organization. Moreover, Parker's observation last night of a liaison between the auditor Jeremy Wilson and Natasha, while her husband remained bedridden, added another layer of likely deceit to what was going on among the leadership at Regular Solids. Parker also wondered how much Miles knew about Natasha's relationship with Jeremy through Paula's eavesdropping.

Parker then called his other friend, Jim Rowdy, and updated him. He asked him to start watching Jeremy Wilson and do some research on his background and possible involvement with Natasha. Parker hoped to coordinate his work with Ray's surveillance of Miles to get a better understanding of what was happening. Parker wondered about Natasha's recent request to talk to him about her double. Why had she called him months after he'd failed to find any dirt on Miles? Did Paula's eavesdropping and her possible involvement with Miles have anything to do with Natasha's recent request to him about a double?

Parker's thoughts were interrupted when Sergeant Boyle called and asked him to stop in at the Area Six unit to discuss the murder of Dave Curtis. Parker needed a break from the developments at Regular Solids and put that case on the side as he drove to the Damen Avenue police station. As he walked into the building, Office Wojcik asked to talk to him once he was done with Sergeant Boyle. Parker nodded.

Sergeant Boyle was thumbing through his black book as Parker took a seat by his desk. He started summarizing the case, "It's Wednesday morning and forty-eight hours after discovering the murder of Dave Curtis. We have only found evidence of two people in the apartment, Dave Curtis and

Nicole Elkhart. Her fingerprints are in every room, as are his. We have dusted but cannot find any other prints. Also, we haven't found the murder weapon, a knife or switchblade with a blade long enough to reach Dave's heart. Based on the testimony of Nicole and Richard Blackburn, Nicole ran out of the apartment around 11:30 p.m. Saturday night, and the coroner has placed the time of death between 11:00 p.m. and 1:00 a.m. It's possible that, after Nicole left, Blackburn went up to the third floor and murdered Dave because of a grudge he had against Dave or for some other reason. Possible but not likely, and that leaves us with Nicole." Boyle sat back in his chair and looked at his son-in-law.

"Do you think she's the one who murdered Dave?" Parker asked.

"Right now, it certainly looks that way. Nicole appears to be uncontrollable. She may be promiscuous. She may be emotionally unstable. She may have some other problem. After she moves in with her lover, Dave Curtis, they quarrel, and it turns to violence. She kills him during an emotional moment and runs away. That's not that uncommon in cases when young people quarrel, except, here, we have a quick murder; usually, the police are called in after the guy starts beating up the girl."

Boyle cocked a suspicious eye at Parker. "You don't think she did it, do you? I can tell. Did you have one of your insights?"

Parker shrugged his shoulders. "No, I just think this woman isn't a murderer. Though there's something bothering her, big time. Regarding sex, Mrs. Meyer doesn't think they were sleeping together."

"Mrs. Meyer is removed from their generation by forty years and didn't grow up in the 1960s."

"That's true, but I found her to be a perceptive person."

"She also likes Nicole and likely thinks of her as the daughter she never had."

"Yes, that also appears to be true. She does have a bias in favor of Nicole."

Boyle scratched an ear, like a cat bothered by a flea, "I tried to get Nicole to tell me the nature of the argument she had with Dave. Did Dave try to force himself on her, and she refused? That's when she really broke down with tears and anger, but then instead of confessing anything romantic, she stopped the crying, became very coherent and adamant that nothing untoward had happened between them. They just had another argument, and she was tired of him, and so she said good-bye. It was two different incompatible personalities, and she ended it by walking out. That's her story. Our talk was intense for a few minutes, and I let her go back to her apartment. How did you manage to get Nicole to come in and talk to me yesterday?"

"She may be emotional, but she's also intelligent. I reasoned with her. I told her the police would have to question her, and the best way to get to the truth about the murder was for her to tell you the truth."

"How did she react when you first told her about the murder?"

"She screamed, pounded her fists on the table, and got angry, but she snapped out of it quickly when I told her I was sorry to be the person to deliver the news of Dave's death to her."

"Exactly. It's the same pattern I just described to you. She started crying when I asked her about Dave and their argument, but then, on a dime, she stopped and became calm. That's not normal behavior. It's erratic. I can easily believe she briefly lost control in an argument with Dave and killed him."

"And she just happened to have a knife on her?"

"She grew up with knives and guns. You saw George's trophy case prominent in the Elkhart living room. I didn't mention the murder to him, but I got George to talk about the weapons in his trophy case. He was an avid hunter and indicated the stuff in his trophy case was only a third of his total collection. The remainder is in storage at his summer house at Fox Lake. Thus, Nicole could have taken a knife from there and had it with her in Dave's apartment."

"You're certainly starting to build a case against her. What did you say to Nicole last night after she stood by her incompatible personalities story?"

"I thanked her for coming in, told her she should stay close to Chicago and let us know her whereabouts if she has to go anywhere. I said we would talk again if there were any further developments. I then put a tail on her." Sergeant Boyle laughed good naturedly and continued, "Last night she went back to her apartment, and this morning she's working at Continental. I want to talk to her roommate, Denise, when she returns. I also need to figure out a way to get Nicole to take a psychological test, and there I wonder if you might be able to help."

Parker now understood why Sergeant Boyle asked him to come into the station instead of just talking on the telephone. Face to face is always better when you're asking for a favor, even when it's family. "In what way can I help?" asked Parker.

"Well, since you convinced her to come to us and then gave her your calling cards, perhaps she will listen to you. There's some evidence she already recognizes she needs help because she says things like, 'I don't know what's wrong with me, and I'm all screwed up.' A gentle talk by you may get her to submit to a psychological test and perhaps a psychiatrist."

"Okay, I can make an attempt at that."

Sergeant Boyle continued, "We released Dave's body to his mother and sister. There's a wake for him tomorrow night in Forest Park, and he's going to be buried in Woodlawn on Friday morning. My guess is Nicole will be at the wake tomorrow night, if you can make it."

The father-in-law was really moving things along. To Parker, Nicole seemed to be mixed up, but he was uneasy about the idea of her stabbing Dave in the back. He asked Sergeant Boyle, "Have you talked to this guy Carlos Able? Apparently, he and Dave were enemies, and his name has come up a couple of times as someone who might have a motive for attacking Dave."

"Yes, Carlos is a tough, streetwise gang member, and we talked to him and others who know him. However, he has an alibi for Saturday night at the time of the murder. His girlfriend claims they were together in her apartment from eleven onward. That may be an obvious lie, and thus I have not ruled him out as a murder suspect; however, it's difficult for me to think of Carlos going to Dave's apartment to murder him. He would murder Dave in some street or alley but not in his apartment around midnight on a Saturday night."

There was no doubt Sergeant Boyle was on top of this case, and Parker saluted the Sarge with respect, saying good-bye to his father-in-law. On his way out of the police station, Parker found Officer Wojcik, "Chet, you wanted to talk to me."

"Yes, thanks for stopping on your way out, Parker. I was thinking about what you told me, about dating women who are stable and intelligent, rather than merely looking at their physical attributes, and obviously that really makes a lot of sense. The problem is the two women who are in that category, and who I really like, are already engaged. I don't know anybody else, and I find it difficult to go to social events and make small talk with the hopes of finding someone. I don't really know how to make small talk and then how to proceed once I've met someone. Nevertheless, I appreciate what you said about not letting someone good slip away, and, unfortunately, I think this has already happened to me."

"Chet, you're talking to me freely and easily. Now if it's a woman you're talking with, just forget that and start talking freely and easily about something of interest to you and her. It's that simple. Of course, you'll have to go to a place where there are eligible women—you mentioned social events. Do you dance? That's a good place to start."

"I go to visit my parents in Evanston on weekends, and our church up there, St. Joan of Arc, usually has events—dances, card parties, and other gatherings. Summer is over, folks have returned from vacations, and the parish is starting up new events. I could start attending some of them with the hopes of meeting someone special."

Parker smiled and shook Chet's hand, "That's a good plan, and I'm certain you'll find that there are a number of young ladies who have the same idea. I met my wife, Rosemary, at a parish dance. And let me add that, if you persist in your search, you shouldn't worry because it will become clear to you as to how you should proceed once you've met her because an interested woman will always guide you." Chet, as he'd done the last time they talked, looked amazed at Parker's words.

That afternoon, as scheduled, Parker went to the offices of Manan and Son and certified some of their reserves. There was a glitch in one of the exhibits that was quickly corrected, and Parker signed and made it home early for supper, avoiding the thunderstorms that marked the first day of autumn. Anna showed him the drawings she and Nana had made that day. Peter had started another Hardy Boys mystery and told his father that soon he'd write a mystery story. Grace was studying for her first big history test of the new school year while John was struggling to understand wave-particle duality, especially for electrons, which he always understood as tiny particles revolving around a nucleus, like the earth going around the sun, but that was an incorrect and a misleading way to think about electrons. Meanwhile, Rosemary had made her meatball spaghetti special, giving Parker an excuse to open a bottle of red wine.

That night Rosemary and Parker retired early to bed, and, with the bedroom light still on and after her evening prayers, Rosemary started talking about God's unconditional love and an article she'd read in a Catholic newspaper that was discussing the topic. She read a portion of it out loud, "Unconditional means without any conditions, and yet God's love includes commandments, which are conditions on how we are to live. For the fully convinced believer, the commandments are not thought of as imposed from without but joyfully reflect the believer's own will, having found God's reality; however, what about those individuals who are genuinely confused or undecided or those who waiver and remain on the fringes of faith? For such a person, the notion of unconditional love can be a rationalization to remain unrepentant and unchanged because God loves me anyway. Pastors should be careful when using the unconditional word." She then looked at her husband and asked, "That's challenging—how would you answer that?"

Parker said, "My understanding is that God's love is always there; however, a person has free will and has to respond to it. The condition to respond is on the person not on God."

"My darling, husband," said Rosemary sweetly, "The columnist also points out that some priests preach about God's unconditional love and then say people are going to hell for all eternity. That is a strange sort of love, allowing someone to spend *forever* in hell. What do you think about that conundrum?"

Parker thought about his classical background and the discussions that had occurred in collage philosophy, especially when studying Plato. Justice is another transcendental, and Plato's concept of justice led him to accept the immortality of the human soul because justice is never complete or fully achieved in reality, and yet justice is one of the deepest longings or desires in all of humanity. Thus, justice not rendered here in this life will happen to the immortal soul. This can lead to the notion of reincarnation if a human body is required for justice, but Christianity doesn't accept reincarnation, and, given His glorious resurrection, Jesus understands it's *your body* that did justice or suffered at injustice; therefore, it's *your body* that's resurrected, either glorious or not. Rosemary and he had had this conversation before; however, tonight she was bothered by the concept of *forever*. Recalling the Boethius lecture, Parker responded that eternity for the Christian should not be confused with perpetuity. Eternity is not time stretched out forever. God is *outside* time, and eternity is the whole of unlimited life possessed at once.

"What are you talking about?" Rosemary now raised her head from the pillow, and her elbows supported her body position as she looked at her husband with her beautiful blue, inquiring eyes.

Parker knew this was a difficult concept to grasp because we experience time sequentially, and time was part of the physical world that would pass at our death. There was no such thing as time in the spiritual world, "Rosemary, imagine seeing your whole life at once. That includes all the free decisions you made. You've chosen God and love, or you have not. It is what it is. That's eternity."

She groaned and put her head back on the pillow. Turning off the light, she said, "That's either profound or a totally evasive answer when it comes to the adjective *unconditional* applied to the words God's love; however, I do love you. Only God knows why, but I do." Parker smiled when she said, "totally evasive" and "only God knows why."

He said, "I love you, Rosemary" and closed his eyes for another night of sound sleep. However, it didn't happen that quickly. He started thinking about his morning conversation with his father-in-law, who had Nicole in his sights as the person who murdered Dave Curtis. Conceptually, that was possible. Nicole may have killed Dave in an emotional state, but this went against Parker's instincts, and he attempted to figure out why. Parker had long ago identified beauty as one of the chief characteristics of God, who is the source and reason for all that exists. Parker saw beauty in nature, mathematics, art, music, rational thought, and women. He decided it was Nicole's physical beauty that was influencing his thoughts about her innocence and resolved not to allow her appearance to sway him. He would make an extra effort to objectively understand her and decided to approach her through the mathematics they had in common. She'd shown Parker determination in studying, and math was the way to gain her confidence and make progress in figuring out her involvement in the murder. With those thoughts—that he would use Nicole's upcoming exam as a way to connect with her—Parker fell asleep.

(16) Nicole Comes into Focus

The next morning, Parker talked on the telephone with Ray, who reported Miles worked late on Wednesday and then returned home alone. There was no evening contact with Paula, who went grocery shopping and then home to her apartment. Parker asked Ray to try to figure out when Miles and Paula first started seeing each other outside the office. Miles had been with the company for years, but Paula started when Natasha was made president of Regular Solids after William Pillsbury's stroke and semi-retirement. Parker's last suggestion to Ray was to focus a search on Paula from that point in time. Parker then called Jim, who said Jeremy spent the entire day at work in his office and went home late without any direct contact with Natasha.

That afternoon Parker went to the wake for Dave Curtis. He gave condolences to Dave's mother and to his sister and her husband. This was his only immediate family, as Dave's father had died a few years earlier. Some of Dave's colleagues from where he worked showed up, and then Mrs. Meyer and Richard Blackburn came to the funeral parlor together. She spotted Parker, and, after talking to Dave's family, she and Richard came over and sat next to him. Parker nodded to Richard, who returned the greeting.

"Richard was kind enough to take the afternoon off from work and gave me a lift here. I don't like going out at night," said Mrs. Meyer. Parker said he wanted to discuss something with her, and if she and Richard didn't mind, he would drive her home. Richard nodded and Mrs. Meyer agreed. For his part, after about a half-hour, Richard excused himself and went to say good-bye to the Curtis family. Parker also got up and told Mrs. Meyer he wanted to stretch his legs in the lobby of the funeral home, and that he would return. Thus, Parker was in a position to greet Richard as he was leaving the funeral home.

"Have a pleasant afternoon and evening, Mr. Blackburn," said Parker.

"Oh, it's you again. Any luck as to who killed the kid?"

Since he seemed friendly, Parker pushed his luck and tried again to find out about Nicole, "Please tell me again about the first time you saw Nicole hysterical."

"No," growled Richard, turning away.

Parker touched him lightly on his arm and pleaded, "It's important you tell me, Mr. Blackburn. Dave was murdered. The police suspect Nicole may be responsible, and your full testimony is crucial, especially if it has something to do with Nicole, and something that may have happened between you and her. Please, don't be afraid." Here, Parker was thinking of what Nicole had told him about Blackburn making a pass at her. Parker's words affected Richard. He paused. He was a good guy, he understood, and he nodded his head in agreement.

He spoke softly. "I'll tell you. I'm not proud of this, but I'll tell you." He looked at Parker with sad eyes. "It happened months ago, after Nicole started working at Continental. She kept saying how grateful she was to me for telling her about the job opening, and the way she looked at me up close with those big blue eyes and smiling red lips, she made me believe that—that I could have her. Me, half bald and fat, and more than twice her age, she had me convinced I had a green light with her." He hung his head and glanced down at his feet. "When I tried, she cried like a baby and ran away. That broad is a tease." Remembering the unpleasant incident, Blackburn's face contorted as he spoke, "I felt like a monster. What a stupid tease! But I was dumb. Perhaps I was trying to get back at Dave because he'd taken one of my girlfriends, but I don't think so. I just thought I was going to have some fun with a beautiful woman, and that I had a green light. That's all there was. Nothing happened except distress when I acted like a dumbass, and she went crazy. Does that help you?"

"Yes, it does. It gives me a clearer picture of Nicole. Thank you for telling me that." Richard nodded and then walked out of the funeral parlor, shaking his head sadly.

Parker went back to the wake and sat next to Mrs. Meyer. After a few more minutes, they were ready to leave, gave final condolences to the family, and made their way to Parker's car. It was late afternoon, and rush hour traffic in the western suburbs of Chicago had already started. The rain and thunderstorms continued for a third day. The Eisenhower Expressway was packed, but Parker was in no rush because he wanted to learn more about Nicole from Mrs. Meyer, "You said before you had many long talks with Nicole. Perhaps you could tell me something about her so I can better understand her personality. I would like to know about her attitudes, what she really thought, and some personal things, especially toward men and love, if you can share that with me."

Mrs. Meyer stared at Parker. She seemed to hesitate.

"It's important to the case and for Nicole," he quickly added.

Mrs. Meyer nodded. "She's a beautiful woman and a very friendly, outgoing person. We spoke to each other like a mother and daughter. We could really communicate with each other, despite the age difference. I never had a daughter, and I tried to listen and to understand. Some of our talks were about evaluating her male friends and admirers. Many times, it seemed to me, she arrived at a wrong decision about a man or was indecisive. For example, a month ago, she was going to break up with Dave. I talked her out of it." Mrs. Meyer stared at the roof of the car. "Apparently, it would have been better if they'd separated." She lowered her eyes.

"Why did she want to break up with him?" Parker asked.

Mrs. Meyer sighed and shook her head. "Down deep, I think she's afraid of men and of being loved. She always shied away whenever a guy tried to develop a meaningful relationship. She and Dave had been dating a couple of months, and he seemed to understand her; he was taking his time so they could develop a better rapport. I tried to get her to gain confidence in herself and to recognize Dave as a caring person. I thought it was working."

"Did you ever see her hysterical or emotionally out of control?"

"Why yes, I did. How strange you should mention this. It was just about a week ago—I think a week from last Monday night. She'd just moved into Dave's place because her roommate was going to be gone for two weeks. She was also starting her study time from work for the upcoming actuarial examination and came to my apartment to talk to me about it. We sat in my living room and talked about the pressure of the job and the importance of the examinations to the actuarial profession. Then we went on to talk about other things, and all of sudden she seemed to become upset over nothing."

"It would be helpful if you could go into some details about those other things—and in particular what you were discussing at the moment when she got upset."

"Well, let me think—as I said we were in my living room talking—Dave was working late and not around. Nicole mentioned the cottage that her parents own on Fox Lake. She mentioned it in some past discussions since she'd spent many happy summer days growing up there as a young girl. Nicole was recalling some of the incidents that had occurred there when she stopped talking and looked distressed. I asked her what was wrong. She said she was trying to remember the details of something from the past, and just at that moment my telephone rang in the kitchen. I excused myself and got up to answer it. It was my dad, calling long distance from Arizona, where he retired and moved years ago."

Parker recalled the portrait of Mrs. Meyer's father on her living room wall, with his dignified face and smile. Then unexpectedly his mind went back to Nikki's photograph in the Elkharts' living room and the terrible look George Elkhart, Nicole's father, had given him.

Mrs. Meyer continued, "Dad and I talked for about five minutes. When I returned to Nicole, she was crying. She bawled like a child. I tried to calm her, but she kept sobbing, saying she didn't really remember. I made her some tea, which she drank. Finally, she stopped crying and excused herself. I still don't understand what caused such a scene. It frightened me. Nicole is normally such a cheerful and outgoing individual, and that sudden tearful mood presented such a sharp contrast."

"Did she ever offer an explanation?"

"No, she never mentioned the incident. I don't think she knows exactly what happened. Apparently, there's some very unpleasant experience buried in her unconscious."

"Yes, the police noticed erratic behavior on her part when they asked her about Dave's death. They would like her to take some psychological tests and perhaps be evaluated by a psychiatrist. Do you think there would be any chance of her doing that on her own?"

"Oh my, I don't really know. She told me Tuesday night when she called me that the police had questioned her. She also mentioned you were helpful in seeing that she got to the police station; however, she's worried the police will try to pin the murder on her since she admitted she had a fight with Dave and ran out of the apartment, making her the last person to see him alive. I can't believe the police really think Nicole killed Dave. I hope they'll find some real evidence as to who did it. As far as a psychiatrist goes, I don't think Nicole needs one. Young folks get emotional and sometimes confused if they're around someone they're attracted to and usually need time to figure things out and settle down. I'd just keep talking to her, and she'll figure it out." Parker said nothing. He thought perhaps Nicole was trying to work things out but was not able to do so by herself.

They arrived at Mrs. Meyer's house, and she got out of the car, "Thank you for the lift. Please let me know if there are any developments, and I'll keep you informed if I hear anything from Nicole."

The evening wake was at seven, and rather than going home for supper, Parker stopped in a diner to eat and then made it back to the funeral home in plenty of time. He hoped Nicole would come to the evening wake after work because he wanted to talk to her. He sat at the rear of the funeral parlor and waited. Nicole eventually arrived and spent a long time talking to Dave's mother and sister, sitting with them in the front row. For the first time, Parker saw her wearing a long dress instead of a miniskirt or hot pants. He thought she was equally beautiful wearing a dress, which shifted the emphasis to her face and hair, rather than her stately legs. Rick Henderson and a young woman arrived and offered their condolences to the family and then talked with Nicole. Parker presumed the young woman was Susan, Rick's girlfriend. Like Rick, she had brown hair and eyes, and standing together interacting with Nicole, she and Rick seemed to be a perfectly matched couple, not only physically but also emotionally. Parker tried to envision what type of man would be a good match for Nicole. Rick and Susan took seats behind the first row while Nicole sat next to Dave's mother and sister. Nicole dabbed her eyes with a hanky as she spoke to them. She noticed Parker sitting behind her toward the back of the parlor and inwardly became excited and happy to see him and decided she had to talk to him. Parker saw her glance and waited for her.

Time passed, and eventually Rick and Susan got up and left the funeral parlor. Rick on his way out noticed Parker and waved. Parker waved back. Finally, Nicole got out of her chair and walked over to Parker. Her opening line was, "Are you part of the police detail following me?"

"If I was following you, you wouldn't be aware of it," Parker replied, smiling. "You're seeing me because I want to talk with you."

"Okay, I'm here. Let's talk." She took the seat next to him, obviously happy by his presence. Inside her mind, she felt a definite attraction to this middle-aged actuary and detective.

Parker continued smiling, "You may want to consider hiring a psychiatrist to find out what has been bothering you emotionally since you're not able to figure it out for yourself. Sometimes these internal struggles can only be resolved when you have the right person talking to you."

She let out a gasp, "Wait, are you serious? I can't tell if you're joking or serious."

"I really don't know if it's the right thing for you to do or not, Nicole, but you need to think about it." Parker was no longer smiling and paused. "I know you're worried about the police arresting you for Dave's murder on circumstantial evidence. If that happens, they'll have a police doctor, and the record will be public as part of a crime. If you hire one of your own, it will remain private. It might reveal something your unconscious has been repressing, and once it's revealed to you in private, you'll be able to handle it."

"Repressing? Able to handle it? That sounds like some of that Freudian nonsense I learned in college." She paused and looked inward. "I don't think I'm repressing anything," she said quietly. She didn't sound convinced. "That's one of the reasons I chose to be a math major. Math is straightforward and logical, and I can handle it. I love to solve actuarial problems."

"If logic or math can help you with whatever is bothering you, then go for it. Anyway, that's all I have to say except please remember I found Dave's body, and now I really would like to find the person who murdered him."

"Wait, I told you—it's not me, and I don't have any knowledge of who did it or why." When she said, "it's not me," her open right hand went to her heart. She'd also leaned in close to Parker. He thought to himself that Nicole was not only physically attractive but now vulnerable, and this time he didn't back away from her as he did on the Fox Lake porch but moved closer, smelled her perfume, and softly whispered into her ear, "I believe you when you say, 'it's not me'; however, my intuition is that you may not realize what you have hidden within you."

"Intuition—what intuition could you possibly have about me? Or what's hidden inside me?" Nicole had a frightened look in her eyes, and now it was her turn to quickly pull back from him. She thought this man couldn't possibly know her past, and that immediately calmed her. However, Parker had caught her frightened look and remembered she'd mentioned a dark secret to Frank. He now realized she did have a dark secret, and that it wasn't made up as an excuse on her part to get rid of Frank.

Parker assured her, "My intuition about you isn't clear to me; however, if you proceed and talk to someone who can help, things are likely to become much clearer for you."

"Hire a psychiatrist—I couldn't afford a psychiatrist even if I wanted to see one, especially now." She sadly shook her head sideways. "My roommate Denise just told me she's leaving Chicago for Santa Fe, which means I'll be paying the full rent for the apartment."

"So, Denise has returned. When did that happen?" Parker asked.

"She won't return until Saturday, but she called me at work today to say she's leaving on a plane this Sunday afternoon. She's getting a ton of extra money for her gig and can now make the move to Santa Fe that she's been talking about for months."

It had been a rough week for Nicole. First, the shocking death of Dave, then the police investigation into her possible role in the murder, and now Parker's suggestion to her to seek professional help for whatever was bothering her emotionally—and all of this at the same time as Denise announcing her sudden departure was enough abrupt change to make anyone anxious, if not depressed. Parker decided it was time to take her mind off all these difficulties and talk to her about the upcoming exam, as he'd originally planned. Besides she'd just told him she wasn't into Freud but could handle logic and math. "Nicole, you need to take care of yourself. You have Part Three of the actuarial examinations coming up, and you know how difficult the exam is and how many practice problems you must solve before the examination to have any chance of passing it.

Thus, put all the bad stuff that has happened behind you and solve actuarial problems. You like to do that, and it'll help you pass Part Three. Here I have a problem for you to solve: At what effective rate of interest will payments of $100 at the end of every quarter accumulate to $2,500 at the end of five years?"

Nicole was suddenly overjoyed; tears of happiness started to form in her eyes, "You're so right, and you—you understand me. Thank you!" She sat up straight, with a bright smile on her face and started to move forward as she'd done in Sergeant Boyle's office when she kissed him, but this time she stopped herself and merely offered him her right hand. They looked into each other's eyes, hers were sky blue and very moist, his were brown and very clear. Catching Nicole's genuine emotion and how correctly he'd understood her, Parker now leaned forward but stopped short of kissing her. He recognized he had to extract himself from a developing situation; he merely accepted her right hand and shook it. "I'm happy I was able to help you with my suggestion and the interest problem. Now, if you'll please excuse me; I should be getting home." And with that, Parker quickly left the funeral parlor. He knew it was going to be very difficult for him to be objective about this woman. Meanwhile, Nicole sat in the funeral parlor, excited that Parker had just shown he cared for her.

That evening, as Parker and Rosemary got ready to go to sleep, and after her evening prayers, Rosemary again started talking about unconditional love and why she agreed with the columnist that the unconditional word should not be used as an adjective to describe God's love. From the newspaper, she read his additional comments, "Unconditional is a poor word to describe God's love because it can inadvertently lead people astray. In Luke, chapter 15, we read that the Prodigal Son after living a dissolute life says, 'I will break away and return to my father, and say to him, Father I have sinned against God and against you; I no longer deserve to be called your son.' Now this is repentance, and the father responds, 'He was lost and is found.' Then the celebration began; there was no celebration before repentance. In an earlier parable, Jesus says, 'I tell you, there will likewise be more joy in heaven over one *repentant* sinner than over ninety-nine righteous people who have no need to *repent.*' The joy is for the repentant sinner, and the celebration begins when the lost son is found. That's what I was trying to understand last night before you hit me with God is outside of physical sequential time."

"Wow," Parker replied, "I see you've been thinking about this all day."

"Yes, in between raising our four children and dealing with daily events. So, darling husband, what do you think about the unconditional word as an adjective describing God's love?"

"Love in the English language has many different meanings. You recall in the Scripture an exchange between Peter and the resurrected Jesus has Jesus asking Peter three times if Peter loves him, and, in the Greek translation, Peter's love response is always *phila.* The first two times, Jesus uses the word *agape*, and finally in the third question Jesus accepts *phila*. Thus, I think English needs an adjective to describe God's love. Do you have a word to replace unconditional?"

"I would use unwavering love," said Rosemary, without hesitation.

"I think unwavering works. Of course, remember unconditional in the original formulation is only being applied to God's love. To think unconditional love allows us to do wrong and to deliberately break God's commandments because God loves us anyway is a mistake in logic."

Rosemary went into a long think before answering, "Yes, I see what you mean. The trouble is that I, along with millions of other folks, sometimes have a problem with logic. I'm going to avoid those problems and think, 'God's unwavering love,' whenever I hear 'God's unconditional love.'

I'm not going to object if a priest uses 'unconditional'; however, the commandments need to be followed, and I don't need verbal distractions. Besides, I think of my love for my children as unwavering, and I'd be really upset if any of them went astray. I'd try to bring that child back to common sense." With that, Rosemary climbed into bed and offered Parker her hand, which he took. They looked into each other's eyes—hers soft blue and clear, and his brown and moist over what she'd said.

Parker kissed her on the lips and gave thanks for Rosemary's unwavering love for him and their children. His mind went back to when he proposed to her. He had a ring for her and dropped to his knees, acknowledging he loved her and would always be there for her – that was an outward sign of his unwavering love.

"Here are four kisses, my love, one for each of our children," said Parker. He then started kissing Rosemary, slowly and carefully, with each kiss lasting longer than the prior kiss. At the end, Rosemary was very happy, smiling and removing her pajamas, saying, "Twice in one week is good, and I'm still in the safe part of my period. Even if I weren't, I wouldn't mind a fifth child with you."

(17) The Second Murder

The next morning, Ray called Parker on the phone to report there was no contact Thursday night between Miles and Paula. Ray, by taking a close look at all the photographs of Miles in his personnel file from the prior investigation, noticed there were two photos from the Christmas party the year Paula joined the firm, showing her and Miles dancing in one photo and holding hands at their table in the second photo. This certainly wasn't conclusive proof that they were a couple back then, but perhaps an indication that something had subsequently developed. Meanwhile, Jim had been following Jeremy and reported he and Natasha didn't meet on Thursday night. However, he found out a few things about Jeremy's background. He had gone to a Catholic high school, where many of the men went on to become priests. That certainly was not the case for Jeremy, who discovered women, or they found him, and he stopped going to church. He majored in accounting at college, and since then his life had been all women and auditing finances.

Parker thought of various ways to jump start an investigation into what was happening at the board of directors of Regular Solids and where they were in their thinking about the appointment of a new leader once William

Pillsbury stepped down. He called the offices of Benjamin Q. Damon, who oversaw the independent auditing firm that handled Regular Solids. He'd done actuarial consulting work for him in the past, and Benjamin had recommended Parker to Mrs. Pillsbury, which is why she called Parker in the first place. Moreover, Mr. Damon was one of the six hand-picked members of the board of directors of Regular Solids and helped William Pillsbury run the private company. Parker thought he might gain some overall insights as to what was going on with Regular Solids if he had the opportunity to talk to Benjamin directly. Parker was able to get on Benjamin's calendar for a meeting Monday afternoon in Damon's office at four o'clock.

Parker then called the office of Natasha Pillsbury with the same idea. However, to get her away from the office and the ears of Paula's eavesdropping, he decided to invite Natasha to lunch.

Paula answered the telephone, "Oh, Mr. Spooner, Natasha isn't in the office today. Tonight is her big gala at the Art Institute. May I have her call you on Monday, or do you wish to leave a message?"

"That's okay—I'll try again on Monday, and there's no message—thank you."

Parker looked at the morning papers and saw the Art Institute was holding a special Friday evening fundraising gala hosted by Natasha Pillsbury. It was by invitation only, closed to almost everyone except the rich donors and expected to raise at least two million dollars. These were the events that kept Natasha in the news. She would circulate among the invited, making casual talk, sipping wine, and munching expensive snacks as docents led the small but elite crowd through the museum.

However, that night, everything changed. Parker's home telephone rang about eleven o'clock. He was reading in bed, waiting for Rosemary, who'd just finished showering, "Who in the world would be calling at this hour?" she yelled from the bathroom.

It was Ray Ulster. "Sorry to bother you and your family at this late hour, Parker, but it looks like Miles Clayton has been shot and murdered in a motel room near O'Hare Airport. The place is called the Open Doors Motel, and there are a whole bunch of police and an ambulance here in the parking lot. I'm waiting for confirmation that it was Miles. The police haven't said anything official, and it looks like it's going to go on for some time, so I thought I'd call and let you know before you went to sleep."

"Okay, thank you for letting me know. Will you be able to stay as long as the police are there?"

"Yes, there's no problem for me to stay. I also thought you'd want to know what I've already observed."

"Absolutely, please continue."

"I was following Miles this evening after he left his house around eight. I thought he might be on his way to Paula's, as he did last Tuesday night. Instead, he came to the motel by himself, parked his car, and checked into one of the rooms. After some time, I entered the place and asked the clerk for Miles Clayton's room number. She gave it to me, number sixty-one, and I located the room, which was an inside room. That is, the door to his room opened to an inside corridor, not to the outside. That made it difficult to watch since I couldn't stand in the corridor without giving myself away. I put my ear to the door, and I heard the television was on. I went outside and located his window. The drapes were closed, but the light was on. The motel was starting to fill up, and the place was noisy, not only on the inside but also the outside, with traffic and low-flying planes landing at O'Hare. I went back to my car, which had a clear view of Miles's car. I figured Miles wasn't staying the entire night since he didn't have a bag when he walked in. As a matter of fact, the only thing he was carrying when he walked into the motel was a home movie camera. I thought he might be coming out late, and I might see who he was with. I was prepared to stay there for some time; however, about ten o'clock, I heard a police siren. The first patrol car stopped at the motel's front entrance, and both policemen drew their guns and ran in. That was followed by more police cars and an ambulance and then detectives. I tried to get back to the room sixty-one corridor, but barriers were set up, and the police asked the crowd to disperse and keep moving as they emptied the motel of guests. I circulated around the building to its side and talked to people who were inside the motel where the shots happened, and they said a man in room sixty-one was shot dead. I'm assuming it was Miles."

"Okay, Ray, thanks for the information. I think you should give the police on the scene that information as soon as you can, especially since you asked the clerk for Miles's room number, and they're going to be looking for you as a possible suspect. Tell the police detectives you're working for me, and you were following Miles on a case."

"Do I tell them everything?"

"Yes, absolutely, tell them everything you observed tonight. They can contact me tomorrow for the details about the case."

"Call you directly?"

"Yes, that's good, and we'll talk again after I meet with the police. Have a good night."

Rosemary had come into the bedroom and sat on the bed in her pajamas, "More trouble with the Real Solids company and Natasha?"

"Yes, it appears Miles has been shot and murdered in some motel room. I was going to take the kids to the movies tomorrow afternoon to see *Airport*, but I'm probably not going to be able to do that because the police will want to talk to me."

"If Anna can go, then I'll take all the kids," said Rosemary. "Is this a movie we can take a four year old to see?"

In 1968, a rating system had been introduced to help individuals determine if the movie was suitable, especially for children. Parker responded, "It's rated G, so it's probably okay for Anna from that point of view; however, I don't know about its length because it's a long movie, nearly two-and-a-half hours, and that's a long time for Anna to sit in a darkened theater. It's also a drama about a bomber on an airplane, so it may be too much for her, but most of it will be beyond her understanding. It has an all-star cast, but she doesn't know and wouldn't recognize Burt Lancaster, Dean Martin, or any of the other actors. On the other hand, it's in color, with a large screen and shows airplanes, snowstorms, and lots of people moving around."

"What kind of reviews has it gotten?" asked Rosemary.

"Your favorite movie critic, Roger Ebert, only gave it two stars but admitted it held his interest for a couple of hours before the movie became ridiculous. Generally, it has mixed reviews but seems to be a blockbuster and is making a lot of money. It's been playing in theaters since spring and is likely to be gone if we don't go see it soon."

"I think it would be good for Anna. I've been talking to her about growing up and being a big girl. She can sit next to me, with big sister Grace on the other side. I think she'd love being with us."

"Okay, my love, we'll plan on you taking the four children tomorrow to the movies." And, with that, Rosemary said her evening prayers, and the Spooners turned off the bedroom lights. Parker found it difficult to sleep because he'd now become entangled in two murders, first Dave and now Miles. Ever perceptive, Rosemary knew discovering Dave's murder and then locating Nicole had impacted and troubled her husband in a different way because she intuitively understood her husband was physically attracted to Nicole. He was a man and had to deal with beautiful young women all the time in his investigations. One of these days, she knew, one of those ladies would likely catch his fancy because he loved beauty. Knowing Parker, he'd be able to handle it, but, nevertheless, she had to be there for him, to support him, and to remind him of what he'd already accomplished, and what he already had.

Meanwhile, Parker wasn't asleep and was thinking about Miles's murder. It sounded like a hit job, and he wondered what the police had discovered. He thought Natasha certainly had a motive to kill Miles because she'd gain control of the company, but hiring a hit man wasn't something she'd do. She was smart enough to know, as the president of an investment company, she'd forever be a blackmail target if she approached a hit man or the mob. It was also possible the murder had nothing to do with the Regular Solids company. Ray said Miles carried a movie camera into the motel. That would indicate he was planning to film something or someone at the motel, and that sex was likely involved in this crime. It was useless to speculate at this point, and thus Parker put the murder out of his mind.

The thought of sex, however, started Parker thinking of his lovemaking the prior night with Rosemary. She'd surprised him with the idea of a fifth child. If that was going to happen, it should happen soon because she was now at an age where it was more difficult to conceive, even if they sexually engaged every day during her fertile period. Parker would raise the issue directly with her, and they'd decide. Parker's thoughts then turned to Nicole and how happy she became when he gave her an actuarial problem. It reminded him of how much he enjoyed doing mathematics. Parker turned over in bed but didn't immediately fall asleep because he kept thinking about both Rosemary and Nicole.

(18) Earlier in the Night, before the Second Murder

Miles parked his car in the Open Doors Motel parking lot around half past eight on the evening of Friday, September 25, 1970. Carrying only a handheld movie camera, he entered their lobby. He'd made a reservation for room sixty-one earlier in the week, and Mollie, the desk clerk, gave him his motel key. She wasn't surprised he had no luggage and carried only a camera. It was normal for individuals who rented room sixty-one to be traveling light and carrying cameras.

Once in his room, he turned on the lights, closed the window drapes, placed the camera on the bed, and removed the light jacket he wore, hanging it on the back of a chair. There was an empty closet on the left side of the motel room near the door, then a dresser with a lighted lamp, followed by a TV on a stand. The far end of the room had a desk and a chair beneath windows covered by the drawn drapes. On the right side of the room was a Queen size bed with a large wooden piece of artwork over it. The bathroom was situated near the entrance and opposite the closet. Miles was wearing a white, short-sleeved shirt, gray slacks, and black shoes. He turned on the black-and-white television and sat on the bed next to his camera. He touched his goatee, looked at his watch, and thought he'd arrived early and now had a good hour to wait.

He wasn't aware Ray Ulster had followed him and had asked Mollie for his room number and then checked out the location of room sixty-one from the inside hallway and then outside the window before returning to his car. Shortly before ten, there was a knock on the door. Miles stood up and answered it. The tattoos on his arms were partially hidden by his shirt but still clearly visible as he opened the door to two bullets pumped into his chest. He fell back dead into the room. The door of room number sixty-one remained ajar, as the unseen killer ran out of the nearby motel exit door into the parking lot along the side of the motel.

(19) Entanglement/Connections

The next morning Detective Sergeant Kevin Garber called and asked Parker to visit him at the Area Five police station regarding the murder of Miles Clayton. Parker had worked with Kevin before, and, as a homicide detective, Kevin Garber was in the same position in that police area as Michael Boyle was in Area Six. Parker glanced at the Saturday morning newspapers to see if Miles's murder had made it into print. They didn't have details or the name of the murder victim but merely reported in a side column—that a man had been shot and killed at the Open Doors Motel near O'Hare Airport.

Natasha, however, was in the morning newspapers, big time. The gala at the Art Institute was a huge success—one headline hailed it, writing, "Natasha Pillsbury's Gala Raises Millions for Art Institute." The article showed two photographs of her, both credited to photographer Joseph Johnson. The first, labelled *Arrival at Gala*, showed Natasha getting out of a yellow cab, while the second showed her in a stunning evening dress, wearing a gorgeous sparkling necklace, surrounded by Chicago's smiling art patrons.

Parker put the newspapers to the side and talked to his kids, telling them

he had to work, and their mother would be taking them to the movies on

Saturday afternoon. Anna would be going, and this would be her first

movie. The children were excited, and Anna started strutting around the

house, walking very straight. She was a big girl now. John asked his dad

for a few minutes to talk about physics. The father and son sat together in

John's room. "Entanglement," John said, "Quantum entanglement—can

you explain it to me in your own words?"

"I'll try to explain, but remember I'm not a physicist, and these

phenomena are happening in the micro-world. Entanglement has to do

with the state of particles after they've interacted with each other. You

remember when we talked about Schrodinger, that superposition of states

for quantum particles is an experimental reality. Can you tell me in your

own words what superposition means?"

"I think it means the particle is in two places at the same time," replied

John.

"Good," said Parker, "Now, sometimes, particles become correlated or

connected in some way, and the way physicists describe that in their math

is through one equation. That is, after the interaction or connection, there's no separate wave function to describe each particle; rather, they're described with one equation or what physicists call one joint wave function for the two particles. That's entanglement, and if you had two entangled electrons, and you knew the spin of one, then you'd automatically know the spin of the other electron, without any measurement, even if they're separated by great distances."

John nodded that he understood what Parker had just conveyed, and the father continued, "However, this caused a great debate in physics. Albert Einstein called it 'spooky action at a distance' because his theory of relativity showed information cannot be transmitted faster than the speed of light. He thought something else had to be involved. Then Einstein and others devised a thought experiment to show the wave function of quantum physics was not a complete description of physical reality."

"And what happened? Was this thought experiment accepted?"

"No, it was debated, and, in 1964, another physicist, John Bell, came up with an actual experiment to determine whether quantum mechanics is correct. He devised a way to test if reality is 'spooky' or if there could be a better explanation of the correlations between entangled particles. This research is still going on; however, as of now, the quantum micro-world is real. 'Spooky' is real, and particles separated at great distances can be entangled."

"What do you think, Dad? In the real world, can something that's really far, far away from us somehow have an immediate impact on us?"

"Yes, I think that's possible. Certainly physical distance is not a barrier for God's love and grace to be available for us. Similarly, entanglement involves a connection between particles but not a physical connection." Parker paused and looked at his son before continuing. "It's also possible the sudden insights I have when I'm doing investigations might be some form of entanglement that impacts our macro real world, bringing people and events together."

At this moment, Rosemary called the kids for an early lunch and told them to get ready for the movie. Parker also had a quick sandwich with them and then took off for the police station. He arrived there around noon, and Sergeant Garber asked him to first view the body in the temporary morgue, located in the building's basement. In many ways, Sergeant Kevin Garber was "the spitting image" of Parker's father-in-law, approximately the same age and with similar facial features and gestures. The Area Five homicide site was at the same location as the Fourteenth

District police station. The Fourteenth Police District only covered a small portion of the north side of Chicago, away from Lake Michigan, while Area Five covered the entire Northwest portion of the city, all the way to O'Hare Airport. In terms of population, it was the largest police area in the city.

Sergeant Garber and Parker walked down the stairs into the temporary morgue, where they were greeted by a technician, a young woman in a blue medical gown wearing a name tag that read "Joan." She had a gently pointed face that sloped toward her chin, contrasted by soft brown eyes, a light shade of lipstick, and two pigtails that kept her long blondish hair together behind her ears at the back of her neck. Parker noticed she wore a small golden cross around her neck that had slipped to the outside of her medical gown. Joan opened and withdrew a drawer in the side wall that held the body, allowing Sergeant Garber to remove the sheet that covered the corpse. "Do you recognize him as Miles Clayton, the man you were investigating?" he asked Parker, who nodded yes. The body had been cleaned, but there were two obvious bullet holes near his heart that disfigured the chest area. His eyes were shut, and his face strangely peaceful, creating the illusion that perhaps he was only sleeping. Parker noticed Miles's tattoos on his arms had faded and were nearly invisible. "What happened to his tattoos?" he asked.

Sergeant Garber looked puzzled, but Joan knew what he meant and spoke up immediately, "His two tattoos aren't real and were already faded, and now they have almost disappeared, after I cleaned the body." Parker noted Joan had a distinct French-Canadian accent. At this moment, someone shouted down the steps that Sergeant Garber was needed upstairs for a phone call with the police superintendent. Garber excused himself. Parker looked at Joan, and she continued talking about fake tattoos, "I'm surprised how technology has improved for making realistic looking but not real tattoos. Apparently, there's a market for impressing people that you're serious enough to show a tattoo but not that serious about making them permanent."

"You've seen someone trying to impress another person with a fake tattoo?" Parker asked.

Joan laughed out loud, "Yes, my ex-boyfriend had my full name, Joan Jobin, tattooed on his arm. I got alarmed because I hadn't done anything to encourage him to take what I thought was a serious step. I was relieved it wasn't permanent, and he quickly washed it away."

"Interesting," Parker said, "I've seen old photographs of Miles, and the tattoos are there. He must have periodically replaced them as they started to fade. The tattoos represent the advertising symbols of his company, and, yes, he did impress his boss by having them. Perhaps he didn't feel comfortable with real tattoos but was willing to replace them as the fake ones faded. He was very much involved with his company and it wasn't clear whether having their advertising symbols tattooed on his arms was a conviction that his company had a handle on profitable investments or merely his way of currying favor with William Pillsbury, the founder of the company; however, having fake tattoos was certainly a way of hedging his bets against something permanent."

Sergeant Garber's telephone call was taking longer than expected, and Parker continued his conversation with Joan by asking her if she was a full-time forensic morgue technician.

"Yes," she replied. "I graduated this spring with a degree in biology from Northwestern University, and the city of Chicago hired me. I live in Evanston, and this location is more convenient for me than the main morgue, which is further south. Here we start early at 7:00 a.m. and finish by 3:00 p.m., so I miss the heaviest traffic, both coming to work and going. I work Tuesdays through Saturdays, so tonight is party time, and I love to dance. C'est si bon!"

She was young, enthusiastic, and a joy to behold. Parker continued, "Dancing is wonderful. Do you go with someone special, or does a group of your friends go together?"

"I go with a couple of my girlfriends. We're always hoping to meet someone, but even if that doesn't happen, we always have a good time out on the floor by ourselves."

"Joan," Parker replied, "Now this is an interesting coincidence, but I was having a similar conversation last Wednesday with a young policeman who grew up in Evanston. He visits his parents there on the weekends. He just finished his bachelor's degree in engineering from Northwestern University and said to me he was going to start attending some parish events at St. Joan of Arc parish."

Joan's brown eyes opened wide, and she gasped, "That happens to be my parish, and, by the way, my parents named me Joan for Joan of Arc. Do you think your police friend will be there tonight? What's his name? What does he look like?"

"His name is Chester Wojcik, and he's about 6 feet tall, brown eyes, and brown hair with a clean, open face. I don't know if he's going to be there, but he said he was thinking about it."

"Oh," cried Joan, clasping her hands together, "I'm going to say a prayer that, if this is God's will, to please push Mr. Wojcik out of his door tonight in the direction of St. Joan of Arc parish."

Parker heard Sergeant Garber on the stairs returning to the basement and immediately decided to give Joan his calling card, "My name is Parker Spooner. You can use this card to introduce yourself to Chet if you meet him, and I hope your prayers are answered and that you and Chet have a wonderful time tonight dancing and talking." Parker thought that, in our macro-world, this is one way people become entangled. There's no wave function to describe entangled people in the macro-world, but almost every person is connected to other people or things in some specialized way that reflects their desires. The coincidence of Joan and Chet belonging to the same parish and then meeting at a dance because of his actions might be called chance, but Parker reminded himself that not even chance occurrences fall outside the scope of the universal cause.

"Sorry for the delay, Parker," said Sergeant Garber. "I wanted you to see the body and confirm this is the guy you were investigating. As you can see, two bullets in the chest—we don't have the murder weapon, but we'll be able to identify the gun if we find it. Let's go to my office."

With that, Parker said goodbye to Joan and followed Garber to his office. At the top of the stairs, Parker glanced over his shoulder and saw the vibrant and very much alive Joan Jobin enclosing the still—and very much dead—Miles Clayton back into the wall.

(20) The Double Appears

Detective Sergeant Kevin Garber's office space was a mess. There were papers, files, and boxes everywhere—on the floor and on the chairs in front of an immense wooden desk that had two televisions connected by wires that looked like coiled snakes—some that went to outlets in the wall and others along the windows and out to the antennas on the roof. He moved a box off a chair to the floor and motioned Parker to sit. Parker sat, and Garber started, "Thank you for coming out to talk to me directly. I have here the report of your operative, Ray Ulster. He described your prior and recent surveillance of the murder victim and stated Miles visited Paula Dean at her apartment last Tuesday evening. He noted Miles had no luggage with him when he entered the motel, only a home movie camera. Yes, it appeared to our police on the scene that Miles was waiting for a lover and expected to do some filming. When he opened the door, instead of the anticipated sex, he got two bullets. However, there may be much more involved in this murder because Ray's report says Mrs. Pillsbury asked you to investigate Miles months ago because she didn't trust him. Your investigation didn't find any wrongdoing. Is this narrative correct, and, if it is, then is there anything you can add to it to make it more complete?"

"Yes, it's accurate; however, I'll add some details. Paula Dean, Natasha's executive secretary, was spying on her and reporting information to Miles. It's likely we didn't find anything on Miles when we first investigated him because Paula told him about our investigation. I also observed Natasha and her auditor, Jeremy Wilson, kissing in the back seat of her limo last Tuesday night, so there appears to be office romances going on at Regular Solids, which certainly muddy the waters of a murder investigation. Additionally, there was severe competition between Natasha and Miles for the top job at Regular Solids once William fully retires."

"When we talked to Natasha about the reported competition between Miles and her, she brushed it off, saying her approach to the business was different from Miles's approach, and William as the chairman made the decisions. William nodded yes to that and agreed with his wife."

Parker responded, "Did Natasha bring up her doppelganger? She had me in her office last Monday to talk about this double who was bothering her."

Garber shook his head sideways, "No, we didn't discuss a double. However, our police in questioning people who were at the motel last night reported a man thought he saw Natasha Pillsbury running in the parking lot. This woman was in a hurry and carried a purse and wore a long-sleeved white blouse and a black skirt. We dismissed the notion that this woman was Natasha because all the news coverage last night and this morning in the papers has been about the Art Institute Gala, where dozens of people saw Natasha face to face. A Natasha double, however, is certainly a person of interest and adds another dimension to our investigation. Additionally, the fact that Mrs. Pillsbury asked you to investigate Miles months ago also raises the question as to whether her suspicions of him back then have any connection with his murder last night. Why did she want you to investigate him?"

"Natasha told me she didn't like him and didn't trust him. She thought he might be doing something illegal with the company's money but said her auditor Jeremy Wilson kept telling her that wasn't the case. Thus, she hired me to find some dirt on Miles. We didn't find anything wrong with him, and, she, in turn, stopped the investigation. Then suddenly last Monday she asked me to visit her office, and she talked about a double who's been bothering her, and I observed that Paula, her secretary, is likely eavesdropping on Natasha."

"All of this background certainly complicates this murder. However, if I ask who had a motive to kill Miles, then Natasha gaining control of the company obviously comes to my mind," said Garber.

Parker smiled and nodded, "I had the same thought last night; however, company executives don't physically kill their internal competition for a job position. They just show their talent in running the business or use office politics and outclass their competition. Nevertheless, I wonder if Natasha hired someone to shoot Miles?"

Garber responded, "I've asked our mob task force to check this out. Guys are usually brought in from Vegas or Florida to do the hit. We would find this out quickly if it happened. If an amateur was hired, he almost certainly left clues, and we should discover that soon." He paused and then continued, "Early information can be the difference in breaking a case, and your information has already added to this case in a significant way. If you have any questions or need anything, please ask me. I know you're Boyle's son-in-law and have helped the police in the past. I welcome your input."

"My only question at this moment is why the people in the motel who heard the shots didn't come out into the hallway and perhaps see the killer fleeing?"

"As far as we can determine, the shooter waited for an overhead plane, and this noise along with the underlying noise created by everyone having their televisions on, was enough to dampen the shots at the other end of the hall. Moreover, the two different couples who reported the shots didn't immediately run out into the hallway but came out of their rooms very slowly. Miles was in a corner room with a side hallway next to his room that led to an exit door at the rear of the motel. The killer probably ran out of the motel using that exit seconds after the shooting. The room next to Miles had been booked for the night but was vacant, so there was no one there to hear the shots. The couple in room sixty across the hall from Miles was getting ready for bed. They said they heard two shots. The husband remarked something about a gun being fired and moved toward the door, but his wife initially stopped him from going out into the hallway. After a minute or so of silence, they opened the door, as did the couple next to them in room sixty-two. They both agreed they'd heard two shots across the hall and observed the door to room sixty-one open. As soon as they approached the room, they saw Miles on the floor of his room, bleeding from the chest with all the lights in the room on and the television playing. They immediately called the lobby and the police to report the shooting."

"Does the motel have any cameras on the grounds that take photographs of the guests coming and going?"

"Unfortunately, they don't. The place is old and has a reputation as being a one-night stand flop house, which is why your man's testimony is our main lead right now."

"Would you give me permission to look at room sixty-one in the motel?" Parker asked.

Sergeant Garber looked pleased at the request. "I can take you there right now if you have time. I want to look it over again."

In his car, Parker followed Garber's police car to the motel. Garber showed him Miles's car in the parking lot, where the murdered man had left it last night. "We went through his car this morning and didn't find anything of interest," said Sergeant Garber, "and we'll be towing it away tonight." They walked through the motel lobby, which was crowded with customers who were checking into the place for Saturday night. They made their way along a corridor to a perpendicular hallway where the corner room was marked with the numeral sixty-one. A policeman was standing by that doorway behind a barrier that said Crime Scene, Do Not Cross. Room sixty-one was the first room in a long corridor of rooms on both sides of the hallway. Garber pointed out an exit door that was at the end of the corridor they'd just walked down. It was the doorway the killer used to escape. "You see how easy it was for the shooter to just run out of the building unseen after pulling the trigger twice? Even if people had come out of their rooms quickly, they wouldn't have seen them," said Garber.

The policeman opened the door to room sixty-one, and Parker and the sergeant entered. The first thing Parker noticed was a huge bloodstain on the carpet behind the door. On the left, there was a closet, a dresser, and a TV stand. A desk sat by the windows at the far end of the room. The drapes had been pulled open, and sunlight streamed into the room. On the right there was a bathroom and a Queen size bed with a large wooden piece of artwork over it. "We dusted for prints but didn't find anything unusual. The killer never entered the room and almost certainly wore gloves while knocking on the door with one hand, pulling the trigger with the other."

Parker walked around the room, looking at the bathroom and the closet. The wooden artwork above the bed then caught his attention. It was rectangular, measuring 4 feet in length and 3 feet in height, protruding about 2 inches out of the wall. Blended into the wood along each side were what appeared to be hinges, and, as part of the design, the artwork was divided equally into two halves, with a left side and a right side. Parker got up on the bed on his knees to take a closer look at the small vertical separation that distinguished the left side of the artwork from the right side. There were two small knobs, one on each side of the separation that served as handles, and when Parker pulled on them, two doors opened outward into the room, revealing a four by three piece of reflective glass flush with the wall. Parker immediately recognized the glass as a two-way mirror that could be used to view the interior of the adjacent room, number sixty-three, which had been vacant Friday night. That is, he knew he wasn't looking at a normal mirror hanging on the wall but a four by three piece of glass that allowed the occupant of room sixty-one with proper lighting to spy on the neighboring room. These mirrors were used in police interrogations and were called one-way mirrors—also known as two-way mirrors by the public.

When Sergeant Garber saw the one-way mirror, he swore under his breath and grabbed the phone on the desk, calling the lobby and demanding the manager bring the key to room sixty-three immediately to him, along with the details as to who booked that room Friday night and failed to show. He then drew the blinds in room sixty-one and turned off the lights, instructing the police officer to stay in the darkened room while he and Parker waited in the hallway. Several minutes later, the manager arrived. He was a short man with lots of hair and dark eyes that darted everywhere. He opened the door to room sixty-three, and they entered, turning on all the lights. The furniture in the room was symmetrical with the furniture in room sixty-one, with one difference; on the left side of room sixty-three, there was no wooden artwork above the Queen size bed, only the mirror flush against the wall. The manager, Garber, and Parker viewed themselves in the mirror. The police office in room sixty-one on the opposite side of the mirror shouted, "I can see the three of you and your room clearly through this glass."

Sergeant Garber growled at the manager, "How many rooms in this motel have a one-way mirror like rooms sixty-one and sixty-three?"

"There are two other combinations like this, rooms twenty-one and twenty-three are connected with one-way mirrors, as are rooms forty-one and forty-three," answered the manager, his eyes flashing back and forth between Sergeant Garber and the mirror.

"I want the names and license plate numbers of everyone who has used rooms twenty-one, forty-one, and sixty-one this year and then also the names and plates of everyone who has used rooms twenty-three, forty-three, sixty-three," snapped Garber, looking directly at the manager.

"I don't think the motel owners would want me to do that. The customers who use these rooms wouldn't want that information known," replied the manager, looking down at the floor.

"These mirrors are illegal because they can be used to either blackmail people or to make pornographic films, both of which are against the law. Tell your owners if I don't have within the next three days the names of the people who recently used these rooms, then I'll get a court order to close the Open Doors Motel. Do you understand?"

The manager nodded yes.

Garber then growled, "Don't just nod. Answer me yes or no that the names and plate numbers you have will be provided to me within three days."

"Yes, sir, you'll have them," he replied, looking directly at the angry sergeant.

"Now tell me who booked room sixty-three last night and remember your answer to this particular question is part of a murder investigation."

The manager thought for several seconds, his eyes darting around the room, but then he quickly looked at Garber, "Some guy booked the room last Tuesday and gave his name as Joe Hall. He paid cash. According to the register, he said he'd provide the license plate number when he arrived on Friday. We don't know who this guy is. He never arrived last night."

"I want to talk to the clerk who took the money and get a description of this Joe Hall."

"That would be Mollie. She works the desk Monday through Friday. She's not here today."

Garber was disgusted. He then turned Parker, "Do you want to ask this manager any questions?"

"Yes," Parker replied. Turning to the manager, he asked, "Has Miles Clayton, the murder victim, ever used this motel in the past?"

"No, we never heard of him before last night."

With that Sergeant Garber told the manager he could go—but to remember his three days deadline for providing names to the police. Parker decided it was also time for him to go and allow the police to continue their investigation. He excused himself.

Back home the kids were all excited about the movie *Airport* that they'd just seen. Peter grabbed one of his play airplanes, flew it around the house, and made a safe emergency landing in his room. Anna, according to her mother, had been particularly good in the theater. "I brought some of Anna's toys, her coloring book, and my little flashlight. When she wasn't watching the screen, she spent time coloring or quietly playing with the toys in her seat," said Rosemary. *What a good mother you are*, Parker thought, *I'm fortunate to have you as my wife*. He then called for a couple of pizzas to be delivered, and the family sat around the table discussing the movie as they ate the pizzas and drank soft drinks. The older kids talked about the different scenes in the movie that had impressed them. The mother whispered to the father, "Not a believable movie. It's pure fluff but very entertaining if you don't take any of it seriously." The father smiled and wished he could have said the same about his afternoon, where his thoughts were of a dead Miles being slid into a wall and a sleezy motel with two-way mirrors.

The Spooner family had a stack of back *Life* magazines in their living room, and Parker found the issue that had a feature on Natasha Pillsbury. He reread the article to refresh his memory and to see if he could get any further insights into her. He couldn't, but a full-length colored photograph of Natasha stared back at him and looked vaguely like another face he'd recently seen but couldn't place.

Later that evening the telephone rang. It was Jim Rowdy. "I tried calling you this afternoon but there was no answer. I followed Jeremy Wilson yesterday after he left work. He was at a house party in his apartment complex Friday night. Anyway, it was nearly ten when I decided it would be a waste of time to sit there all night while the party was going on and took a ride to visit Natasha's condominium, since you mentioned something may be happening between Natasha and Jeremy, and I wanted to get a feel for her place. I parked my car on the street and walked around the condominium. It has outside benches to sit on and a parking garage off the street. Cars go down a ramp into the basement of the building. There's a gate at the bottom of the ramp with an attendant in a booth. A sign at the top of the ramp read, 'No Parking. Temporarily Full.' I walked past the garage to the main building and took a quick look inside the lobby, where there was another attendant before you can even get to the elevator bank. It was a busy place. People were coming and going. I noticed the Pillsburys have their own private elevator to get from the top floor to the basement. That's certainly convenient for them to be able to skip all the other floors on their way to the garage. Anyway, on my way out of the complex, I was on the street sidewalk, heading back toward my car parked up the block and approaching the parking garage ramp when I saw Natasha driving a car into the basement garage. That surprised me because I always thought she was chauffeured around in a limousine, but that wasn't a limo she was driving. When I reached the entrance, Natasha's car had already disappeared into the basement garage. Today I read in the newspapers that Natasha was at the Art Institute yesterday evening; however, I saw her entering the basement garage around half past ten, which doesn't make any sense, and which is why I'm mentioning this particular observation to you."

"I imagine you only saw part of Natasha through the car window and only for a few seconds. Do you remember what she was wearing?" asked Parker.

"It was a white blouse, and you're correct it was only for a few seconds. I only saw her left side profile; however, the entrance is well illuminated, and I clearly saw her distinctive red hair."

"What about the car? I guess you couldn't see the license plate number, since you only saw the side of the car, not the front or back; but what about its make and color?"

"It was a light blue 1966 two-door Food Falcon, and yes, I couldn't see the license plate number from the side," replied Jim.

Parker told him this was an important piece of information, and that he should write it up and get the report to Sergeant Garber immediately. Rowdy said he would and then added that Jeremy went to his office to work on Saturday afternoon, came home, and now was at another house party. "The guy is a real party animal, two parties on back-to-back Friday and Saturday nights, but so far I didn't see any contact between him and Natasha." Parker thanked Jim for his good work. His observation of Natasha driving a car showed the double had returned, and the second

Natasha had been active the night of the murder. Also, Parker thought there were many light blue 1966 two-door Ford Falcons in Chicagoland, but that was the color, year, and make of the car Nicole drove when she followed his Oldsmobile Cutlass to the police station last Tuesday afternoon. That car belonged to Denise, and the thought crossed Parker's mind that somehow Denise, Nicole's roommate, might be connected to or involved in Miles's murder. The next time he spoke to Nicole, he'd ask her about the car.

The next day was Sunday, and the entire Spooner family went to mass and, after church, went out to eat brunch. The afternoon was clear and cool, and they went to the Brookfield Zoo and then supper at a local restaurant. Rosemary was beaming from ear to ear, "This is great— consecutive meals over two days in a row and no cooking. It's like a mini vacation."

"Your cooking is great Mom. The food here is okay but nothing like what you make," said ten-year-old Peter. The teenagers quickly doubled down and supported his statement. Anna smiled at her mother.

The father made it unanimous, "I have to agree with our children, my love. Your cooking gets five stars, but it's wonderful to give you a break every now and then."

Back home Peter got into his pajamas and as usual grabbed a book and started to read; Grace and John were in their bedrooms doing homework for school while the parents put Anna to bed and then looked at the various weekly papers that had arrived with the Saturday mail and the Sunday newspapers. Parker noted the late Sunday editions had articles about the Friday night murder of Miles. They didn't have many details but reported Miles was the financial and operating officer and a long-time employee of Regular Solids Investments, and he was shot twice in the chest at the Open Doors Motel. The police were investigating the crime, but there were no suspects. Parker put the paper down and started to think again about the case.

Rosemary was reading the Catholic newspaper and columnist who the prior week had been opposed to the word *unconditional* to describe God's love, and she started talking to Parker, "The columnist has received a number of critical letters for his view; one letter said God's love is unconditional, and His love for Hitler and Mother Teresa is the same; a second letter called his column questioning 'unconditional' as 'near heresy' and quoted the Prodigal Son parable to show the young son did everything wrong, and yet the father continued to love him, which proved unconditional love; a third letter said God's love is unconditional; however, we have to reach out and grab that extended hand."

"How did the columnist respond?" Parker asked.

Rosemary replied, "He pushed back and wrote: 'Yes, reaching out, repentance, and conversion are all conditions for God's love to become effective. In the parable of the Prodigal Son, the father waits patiently and is always there, but the celebration only begins when the son comes to his senses, repents, and returns home. There's no celebration as long as the son remains lost.' That was the point the columnist made originally—and what I was trying to understand the other night, my darling. Namely, God's love is always there—it's unwavering, as we said before; however, God doesn't love sin, which is harmful. The columnist then makes this clear when he continues by quoting St. Thomas Aquinas in his *Summa*: 'Nothing prevents one and the same thing being loved under one aspect, while it is hated under another. God loves sinners in so far as they are existing natures; for they have existence and have it from Him. In so far as they are sinners, they have no existence at all, but fall short of it; and this in them is not from God. Hence, under this aspect they are hated by Him.' The columnist then concludes by writing that this distinction helps us understand God's love for Mother Teresa asking for blessings and going out to help the poor isn't the same situation as Hitler murdering innocents in World War II because God's hated of sin is also present when innocents are murdered."

"Yes," said Parker, "avoiding sin is important. Sin is a transgression of divine law and sends a person off course. I think sin could prevent me from solving the cases that have been given to me. Certainly, I need to be ready to handle the events that will break in my two recent cases."

"Darling don't worry. I have no doubt that, using your skills, both the reasoning component and your intuitive insights, you'll be led to a satisfactory resolution of both murders."

Parker thought the conversation was over and moved to another topic on his mind. "The other night, my love, you mentioned another baby. Is that something you're seriously thinking about?"

"I've been doing more and more thinking about another child, and, yes, absolutely, I'm ready for another baby—how about you?"

"Yes, I think that would be wonderful," replied a smiling Parker.

And with that they embraced.

198

(21) Frank Explains the Double Slit Experiment

It was early Monday when Parker arrived at his office, and the telephone was already ringing. It was Frank Lawson, who was in a hurry and spoke in his usual rushed fashion, "I'd like to talk to you about what Nicole said to you last week. I haven't seen or called her since her return, as I promised you. I wonder if we could meet to discuss her situation. I'd like your advice as to how I should proceed with her. I have a class at eleven, which will be done at noon. There's a University of Chicago food court outside the Reynolds Club near the lecture building. Would it be possible for us to meet there for lunch today around quarter past noon?"

Parker told him yes.

He arrived at the food court early and took a seat at one of the tables. Frank arrived shortly thereafter and sat next to him. "How did your class go this morning?" inquired Parker.

"Good! I lectured on the double slit experiment. Are you familiar with it?"

Parker smiled and nodded yes as the two men started walking through the food court, selecting their luncheon items. Parker knew the double slit experiment first done by Thomas Young in 1801 was the physics experiment that helped fuel the quantum revolution in the 1920s. In fact, this experiment, with two holes or slits, was at the center of various ongoing scientific and philosophical arguments about reality. "Yes, I'm familiar with the double slit experiment. I recall Einstein had already shown in his paper on the photoelectric effect that light was made up of small particles or photons. At the same time, the double slit experiment repeatedly showed light was a wave. If you shine a light on a wall that has two small openings or slits, a diffraction pattern will appear on the other side of the barrier, similar to water ripples flowing through two openings."

"Yes," replied Frank, "a wave of water will be diffracted at the slits, and two new circular waves will spread out from each hole on the other side. As those waves bump into each other, they create a constructive and destructive interference pattern typical of ocean waves pounding rocky shorelines. If light is wavelike, then you'd expect to see an interference pattern on a screen behind the holes; and, in fact, this is the result of the double slit experiment using a light source. Thus, the double slit experiment first done in the early 1800s shows light is a wave."

Parker then said, "But if you shoot many small pellets at two holes, you get two patches of pellets on the other side, and that's not what you see with light, where you get an interference pattern. Hence, this experiment shows light can't be a particle, yet the photoelectric effect and Einstein showed light was a particle. That's the problem."

"Exactly," replied Frank, "physicists had a problem, a contradiction. The double slit experiment with light showed light behaves like a wave, but the photoelectric effect showed light is a particle. People started thinking of light not solely as a particle but as a particle wave."

The men had returned to their table and started eating in silence.

Frank then said, "Surprisingly, electrons also exhibit interference wave patterns when passing through the double slit, and thus this experiment also showed it wasn't correct to simply consider electrons to be particles. Indeed, to produce the pattern seen on the screen when firing electrons at it, the notion that somehow an electron passed simultaneously through both holes and interfered with itself became a possibility. That, of course, didn't make any sense if the electron was solely a particle. How could a single particle pass through two holes at the same time?"

"Yes," said Parker, "my son is taking high school physics and has been asking questions trying to understand wave-particle duality."

"The explanation I give is that, when you observe or see something, a light photon is involved, and, in the micro-world, the light photon disturbs the electron. By shining light on the experiment, the objective observer or physicist is interfering and changing the results of the experiment. The double slit experiment shows a wave pattern for electrons, but if you start observing the electrons, which physicists did by setting up counters, the electrons behave like particles, and you get a curve consistent with small pellets. The observer, the physicist, is interfering and changing the results of the experiment. If we don't look or count the electrons, we have a different distribution on the screen than we do when we count or look because light photons disturb electrons. Thus, I tell my students to think about it this way: to observe the micro-world, we must shine light on it, and this light interferes with the micro-world, the object of our study, and we generate probabilities, not certainty."

"That's what I said to my son, and this uncertainty occurs when physicists attempt to measure the position and momentum of a particle at any instant," replied Parker.

"Yes, and that's how I concluded my lecture today when I explained Heisenberg's uncertainty principle." And with that the two men finished eating and looked at each other. Parker knew Frank didn't want to talk physics with Parker, even though it was a subject Frank knew and loved. Rather he wanted to discuss Nicole, a person Frank said he loved but didn't know, either intellectually or physically. Frank was uncertain as to how to start a conversation with Parker about Nicole.

Parker smiled at him and offered, "You wanted to meet with me to discuss Nicole, so let's do that."

(22) A Conversation with Frank

"Yes, thank you for agreeing to meet with me," said Frank. He then started to explain why he wanted to talk. Parker sat back in his chair and allowed Frank to continue, "I was really surprised by what you told me last week. The fact Nicole hadn't disappeared but rather wanted to avoid me—and had informed our mutual friends she didn't want to see me—that hurt me. But, after some reflection, I can say she more or less told me the same thing to my face; however, I was so taken with her I didn't believe her. I thought she was just playing hard to get, and so I continued my efforts, and apparently I made a pest of myself. Finally, I went out and hired you to find her when she wasn't really missing. That was stupid of me. But then you did find her, and you gave it to me straight, and that was good. So thank you." Frank cast his eyes down.

Parker smiled and responded, "You're welcome. Of course, by taking your case, I did discover Dave's body—a murder—and I want to contribute to solving his murder. Thus, even though I found Nicole, as you requested, I'm still investigating and helping the police. I hope finding Dave's killer will, in some way, help Nicole." As he said this, Parker wondered why he felt that way—why he wanted to *help her* and what might this feeling mean. He didn't think that way about the people involved in his other cases.

Frank was oblivious to this and continued, "Yes, I think it's important to find out who killed Dave. This has to be devastating to her. Have you talked to Nicole? How is she doing?" Frank then got to his reason for meeting with Parker, "As I told you before, I'm really fond of her, and I'd like some advice from you as to how I should proceed with Nicole."

Parker understood. "I spoke to Nicole Thursday night at Dave's wake. She's under emotional stress regarding Dave's murder; however, she should be all right, short term. She has her actuarial examination coming up and appears to be focusing her thoughts there."

"Wouldn't that examination just add to her stress?"

"No, for many individuals, the exam process acts the opposite way because the actuarial examinations are structured to weed out people, even qualified individuals, to get the very best of an exceptionally good group. Nicole seems to understand this and has taken up the challenge, which means she's willing to put other things on the side when studying for the actuarial examinations."

"I heard those exams are difficult to pass, but I've never heard of them expressed that way," said Frank, pausing a moment before continuing, "When I give an examination, I want all my students to pass, and most of them know enough to pass. Can you give me examples of how an actuarial exam weeds out even qualified people?"

"Actuarial exams are written and administered by actuaries. The subject matter for the first exam is college mathematics through advanced calculus. All the exam takers who sign up for the Part One exam have already taken those courses in college and know the subject matter. The exam problems, however, require a detailed knowledge of formulas and their manipulation to quickly produce an extremely specific answer to a given problem. It's easy to make an error and fall into one of the common mistakes made when solving problems, and if you do, it's likely the wrong answer is on the answer sheet, waiting to catch a sloppy student. Passing the first five examinations shows you can handle not only advanced calculus but all the other mathematics of life insurance and you're accepted as an Associate of the Society of Actuaries or an ASA. Subsequently, if you pass the later examinations, which cover the business and management aspects of life insurance, you become a Fellow of the

Society of Actuaries or FSA. Today, in 1970, there are about 2,000 FSAs, and they're always in demand."

"I didn't realize all of that." said Frank. "Tell me, do you think your actuarial skills help your private eye investigations?"

"Absolutely, as a private investigator I collect many facts about a case, but linking the critical facts and people and then sorting out the relevant facts from the other facts is what solves a case. It takes extra effort and time to list all the relevant facts in time and location, and then to analyze this grid of facts as to understanding, and finally perhaps to reorganize it slightly in order for it to really come into focus. That's also the actuarial process, and it separates Associates who handle the math from Fellows who manage people, businesses, and innovate. It wouldn't surprise me if Fellows could significantly help many police investigations in this respect."

"Interesting," said Frank, "and Nicole is on her way with the first two exams."

"Yes, she is, and we'll see how she progresses. Anyway, you asked for advice about how to proceed with Nicole, and thus I have some suggestions for you."

"Go ahead, I'm listening."

"First, you have to recognize the reality that a woman you find attractive may not find you attractive. This happens to guys all the time in real life. I'm not saying this is your situation with respect to Nicole; it may be, but I don't think so; however, if it is, then you should look for someone else and find yourself another lady. In the meantime, the next time you approach Nicole, it should be slowly and with some thought and understanding."

Frank immediately looked hopeful, "You're saying I still have a chance with her? Why are you thinking that after she told you and everyone else I was a pest and for me to stay away?"

"Because initially you were her teacher, and she liked you and went out with you; however, she has some sort of problem with men, and you unknowingly exacerbated it by thinking of her physically and not intellectually. You need to do both simultaneously. She's not only physical but also a physical soul."

"I'm not sure I understand you when you say a physical soul."

"But you do understand a 'wave particle' in the quantum or micro-world. People are more than a collection of particles. They are reflective and have an inner life. When you approach Nicole, start talking to her about concepts that require reflection. She loves mathematics. Physics, as you've just demonstrated to your students, is loaded with math. Find something in your field of physics that you're interested in and try to talk to her about it."

"When I see Nicole, I'm not thinking about physics but about my desires. She's a beautiful woman, and I'm a man."

"Of course—but please recognize her other attributes and talents. Yes, Nicole's a beautiful woman, and men are naturally attracted to feminine beauty. Nicole's going to have suiters, probably her entire life. Looking at this rationally, I think sexual desire has its origin in biology, where its end is the transmission of genes and new life; however, desires can go wrong, and hopefully you can find people or ideas that correct desires that can become harmful. It helps to strike a balance as you live and to recognize that sexual love is good but transitory and certainly ends when the person dies—if not long before—while other forms of love continue."

"It sounds like you're religious; are you?"

"Yes, my experience has been that, if a man, by the grace of God, successfully integrates sexual desire and understanding into life—that is, finds and accepts the grace to move beyond his own biological desires— then higher forms of love are able to blossom, and good things happen."

Frank responded in a low voice, "Moving beyond biological desires is difficult to do. Sexual desire can be an overwhelming force, and sometimes not at all rational."

"At the same time, you're an intelligent person, and you should be able to figure out a way to integrate the force of sexual desire into your life so positive outcomes are actualized."

"How do you do it, Parker?"

"Rational desires, including sexual desire and the desire to do good for others, are gifts from God, and, if ordered toward their end, produce happiness. You don't want personal desires to turn to evil, and thus you must use your free will, strengthened by prayers, church communion, and reflective thought, to keep them good. Romantic love must focus on friendship, commitment, and family rather than sexual gratification or attempts to control the relationship. This focus is necessary for romantic love to last and grow into the other forms of love that impact life, such as the caring and raising of children. I'm fortunate I have a good wife who understands and agrees with this evaluation. I'm blessed."

Frank was now sitting up straight and giving Parker an amazed look. It was the look that Chet Wojcik had given Parker when he started talking to him about women. Parker continued, "Many folks have this notion of perfect love because they can easily recognize every imperfection in love in others and in their own life. Where does this awareness come from if not from perfect love itself. Yes, I'm religious, and love, along with truth, beauty, justice, and being, is one of the five transcendental desires that people have."

Frank initially shook his head sadly at Parker's words but thought for a few moments as he assimilated what Parker had said. Slowly his face brightened, and he responded, "I don't know about all of that, but let me try to summarize your suggestions for me about Nicole."

"Go ahead," Parker replied.

"With respect to Nicole, I should approach her slowly and with understanding. I should be open to other women if Nicole won't accept me. Yes, that makes sense. When I'm with her, I should pursue and discuss what both of us are intellectually interested in, which involves some form of mathematics. That also is reasonable, and that should be fun because Nicole isn't just beautiful but has the capacity to understand higher forms of math. Finally, I should focus and reflect upon the higher aspects of romantic love rather than the obvious ones, and this will open additional avenues of love for us." Frank looked at Parker and then added, "I know, after listening to you, that I need to do more thinking about the higher aspects of romantic love you mentioned—namely, friendship, commitment, and then children and family."

"Yes, I think that would be a good reset for you and also for Nicole," replied a smiling Parker.

(23) A Conversation with Two Brothers

The conversation with Frank was over, and, at that moment, his brother, Thomas Lawson, holding a tray of food came by and asked, "Do you mind if I join you?" He sat down when Frank acknowledged yes. The contrast in appearance between these two fraternal twins was again noticeable. Frank was pale and gaunt, with horned-rimmed glasses, wearing the same tan pants and blue, short-sleeved shirt with a pen in its pocket that he'd worn the prior Monday when he first came to Parker's office, whereas Thomas had a ruddy, fuller face, no glasses, and was dressed in a suit different from the one he wore at last Tuesday's lecture. "What brings you to our food court?" asked Thomas, looking at Parker.

"I went to school here at U of C as an undergraduate and live in Hyde Park. It's a convenient place for me, and, when Frank wanted to talk, I came here at the end of his physics class, where he was discussing the double slit experiment and Heisenberg's uncertainty principle."

"Ah, yes, quantum mechanics, the great revolution in twentieth century physics—determinism dethroned."

"Yet," Parker remarked, "it doesn't seem to have made much of a practical impact on the way people view physics, and I think I understand why."

"The way physics is viewed," said Thomas, "Can you elaborate?"

"As you implied before quantum physics came along in the 1920s, physicists expected their theories to be deterministic, generating predictions for the outcome of experiments with certainty. Quantum physics appears to be inherently probabilistic. The textbook explanation, called the Copenhagen interpretation, states that, until a system's properties are measured, they encompass a multitude of values. Superposition of states collapses into a single state as the system is measured or observed, but physics can't predict what that state will be. However, even when people thought physics could predict everything exactly, there was recognition that, in practice, for most situations, this could never be done. For example, a person standing close to Niagara Falls gets a drop of water on his arm. In theory, if he had all the forces, including wind, sun, and gravity on that drop, then classical physics could have told him to expect that drop on his arm—while all the other water flows over the falls. Of course, in practice, everyone knows such a prediction is impossible."

"Yes, I see what you mean," replied Thomas, "but physics took a step back in its claims about an exact understanding of nature. After quantum physics, an electron can no longer be predicted to be at a certain location under given conditions. Now we compute the probability of it being there."

"That's correct," said Frank, "after the fifth Solvay Conference of scientists in 1927, physicists generally accepted the notion that, in the micro-world, reality doesn't exist separate from observation. An electron is not in any fixed place before it's measured. However, I don't know why you call that a step back. It is what it is, and that's a step forward in understanding."

"I agree that seems to be the reality, the way nature really *is* at the micro-level," Parker said. "I'm also amazed at the other Newtonian components that are no longer valid in the quantum world, such as velocity, momentum, and energy. These variables, along with the position, aren't well defined and don't take on one specific value."

Frank nodded vigorously, "Yes, and these variables are no longer smoothly varying continuous values. Energy, as an example, is restricted to certain discrete or 'quantized' values."

"Yes," chimed in Thomas, "and particles don't follow a definite trajectory."

"Because of all this, Thomas, with respect to philosophy, have you seen a shift away from determinism and the clockwork or Newtonian universe?" asked Parker.

"Among philosophers, there are several different ideas, but the slot machine universe hasn't replaced the clockwork universe—although we're well into probabilities," he replied laughing. "However, as we've already noted, among physicists, the Copenhagen interpretation, as given by Bohr and Heisenberg in 1927, still holds sway."

"Absolutely," replied Frank, "but young physicists are uncomfortable with many things and are out there trying to come up with a theory of everything, which will be some sort of grand unification of quantum mechanics and general relativity, even if it involves probabilities."

"Let me ask the two of you something," Parker said, "I think we agree the world of science is the world given by our senses and by instruments that can expand our senses. Now this world of the senses is sustained and directed by the laws of nature. These laws are the unifying principles that regulate events in the physical world. These laws are described by mathematics, which requires intelligence, but doesn't that imply life? You must be conscious to be doing this, and yet somehow science thinks of these laws as lifeless. Will that change as we learn more?"

"I think so. I'm a theist because of the structure and order in nature, and a Christian because of God's revelation in Jesus," replied Thomas. "The reality that most of my friends and colleagues operate in seems to be at best conditioned by a Deist view of God, whereby God is construed as some sort of distant object only vaguely related to our world. In this construct, God doesn't actively involve himself in the affairs of science, economics, politics, or culture. That, of course, is contrary to a biblical understanding, where God acts in and through all the ordinary events and dynamics of life. Sadly, in all of this, my poor brother over here remains an unhappy agnostic." With that Thomas looked at his brother, waiting for a response.

"Yes," said Frank, "I'm an agnostic. I think the universe is space-time, matter, and energy, and this gives rise to intelligence."

Parker picked up on the word, *time*, and turned to Thomas, "In your presentation on Boethius and the Big Bang last Tuesday, how did you come up with that two-dimensional diagram that illustrates timeless reality at negative infinity? That was an interesting formulation of God being outside of time."

"It literally came to me in a dream. One evening I was in and out of sleep, and I saw the diagram on the bedroom wall. Over the next couple of days, I put it together and wrote it up."

Parker offered, "Another way to view the timeless is that it provides the time world with a set of potentialities. The choice as to which potential will be actualized in the sensible world is a transition from the timeless to the time-bound world. In quantum mechanics, there's a similarity as one moves from the probability curve to an actual value."

Frank nodded, "However, in the quantum world, I don't think observation causes the wave function to collapse. It happens because that's the way nature works. I do wonder how long it'll take for all of this to become clearer. It's really a puzzle, and I'd think it's going to take a long time, perhaps another fifty years or so, somewhere around 2020, where physics will have figured it out, and it'll be fully understood."

Thomas demurred, "That won't happen because physics only looks at the material and what it can measure. This goes beyond the material to what is called spirit. God speaks, and His Word enters and makes the reality we experience, and that needs to be considered and acknowledged. I'm not saying the Big Bang, which shows that our observable universe had a beginning, demonstrates the existence of this God; however, it does force us to think clearly about creation."

"What do you mean by creation?" asked Parker.

"Creation is a metaphysical—a theological way of saying everything that is depends on God as a cause. Science and, in particular, physics and cosmology, have as their subject the world of changing things, from subatomic particles to galaxies. Whenever there's a change, there's something that changes. Creation isn't a change. To cause something to exist isn't to produce a change in something. Creation doesn't work on existing material. Creation is the cause of the whole existence of whatever exists. Creation isn't a distant event from the past, rather the ongoing cause of all that is. Creation concerns the *origin* of the universe, not its temporal beginning, and it's important to recognize the distinction between origin and beginning."

Thomas saw Parker looked puzzled at this last statement and paused, allowing the question, "What's the distinction you're referencing?"

"Origin means the complete and continuing dependence on God as the only cause. Whatever is created has its origin in God. But that doesn't necessarily mean that, if something is created, it has a temporal beginning. Indeed, the notion of an eternal created universe isn't a contradiction because, even if the universe were to be eternal without a beginning, it still would have an origin, it still would be created."

Parker sat back in his seat. "Yes, that's part of classical Thomist philosophy. An eternal God could have created an eternal universe. Catholic theologians and philosophers have always accepted that God exists outside time. I wonder if any human can fully understand timeless life. I certainly can use my imagination and think of myself as a photon of light, moving at the speed of light, and that speed would free me from time."

Thomas passed on Parker's comments about light photons being outside of time and continued, "The Big Bang theory shows our universe isn't infinite in time. The eternal universe, as presented by the steady state theory, has been replaced. All material things, including time, started from something smaller than an atom. This isn't creation from nothing, so it doesn't prove the biblical account or the Christian understanding of creation, which is 'creation out of nothing' or 'creatio ex nihilo,' but the big bang theory certainly isn't inconsistent with that understanding. Indeed, the labeling of that theory as the 'Big Bang' was originally meant as a put-down by skeptics, and now it's very refreshing to me. The evidence for a temporal beginning of our universe seems inconvertible."

The two brothers glanced at each other, and Parker figured they had talked about these subjects in the past and were about to continue a long-standing discussion; thus, he looked at his watch, saying, "I know I'm not going to shout eureka this afternoon when it comes to understanding quantum physics or the Big Bang; however, I'm working on a case and might have such a moment there. I hope you gentlemen will excuse me, as I have a meeting to go to at four o'clock." With that, he left the two brothers in the food court to speculate about the future of physics while he drove to the Damon Building to talk to Benjamin Q. Damon about what was going on with the Regular Solids Investments firm.

(24) A Conversation with Benjamin

Benjamin Q. Damon was a short, bald man with a white moustache and white hair along his ears that highlighted his white framed glasses, and he was dressed in a light brown suit and tie that matched the color of his eyes. He welcomed Parker and immediately said, "When you called last week to set up this appointment, I couldn't imagine why you wanted to talk to me about the Regular Solids firm, but after the shocking murder of Miles Clayton this past weekend I assume it has to be related."

"I called you last week and asked for this appointment because I wanted to gain some insight as to what was happening at Regular Solids. I had no idea a murder was about to happen. What I knew when I called is that I had investigated Miles Clayton months before at the request of Natasha Pillsbury and found nothing irregular. However, last week, I discovered Miles may have known about the investigation and subsequently changed his behavior to keep his life private. Now someone has murdered him, and whether the murder has anything to do with the Regular Solids firm is an open question. Has the board of directors of Regular Solids met to discuss the situation?"

"We met this morning. Miles was our chief financial and operating officer and our future leader once William Pillsbury was fully retired. Miles will be difficult to replace, but we did discuss the idea."

"I thought the future chairman or whatever title you decide to call your executive leader was a race between Miles and Natasha?"

"Natasha is great with external publicity and getting the company's name out there, but Miles was William's protégé and knew the business. I don't know anyone on the board who would have picked Natasha over Miles for the top job."

"What about Natasha—did she understand this? My understanding is she came across as someone who thought she was already the head of the firm."

Damon chuckled out loud, "She has a strong personality that loves to dominate and, as president of Regular Solids, acts on it. However, she knows she's not going to be the person who replaces her husband. The company will be looking outside the firm to find a replacement for Miles and a future replacement for William. At today's meeting, Natasha even nominated someone, a good and logical choice, one of my partners, Jeremy Wilson, who's been auditing Regular Solids for a long time. I would hate to lose him, but he's qualified and worked closely with Miles over the past years. He does have a reputation as a lady's man; however, that doesn't bother me. If he does his auditing and financial job, he can have as many girlfriends as he wants. Anyway, the board at Regular Solids Investments has other possible successors to Miles, and, after a suitable period of mourning for him, we'll begin the interviews and vetting."

"The reported tension and in-fighting between Natasha and Miles wasn't accurate?"

"No, it was accurate. They didn't like each other and argued over many things, sometimes trivial things. William had to separate them and make the final decision, usually favoring Miles."

"I want to thank you for clarifying that the board thought Miles was eventually going to take over William's position, and Natasha knew that. But do you think she accepted that fact, or was she trying to change the situation?"

"I don't think she accepted it because, in her mind, she thinks she was better than Miles. She's an extremely driven woman and took every opportunity to embarrass or undermine him."

"Was the board aware Natasha hired me several months ago to investigate Miles because she didn't trust him?"

"Natasha told us about that particular episode of hers after she stopped your investigation. We didn't know about it before or while it was happening. Also, you just mentioned something you discovered last week about Miles being aware of the investigation as it was happening. I never heard about that."

"The fact that Miles likely knew about my investigation is new information, and I just started looking into that possibility. At this point, his murder and events prior to it are all going to be part of an ongoing police investigation, and we'll have to wait and see what the police find."

Parker thanked Mr. Damon for his time. He had confirmed Parker's own opinion of Natasha when he said she loved to dominate. Parker couldn't come up with a word from classical languages that described that type of love.

As Parker made his way out of the building, he passed the office of Jeremy Wilson. Jeremy was seated at his desk in a very upright position, with his eyes closed, apparently thinking about something unpleasant, given the troubled expression on his face. There was no one in his office, and, as Parker passed, he heard him moan. Jeremy was in some sort of distress, quite different from the mental image Parker had of him. His long stepping walk, passing swooning women, and the lingering kiss he gave Natasha were in stark contrast to what was happening today in his inner world. Today, he was a deeply troubled man. Parker thought *he worked closely with Miles, and the murder has adversely impacted him.*

(25) First Nicole Insight

Back home for supper, Rosemary mentioned she was thinking of taking the kids to visit her parents' summer home in Twin Lakes, Wisconsin, this weekend, leaving late Friday afternoon after school, and was wondering if Parker would be needing their second car, a Chevy station wagon. Parker told her he didn't think he'd be using the station wagon and that the Oldsmobile Cutlass would handle whatever travelling he'd have to do on the weekend.

"Let's plan on my trip then," she said. "It's an easy drive up there for me with the kids, and I think my parents will be closing the place early this year and not waiting for Halloween. This would be a good weekend for us to visit." The family sat for supper, and the kids were excited to learn about going up to Twin Lakes. Rosemary's parents had a croquet set and a large lawn, and Grandpa Boyle had a horseshoe pit along the side of the house.

"This is wonderful!" shouted a happy Grace. "I'll get to play croquet with Grandma one more time this year. It's a long time to next spring."

"And I'll be able to use Grandpa's horseshoe pit! I'm getting better every time I play," said John.

"And Anna and I can go swimming in the lake since the water is still warm," responded Peter.

Anna started clapping, "Yeah! Yeah!"

"Then it's settled. We're off to Wisconsin this weekend," said the smiling father, and with that all the kids broke into applause and started to help their mother by clearing the dishes from the table.

That evening, Parker decided to give Nicole a telephone call because of Jim's observation that he'd seen Natasha driving a 1966 light blue two-door Ford Falcon. Nicole answered the phone, recognized his voice, and immediately said, "The effective rate of interest is 9.44%."

"Excuse me, what are you talking about?"

"9.44% is the answer to the problem you gave me the last time we talked. You remember, at Dave's wake, you asked, 'At what effective rate of interest will payments of $100 at the end of every quarter accumulate to $2,500 at the end of five years?' The answer is that the effective rate of interest is 9.44%."

Parker smiled and thought Nicole's mind matched her physical beauty. "That's great—it sounds like you've been working interest problems this past weekend."

"Yes, except Denise finally came home on Saturday, packed a couple of bags, and I drove her to O'Hare Airport on Sunday. She's off to Santa Fe to set up a new life. She's going to hire a moving van to clear out the rest of her belongings here in Chicago."

"That brings up the reason for my call. I wanted to ask you about Denise's car, the Ford Falcon."

"Actually, the Ford is my car now. Denise surprised me and signed the title of the car over to me on Sunday. She said she wouldn't need a car in Santa Fe, and, if she did, she'd just buy a new one. She said she felt guilty about leaving me to pay the full rent on our apartment for the rest of the year, and, if I wanted to, I could sell the Ford and probably come out ahead. That was a very nice gift and gave me a big boost. Wait, what did you want to know about the car?"

"I was wondering where the Ford Falcon was on Friday night. Did you use it or was it parked in your apartment's parking lot?"

"The car was with Denise on Friday night," said Nicole. "When she called me on Thursday to tell me she was moving, she also said she needed the car on Saturday to come home and would send someone to pick up the car on Friday afternoon in our parking lot. She had the other set of car keys, and, when I got home, the car was gone. Denise came back on Saturday afternoon with the car loaded with a lot of stuff, some of it quite nice— artwork, decorative pieces, and dozens of Hummel figurines, which are quite expensive, each individually wrapped in paper. I told you she's an actress, has worked extensively at Second City, and bumps into a lot of rich folks who give her nice gifts, like Hummel figurines. Anyway, the car is now mine, and I have it in the parking lot, but it wasn't there on Friday night. Does that help you?" Nicole enjoyed talking to Parker and by now had completely admitted to herself she was strangely attracted to this middle-aged man. She wondered if he was interested in her but was bothered by the fact he was married and had children.

"It answers my question, but unfortunately it isn't the answer I hoped for. A 1966 two-door light blue Ford Falcon was seen on the near north side of Chicago Friday night in another murder case that I'm investigating, and, unfortunately, I don't have its license number. I know there are many 1966 light blue two-door Ford Falcons out there, but I wanted to eliminate your car. Now I can't do that."

"Wait, you're telling me my car, Denise's car, could be involved in some sort of crime? Why would you even think that when, as you said, there are so many of them on the road?"

"It's a real long shot, I know, but sometimes coincidences involve more than chance and can reveal order. Can you tell me something about what Denise was up to during the days when she wasn't with you?"

"She was rehearsing for some performance and told me she was getting a lot of money for one night's work. That's all I could get out of her, which was nothing new for her since, as an actress, she was constantly rehearsing for some performance, and thus I wasn't surprised to hear it was happening again. I'm sorry I can't help you, but that's all I know."

Parker's eyes blinked, and the expression on his face changed. He'd just experienced one of his insights. "Okay, thank you. I'll be in touch if something comes up. Take care."

"No more interest problems?" she teased, wanting to keep him on the phone. "That last one was a good one because it involved more than one step or one equation. That's exactly what they give you on the exams."

"Unfortunately, I have nothing off the top of my head, but I'll try to come up with something for the next time we talk."

Nicole was disappointed because Parker seemed eager to go, and thus she reluctantly said good night and hung up the telephone. She didn't know she'd just given him an important insight. He now knew Nicole had a connection not only to the murder of Dave Curtis but also to the murder of Miles Clayton. Moreover, he thought Nicole and he would be part of the solution to both crimes. He'd been praying for an insight and also came to believe these sudden insights were likely linked to his prayer life. As long as he continued to pray, he'd have these experiences and would have to sort them out because they were never completely clear or explicit. He didn't know precisely how Nicole was connected to the murder of Miles, but he now realized this case could become dangerous to him in a different way. "I have to be careful around her," he said to himself, thinking about Nicole and how he felt about her, finally acknowledging that he was attracted to her.

(26) Steady Progress

The next morning, Parker stopped in the Area Six police station to visit his father-in-law. Chet greeted him with a huge smile, "Parker, thank you, thank you, I couldn't believe it! Last Saturday night I went to the parish dance, and Joan Jobin came up to talk to me. Somehow you met her, realized we were both part of the same parish, and told her to find me at the dance. She's great, and we're going out this weekend. I still can't fully believe this has happened."

Parker responded, "I'm also surprised. I wasn't certain you'd be going to the dance because the last time we talked you seemed a little apprehensive. What made you go?"

"I don't know. I really had nothing to do and decided to take a look at the dance. If it hadn't worked out, I would have left and joined my buddies at the tavern."

"Looks like you had an opportunity to change your routine, and it turned out well. Something that was only a potential became actualized," Parker philosophized.

"Yes, and, after talking to Joan, I went to the library and got this book on St. Joan of Arc." Chet reached under a desk and came up with a book called *Personal Reflections of Joan of Arc* written by Mark Twain. "Joan Jobin is named for St. Joan of Arc, and she recommended this book. I didn't realize Mark Twain had written a historical novel about Joan of Arc. I started the book last night. It's involved, but I'm a fast reader and have gotten through half of it."

Parker took the book from Chet, started thumbing through it, and replied, "I've never read this book, but I've heard about it. It was Mark Twain's last novel, written, I see, in 1896. Joan of Arc hadn't yet been canonized as a saint when Mark Twain wrote this book. I've heard he spent years researching Joan's trial and life and apparently thought she was the most extraordinary person humanity has ever produced."

"When I'm done with the book you can borrow it if you want," replied Chet.

"Thanks, I'd like to read it and will take you up on your offer." After a few more pleasantries the conversation ended, and Parker walked up to the third floor to see Sergeant Boyle. "Any developments in Dave's murder investigation?" Parker asked, taking a chair next to his father-in-law's desk.

"We've been asking people in the neighborhood if they saw or heard anything unusual in the street late on that Saturday night or early Sunday morning, and thus far we've come up empty. Some guy was walking a dog around eleven; a car with a bad muffler woke up two families around midnight; a drunk was singing loudly at one in the morning. If some stranger entered Dave's apartment by the street, killed him, and then left by the street, no one noticed. This leads us back to the two people in the building besides Dave; namely, Richard Blackburn and Nicole Elkhart."

Parker shifted in his chair as Sergeant Boyle continued, "We're going to get Richard Blackburn in here tomorrow afternoon for a second detailed statement. We'll learn if there are any significant changes in his story. Right now, he says he heard arguing in the upstairs apartment before Nicole ran down the steps crying. Now if she stabbed Dave, and he fell dead on the floor; then why didn't Richard hear that? It appears his testimony shows Dave was alive when Nicole ran away. That makes it possible he went up there to find out about the commotion. We know he'd been drinking in a pub that evening and may not have been fully sober.

We know he once made a pass at Nicole, and she rejected him, but now he hears her crying and running away from Dave. Let's imagine Richard sees a chance to get back at Dave because Dave once stole Richard's girlfriend, and he hasn't forgotten. Long jealous of Dave, Richard has had enough, tells him off, and they get into a fight, and Richard kills him. This is a possible case against Richard, and I must test that possibility before I get back to questioning Nicole. I want to eliminate Richard as a suspect in this case before I start grilling Nicole a second time." Sergeant Boyle consulted his black book, turning a couple of pages, and then asked Parker, "Did you have an opportunity to talk to Nicole about seeking some professional help?"

"I did, and she's not going to do that right now. She's taking Part Three of the actuarial examinations in a few weeks."

"What, Nicole is a math whiz?" Boyle said incredulously, remembering when Rosemary and Parker were first married, and the new husband was still taking the Society of Actuaries examinations. The sergeant made some more notes in his black book, looked up at Parker, and said, "The next time we talk with Nicole, I'm going to ask you to join us since you both have an actuarial connection, and I'm also going have her sit with a police mental health professional in a separate session."

"If I can help, I'll be happy to join you," replied Parker, "but tell me are there any other suspects who you're thinking about?

"Yes, I thought of Frank Lawson since he hired you."

"Really? Why Frank?"

"He's in love with Nicole, and Dave was his competition."

"That's true, but it's very difficult to think Frank would murder anyone."

"I agree, Frank doesn't fit the killer profile; however, another person is George Elkhart, Nicole's father. He seems to be an angry man, however, he has an alibi being in a tavern near his house." Parker shook his head and switched topics, asking his father-in-law if he was planning to join his wife at the summer house where Rosemary and the kids were going this weekend. "Absolutely," Boyle responded. "I need a break from this investigation—and all my other active cases. Besides, I'm anxious to see my grandchildren."

Parker stopped at home for lunch. His mother had just taken Anna to the playground, giving Rosemary a chance to start packing for the weekend trip to Twin Lakes. Even though it wasn't a long distance, and for only

two nights, it was still an effort to transport four children in the station

wagon, and Rosemary always started packing early. Each child had

clothes, books, and personal items, along with any games and sports

equipment they might be taking. Rosemary had to be prepared for all types

of contingencies, involving not only her and the children but also the

automobile. They had the routine down well, but every trip was slightly

different. "Thanks for helping me, darling," said Rosemary, giving Parker

a kiss on his cheek after they'd finished packing the suitcases. Parker then

surprised Rosemary by pulling her toward him and returning the kiss on

her lips. Rosemary looked at him and thought his unexpected kiss showed

he was still bothered by "Nicole, the missing woman" and that she,

Rosemary, would have to double her prayers for her husband.

Parker then gave Detective Sergeant Kevin Garber a telephone call to ask

him what his investigation into the renting of the Open Doors Motel rooms

had discovered. "We came up with one name you'll recognize," said

Garber, with some excitement in his voice, "Jeremy Wilson, the auditor of

Regular Solids. He rented two rooms, room sixty-one and room sixty-

three, on four different occasions over the past six months, always on a

Saturday night. Renting both rooms likely indicates he knew about the one-way mirror and was making use of it. We're going to get him in here and pretend we don't know about the mirror. We'll hear what he tells us, but this is exactly what we were looking for, a connection between Miles and someone who knew him and who knows the murder scene."

"What about the motel manager and his staff—do they know Jeremy?"

"Not well, but they'd recognize him if they saw him. He's very tall, well built, and clearly a handsome man to the ladies. Also, Jeremy wasn't the man who made the reservation for room sixty-three and paid cash for it. Mollie, the lady desk clerk, recalls the reservation was done by a black middle-aged man of average height who gave his name as Joe Hall. He was clean shaven and didn't have any distinctive features. In any case, no one at the motel—Mollie, the manager, or other staff—saw either Joe Hall or Jeremy Wilson last Friday night."

"My other man, Jim Rowdy, was going to file a report with you about his observations on Friday night when the murder occurred."

"Yes, I do have this report from your second operative, Jim Rowdy, saying that, on the night of the murder, Jeremy was at a house party. On the other hand, Jim also saw Natasha drive a Ford into her penthouse parking garage. That of course isn't possible since dozens of people saw

Natasha up close at the Art Institute. At the same time, we do have a person who thought he saw Natasha at the motel running in the parking lot. Thus, this other person, let's call her Natasha's double, was active the night of the murder. We must find her and figure out the role she played, if any, in the murder. In any case, right now our best attempt at finding out why Miles was at the motel in that room on Friday night may be Jeremy Wilson. We're going to question him tomorrow morning."

"Paula Dean is another person who may know what Miles was up to that night," offered Parker.

"Absolutely, we're talking to her this afternoon at four o'clock, and we have a police car bringing her from her place of work to the Shakespeare District at four o'clock." The Shakespeare station was the Fourteenth District police station and the location of Area Five headquarters. The building was huge, and Area Five sat on top of the Fourteenth District. Its location in Chicago was on North California Avenue, but a residential cross street was called Shakespeare Avenue, which gave the police station its name. The standard joke among Chicago police officers who worked at the Shakespeare District was that it was named for the literary quality of the police reports they filed.

After a long pause, Garber finally said, "Parker, seeing that you discovered the one-way mirror at the motel, perhaps you'd like to join us behind our one-way mirror when we interview Miss Dean this afternoon and then again tomorrow morning when we interview Jeremy Wilson."

Parker was pleased and thanked Detective Sergeant Garber, saying he'd attend both interviews. He thought it was good to have a father-in-law like Michael Boyle, who had made him known to other detectives. Parker was honored to join the camaraderie and excitement of the detectives and police officers, building a case from scratch. There was always excitement as clues came in and slowly like a jigsaw puzzle the different pieces fell together, often because the police officers worked together as a team with the common goal of solving the crime. It was certainly good to help the police solve a case, and Parker always accepted an offer to volunteer. He knew how to work himself into the mix of detectives and police and contributed whatever he knew to move an investigation forward. At the same time, Parker was careful to remember he wasn't a police officer and had to stay in the background, giving advice if asked, and allowing the police detectives to take all the credit when a case came together and was solved. He had no trouble doing that. His focus was on solving the case, and he never let his personal feelings get in the way.

(27) Parker Prepares

In preparation for the upcoming interviews, Parker decided to review his files on Natasha and the Regular Solids organization. His first folder showed the early days of the company before William married Natasha. He then came across coverage of their wedding in a second folder and saw that Natasha's maiden name was Walters. A photograph of guests surprised him that Denise was present at the wedding. Denise was Natasha's half-sister, and the two women had the same father but different mothers. The sisters apparently were not close because Denise appeared in only one group wedding photograph and her mother was not present. Nevertheless, the fact that Denise had a connection to the Regular Solid organization through Natasha raised thoughts in Parker's mind.

He made a search of his *Life* magazines and found the issue that included Natasha's photograph. Parker then found the playbill with Denise's photo. Placing the two photos next to each other, he immediately saw the resemblance between the two sisters. The differences were in hair and eye color. Natasha's hair color was red while Denise was a brunette. Natasha had blue eyes while Denise's eyes were brown. Otherwise, the two women were the same size and shape.

A red wig and nighttime darkness hiding the eyes might turn Denise into Natasha. Parker's mind raced and he thought *Denise is Natasha's double.* Apparently, she was the person that Jim saw driving the Ford Falcon, which was her own car, the night of Miles' murder, and now Denise was no longer in Chicago based on what Nicole had told him, having left for Santa Fe. Denise had cleared out before the police investigation started. But why would Denise murder Miles? He thought *I don't have enough facts yet to sort this out* and closed his folder.

(28) The Paula Dean Interview

At the Shakespeare police station, Parker sat with two Chicago police officers, one a man and the other a woman, in a darkened side room that had a large mirror allowing them to view the bright interview room next door. In that room sat Detective Sergeant Kevin Garber, a female police stenographer, and another police detective. Paula Dean was ushered in and sat opposite Garber. She was wearing her traditional business gray suit and carried a small purse, but, without her desk and the golden railing in front of her, she looked to Parker very vulnerable, tired, and nervous. Sergeant Garber explained this was a police investigation into the murder of Miles Clayton and thanked Paula for agreeing to be interviewed. He continued with a statement that she and Miles were coworkers in the same office at Regular Solids Investments, and almost immediately Paula surprised everyone by announcing she and Miles were more than coworkers. She was in love with Miles, and he loved her, and they had talked about getting married. She then began to cry and took out a hanky from her purse. The other police detective got up, went over to a side table where there was a container of water, poured some of it into a glass, and placed it next to Paula. She took a sip, wiped her eyes, and took another sip.

Dabbing at her eyes, she said, "I thought Miles and I were going to be married some time ago, but unfortunately he was always afraid of taking that step, afraid of anything permanent." She then nodded to Sergeant Garber that she was ready to continue.

"Miss Dean, I offer you my condolences on your loss. Is there anything you wish to ask or tell me about Miles?"

"Yes, the newspapers said Miles was shot twice in a motel room, and there were no suspects. I'd like you to give me more information about what happened."

Garber nodded and responded, "We know Miles made an earlier reservation at the motel and checked in that night without any luggage, carrying only a home movie camera. He was sitting in the room watching television by himself when apparently a knock on the door caused him to open it, and the person shot him twice in the heart and ran away unseen. Do you happen to know why Miles was in the motel room or who he was expecting?"

"I knew he had something to do on Friday night, but I had no knowledge he was going to a motel room to meet someone, but I believe this meeting had something to do with the in-fighting he and Natasha Pillsbury were engaged in at work."

"Why do you say that?"

"She hated Miles. Miles was in line to run Regular Solids after William Pillsbury fully retired, and she wanted the job."

"Did she tell you she wanted the job? Also, it would be helpful if you could elaborate on the ways in which Natasha hated Miles."

"Yes, she did tell me she wanted to be in charge of the company. She was constantly criticizing Miles and pointing out his faults. She said he was plodding, lacked charisma and imagination, and wasn't creative. I heard her make snide comments about him to the board of directors when he wasn't around. The two of them were rivals and constantly opposed to each other. Moreover, Miles came to my apartment last Tuesday night and said he was going to get some evidence on Natasha Friday night that would show the board of directors she wasn't fit to run the company."

"How was he going to do that?"

"He wouldn't tell me. He also said Jeremy Wilson, the outside auditor, told him he was losing ground to Natasha in the eyes of the Regular Solids' board of directors and that he needed to act."

"Miles told you Jeremy Wilson said that to him?" asked Garber.

"Yes, and I told Miles to be careful with Jeremy Wilson's judgment. I reminded him Jeremy is a notorious womanizer and a creep. He came after me when I first started at Regular Solids, and I dumped him quickly when I saw his harem of women. I like men, but some women are just stupid to fall for an Adonis." With that Paula started to cry again.

"Let's take a quick break," said Sergeant Garber, getting up and leaving the room. A few seconds later he was in the viewing room and looked at Parker. "Paula is very talkative, and I think she's telling us the truth. I'm going to follow up on her last statement about Jeremy. Are there any questions you'd like me to ask her?" Parker immediately gave him a couple of ideas such as to find out why Paula was eavesdropping on Natasha, and to get Paula's take on Natasha's doppelganger.

Garber returned to the interview room, and, when Paula was ready, he started, "You indicated you advised Miles not to believe he was losing ground to Natasha, based on Jeremy's judgment. Was your suspicion of

Jeremy based on a belief that he was supporting Natasha and trying to undermine Miles's confidence? Or was it because you thought he was mistaken in his evaluation of what the board thought about the two of them?"

"The latter—I thought the board supported Miles, and Jeremy, being wrapped up in his own world of women, was just mistaken in thinking the board was leaning toward Natasha."

"As Natasha's executive secretary, did you ever eavesdrop on her private conversations with others and notify Miles as to what was said, and, if so, why did you do that?"

Paula looked surprised at the question, but answered, "I did eavesdrop and warned Miles when Natasha started plotting against him so he could be prepared for her trick questions at board meetings or other things that might make him look bad or inept. Natasha is a spitfire and wants her way on everything. Miles is—was—more laid back, and I loved him and helped him whenever I could."

"Did you ever hear or see anything that suggested Natasha and Jeremy were perhaps romantically involved?"

"No, I didn't, but just as Miles and I kept our romance away from the office, both Natasha and Jeremy could have done the same if they were involved. When Miles and I were at work or used company phones, we only talked Regular Solids business. Similarly, whenever Jeremy was in Natasha's office or on her phone, I only heard them talking about accounting and finances."

"What, if anything, do you know about Natasha's double or her doppelganger who's been causing her problems?"

"I believe the doppelganger is probably a publicity stunt on Natasha's part to keep her in the news. Natasha is a drama queen and needs attention. Every woman probably has someone who looks like her, and I think there may be a woman who looks and definitely sounds like Natasha. I don't know who she is since I've never seen her, but I've heard her talking on the telephone with Natasha in the past, and their voices and speech patterns are similar. I think Natasha just picked up on this double story when a couple of her friends made a mistake, and she's just run with it, keeping her name in the news."

"When did you hear this woman talking to Natasha? And do you remember what they were discussing?"

"This happened several months ago, last winter, somewhere around the time when the doppelganger story first broke. Natasha was always running parties, and this woman was helping her in some way with those events. I haven't heard her talk to Natasha since that time."

With that the interview of Paula Dean was over, and afterwards the two police officers and Parker met with Garber to give him their impressions. The police officers thought Miles was in the room with a movie camera to film a person who was willing to make accusations against Natasha. That remained a possibility; however, Parker thought, given the combination of the one-way mirror and a camera in room sixty-one, the camera was likely to be pointed into room sixty-three, either for pornographic footage or blackmail purposes. Yet, on this Friday night, Miles knew Natasha was at the Art Institute Gala; thus, if he was trying to get evidence to compromise Natasha, it wasn't her he expected to film. The question of why he was in room sixty-one with a movie camera on this Friday night remained open in Parker's mind. Sergeant Garber thanked the group and reminded Parker to return tomorrow morning at ten to view the interview session with Jeremy Wilson.

Parker was still thinking about Denise and her possible involvement in the murder of Miles but he wasn't ready to mention Denise to Sergeant Garber, who certainly had enough on his plate interviewing Regular Solid's employees about Miles's murder.

(29) The Jeremy Wilson Interview

The next morning, Parker was back at the Fourteenth Police District and took his place behind the mirror, viewing the room where Garber was gearing up for Jeremy Wilson. Next to Parker were the same two police officers who'd watched Paula answer questions. When Jeremy walked in the room, he shook hands with Garber, the police detective, and the police stenographer. He then circled the table, pausing for a moment and looking directly at the mirror before taking his seat. He was impeccably dressed in a blue suit, white shirt with cufflinks, and a champagne-colored tie. "He's a real hunk," muttered the lady officer to her colleague, who responded, "I could still deck him, if I had to, with one punch."

After his introductory statement that this interview was a criminal police investigation into the murder of Miles Clayton, Sergeant Garber started his questioning, "My understanding, Mr. Wilson, is that you as the outside auditor of Regular Solids worked closely with Miles Clayton. I need you to confirm that and then answer if you've had any dealings with him outside the normal business cycle? Were you friends with him or have you attended parties with him or sporting events, or gone on vacations with him or have mutual friends that brought you together? Any contact with Miles at all in any of those regards?"

"I worked closely with him on Regular Solids' business, but I had no personal contact with him at all outside the office."

"Miles was shot to death at the Open Doors Motel. Are you familiar with that motel, and, if so, in what way?"

"Yes, I'm familiar with that motel and have stayed there several times over the past couple of years."

"That is of interest to us. Miles was shot in room sixty-one. Would you be familiar with that particular room?"

"Yes, I have rented that room."

"Now please think carefully because this is important. Did you ever mention the Open Doors Motel and room sixty-one to Miles?"

"No, I would have no reason to do that."

"It might have happened in a casual conversation. Perhaps you were at work and took a lunch break and somehow the conversation drifted toward leisure activity, vacations, or pleasure, and you mentioned the motel. Please think. Perhaps it happened some time ago."

Jeremy rested his head on his left hand, leaning forward against the table. "No, I'm sorry. I don't believe it happened. I would not have mentioned the motel to him."

"Why are you so certain?"

"Because it involves my personal life, and I don't go around talking about my personal life to clients." With that Wilson leaned back in his chair and smiled at Garber.

"Okay, I guess we just have a coincidence here," replied Garber. "Two guys who work closely with each other, use the same motel and room, but don't realize it because they don't discuss things like that." He paused to allow the incongruity of that to be registered. Jeremy Wilson didn't blink. The sergeant continued, "Tell me, Mr. Wilson, what do you know about the mirror above the bed in room sixty-one?"

This time there was a blink from Jeremy, and he paused before answering, "It's a two-way mirror, and, if the lighting is correct, you can see inside the room next door."

"And you have made use of this mirror in the past?" inquired Garber.

"I've always rented both rooms at the same time and have the right to view both rooms. I agreed to this interview and wish to cooperate; however, I won't discuss my private life. I don't know why Miles was there last Friday night."

This time Garber paused before continuing, "Let me change the subject a touch and ask you about Natasha Pillsbury. She and Miles were in competition for the top spot at Regular Solids once William, the firm's founder, was fully retired, and Mr. Damon your boss at Damon Auditing, sits on the board of directors of Regular Solids. Did he ever share with you who the likely successor at Regular Solids was going to be?"

"Not really. Miles was William's protégé, and I think most of the board thought he would be the new chairman."

"Did you and Miles ever discuss the possibility that Natasha, being William's wife, would be the one running the company some day?"

"Not really. I think we both thought it was going to happen for Miles at some point in the future."

"Miles wasn't nervous about Natasha beating him out of the job?" asked Garber.

"He was wary of her but thought of her as bringing new clients in and not as running the whole place."

"And you agreed with him?"

"Yes, and the board of directors is now going out to other companies to look for a replacement for Miles, and that person will be the likely new Chairman, not Natasha."

"And could you tell us about your personal relationship with Mrs. Pillsbury?"

"It's strictly professional. We only discuss Regular Solids business," replied Jeremy Wilson calmly.

"Finally, just for the record, where were you on that Friday evening around 10:30 p.m. when Miles was shot?"

"I was at a party in my apartment complex the entire evening and can give you many names who can verify that, if you need them."

"Yes, please do that at the end of this interview. Give your names to the stenographer," responded Sergeant Garber, pointing to the police office sitting at the table, who was taking notes. Jeremy looked at her, smiled, and nodded.

The sergeant continued, "Do you have any ideas or theories as to why someone would want to murder Miles Clayton?"

"No, it's incomprehensible to me. Perhaps the wrong man was accidentally murdered."

It was Garber's turn to give an incredulous smile at the notion that the wrong man had been murdered, as he thanked Mr. Wilson for his time at the police station. With that the interview came to an end, and Jeremy went on his way while Garber gathered the people who watched the questioning for a quick meeting about what they'd witnessed.

The consensus was that Jeremy had to tell the truth about using the hotel and room sixty-one in the past because it was a fact easily discovered from the motel's register of guests. The remainder of his testimony was smooth but less likely to be true.

Parker asked what the Pillsburys said about Miles when questioned about his murder. The answer was that William had to fight back tears to control his emotions when confronted with the reality of the death of his protégé. Natasha said the murder shocked her, and now the board had to find a new chief financial and operating officer. She praised Jeremy and said he could handle Miles's position. Similar to Jeremy, she also raised the possibility that Miles was the wrong target and didn't know why Miles was at the motel that night. Finally she said she was at the Art Institute Gala that entire night.

Garber then reported it wasn't likely that Miles's killer was a professional hitman since the bullet came from an out-of-date revolver, and that part of the investigation was about to close. Interest would then shift to Natasha's double. He said there was an individual who was at the motel the night of the murder who said he saw a woman in the parking lot he thought was Natasha Pillsbury. She was running in the motel parking lot, carrying a purse and wearing a black skirt and white blouse. This doppelganger was definitely a person of interest in the death of Miles Clayton.

Sergeant Garber ended the meeting, announcing a funeral service tomorrow morning for Miles. He was being buried in Woodlawn Cemetery next to his parents. Parker recognized the funeral would be a good opportunity to see all the Regular Solids staff together in one place and an opportunity to talk to Paula Dean.

As the participants went their separate ways, Parker and Kevin went into the sergeant's office to talk. Parker started by telling Garber that Natasha had a half-sister named Denise Walters. The sisters had different hair and eye coloring but otherwise were the same shape and size. Jim's report that he saw Natasha drive a blue Ford Falcon into her parking garage the night of the murder might be explained if Denise was the driver and wore a red wig that night. Moreover, Denise did own a 1966 blue Ford Falcon. Kevin immediately called one of his detectives and asked him to investigate the relationship between the two sisters.

(30) More Progress

After leaving the Area Five police office, Parker decided to check out the parking garage located in Natasha's condominium and drove there. There was a "Temporally Full" sign at the top of the ramp, and Parker pulled his car far enough into the garage ramp to clear the public sidewalk behind him. He activated the parking brake, and, leaving his car on the downward incline, he got out of the car and walked down the ramp toward the entrance gate and the attendant who was waiting in his booth. Parker introduced himself and showed the attendant his credentials. The attendant's name tag read, Edward. Parker told him he was trying to trace a two-door light blue Ford Falcon that may have been in the garage last Friday. Edward remembered the car, "Sure, it was driven by the photographer, Joe Johnson. He drove the car into the garage on Friday mid-afternoon and said he'd picked it up for Natasha Pillsbury and was going to park it next to her limousine for the day. Her space is deep in the garage and large enough for two cars, and that's where Joe drove the Ford. He didn't leave the car keys, and I didn't give him a garage tag since he used Natasha's space." Parker recalled that Natasha had called Joseph

Johnson her gofer, and this information was a confirmation that he did errands for her besides taking photographs.

"Was the car used on Friday night?" Parker asked Edward.

"I didn't work Friday night, so I don't know; however, I saw it leave Saturday afternoon."

"Did Joe drive it out on Saturday?"

"No, it was some young woman. My guess it was one of Natasha's friends, but I don't recall ever seeing her. She was a brunette with short hair, and she waved thank you to me when I opened the gate. A good-looking, friendly woman."

"Do you know who worked the night shift last Friday, and when he might be available for me to talk to him?"

"The night attendant on duty last Friday was Larry, and he should know if the car was used that night or not. He's working tonight starting at six."

Parker thanked Edward and thought the case was coming together. Joe Johnson, Natasha's gofer, had gotten a car for her on Friday, and a brunette, almost certainly Denise, drove the car away on Saturday back to her apartment where she gave the car to Nicole before leaving for Santa Fe on Sunday. Parker now had to track down Joseph Johnson to find where he got the car, and if he knew the brunette. There was a public library close by, and he stopped in to check their telephone books and to use a phone booth. There were far too many Johnsons in the white pages, but it was easy to find Joseph Johnson in the yellow pages under photographers. He dialed the number and was disappointed to find out from the operator that Joe was on vacation and to call back next week.

Parker then dialed his father-in-law directly at the Area Six police station. When Sergeant Boyle answered the phone, Parker asked about the second Richard Blackburn interview. The sergeant said it had gone smoothly, Richard's second statement was consistent with his first, but neither Detective Brendan nor he could rule Richard out as Dave's murderer. However, in cleaning out Dave's apartment and going through each of the items, Detective Brendan had found something of interest to the case, and the sergeant wanted to show Parker what had been found. "Will you be able to come into the station this afternoon?" he asked. It was already well past lunch time, and Parker hadn't eaten anything. Fortunately, he knew of a Wimpy's close to the Damen Avenue headquarters, and he told the sergeant he'd be at the police station after he stopped to eat a hamburger.

The sergeant responded with one of his good-natured laughs, "You and those Wimpy burgers."

Once Parker arrived, Sergeant Boyle, looking at his black book, started talking about Richard Blackburn's two police interviews regarding what he heard the night Dave Curtis was murdered. "Based on his statements, it's difficult to believe Nicole murdered him and then ran out. Richard states there was no sound or screams from Dave, that there was no sound of his body falling to the floor, nor did he hear the lamp hitting the floor. There's no indication that, after the argument with Dave, Nicole did anything but cry, take some clothes, and run out of the apartment. At the same time, it's also difficult to believe Blackburn went up there after Nicole left and killed Dave. Unfortunately, there's not a trace of evidence that anyone else was in that apartment other than Nicole and Richard."

"So, what are you going to do?" Parker asked Sergeant Boyle.

"Take a look at these black-and-white photographs." He handed Parker six postal card size photos. They were photos of George and Martha Elkhart. The first was George by himself, and it had a large X across the photo made by a black marker, but Parker could clearly see George's face. In the other photos of George, his face had been blotted out by the black marker.

Parker could only make him out because he was standing next to Martha, who was untouched by the marker.

"Where did you get these photos?" Parker asked.

"They were stuck between various pages of a calculus textbook used by Nicole and left behind in Dave's apartment," replied Sergeant Boyle. "Apparently Nicole used these old photos as bookmarks and felt it necessary to deface her father."

"Nicole is well beyond beginning calculus and uses that textbook as a reference if she has to look something up. My guess is that these black markings were made a few years ago when she was in college. May I keep this one photo of George with the big X drawn across it to discuss her behavior with Nicole? I'd like to ask her about why she defaced her father and hear what she says."

Sergeant Boyle hesitated but finally said, "Yes, you may borrow that photo of George, but please be careful when you're dealing with Nicole. These photos show she has serious problems with her father, and defacing a photo is another indication of erratic behavior. We've started interviewing many of Dave's friends and acquaintances to find someone who could give us a clue as to the possible murderer. All the men, without exception, who know her have said they thought Nicole came on to them. I'm just pointing that out to you and showing you those defaced photos to remind you you're interacting with someone who may not be stable. Even though Blackburn's statement doesn't implicate Nicole in the murder, it certainly doesn't exclude that possibility. As a matter of fact, based on the evidence we have thus far, you might say she's our prime suspect." Parker was struck that Sergeant Boyle was apprehensive with respect to Nicole and was now warning him to be careful around her. His father-in-law was worried about his safety around her. If Nicole had murdered Dave because she was unstable, then Parker was in danger as well.

"The warning to be careful is fair enough because it's not normal to deface your father's photographs," responded Parker. "With respect to her flirting with men, it seems every guy who has made a pass at her has been rejected—Frank Lawson, Richard Blackburn, and probably Dave Curtis, the night Nicole ran away from him."

"Exactly, but that isn't normal either, if you think about it, and neither is her hysterical crying, and that's why I worry she could go crazy, and, if she did, then murdering Dave in that moment becomes possible, even though Richard didn't hear any sounds of the murder. Anyway, we're going to get her back here to talk next week, once I confirm our psychiatrist is available. I'll give you a heads-up."

"Sounds good, but, tell me, did one of your policemen confirm Richard Blackburn was drinking at a pub that Saturday night before Dave was murdered?"

 "Yes, Detective Brendan went to the tavern 'Jimmy's' where Richard said he drinks, and Jimmy, the owner, confirmed he was there that Saturday, as he is most Saturday nights. Why do you ask?"

"I was thinking again about George Elkhart and Nicole's apparent problem with her father. He went out drinking that Saturday night, according to Martha, after he tossed Frank Lawson out of the house. I wonder what tavern he goes to when he goes out drinking."

"We checked that out and he was at a local pub near his house. George lives on the South Side, and that's a long way from where Dave lived and Jimmy's."

Parker mentally agreed it would make no sense for George to be in Dave's neighborhood; however, if he was in Dave's neighborhood the night of the murder, perhaps later after leaving his local pub, then that fact would be a significant development for the case. Parker had George's photograph and decided to visit Jimmy's tavern to see if anyone would be able to identify him.

(31) Gathering More Evidence

"Parker, I have the Joan of Arc novel, if you want it," said Chet, holding the book, as Parker made his way out of the Area Six headquarters.

"Sure, I'll borrow it. You finished it quickly, in just a couple of days," Parker replied taking the book from him.

"It's an amazing story, especially her trial, where they tried to trick her with loaded questions such as 'was she in a state of grace?' She gave beautiful and honest answers such as 'If I'm not, may God put me there, and if I am, may God so keep me.' I couldn't put the book down last night and had to finish it."

"Thank you, Chet. I'm looking forward to reading it." Parker was wearing a sports jacket, and the book was thick in depth but not that wide, and it slipped comfortably into the inside left pocket of the jacket.

Parker then drove his car to Mrs. Meyer's block and found a parking spot. She was surprised but happy to see him, "What a pleasant surprise! What brings you back here?"

"I'm going to be checking out a couple of things in this neighborhood and thought I'd stop in to see how you were doing."

"I'm doing fine, thank you. The police are still looking at Dave's apartment. Has there been any break in the investigation?"

"Not yet. They're talking to all of Dave's acquaintances with the hope of discovering something."

"Nicole called me, and she seems like she's also doing fine. She has her job and studies to keep her mind on something other than Dave's murder. She also thinks highly of you. You've helped her during this difficult time, and, with your advice, you've become like a father figure to her."

Parker winced at the thought of being Nicole's father figure, thinking of the disfigured photos of her actual father. "Has she ever mentioned her parents during any of her recent talks with you?"

"No, other than that incident I told you about when you drove me home from the funeral. What ever happened in the past seems to have permanently separated her from them or at least from her father, but exactly what that was is something she hasn't been able to talk about."

They chatted for a few more minutes, and then Parker told her to take care of herself and that he was going up to say hello to Richard Blackburn.

"He's not there," said Mrs. Meyer. "Richard has been working late every evening to make up the time he lost being interviewed by the police."

Parked smiled, thanked Mrs. Meyer for the information, and went to his car. It had been a long day, but Parker had one more thing to do before he went home, and that was to return to Natasha's parking garage and talk to Larry, the night parking attendant. He again parked his car on the incline and walked down to the gate, identified himself to Larry, and asked about the Ford Falcon that had been parked next to Natasha's limousine last Friday night. "Natasha took the car out about half past eight that evening and returned it a couple of hours later," replied Larry in answer to Parker's question.

"You spoke to her and recognized her?" Parker probed further.

"We didn't talk, but you can't mistake her red hair. I was surprised to see her driving. She's usually chauffeured in her limousine, but there she was in the blue Ford Falcon."

"Natasha was at a gala fundraiser last Friday night, according to the newspapers," Parker replied.

Larry looked confused and shook his head. "I don't know anything about that. Perhaps at some other time in the evening she was at a fundraiser because she was definitely here taking the car out and returning it."

"Could it have been another woman who looks like Natasha, wearing a red wig?" Parker persisted.

Now Larry hesitated, "I really don't think so . . . it was Natasha's face," he finished weakly.

"How did she get to the car?" Parker inquired. "Did she walk down the ramp like I did and then exit that way?"

"No, of course not, all the tenants use the elevator, which comes down to the basement. You can see the start of the elevator bank around the curve over there," replied Larry, pointing further into the garage.

"And when she returned the car, she drove it in, and she didn't walk back this way?" asked Parker.

"That's correct. Once she drove the car in, I didn't see her. She used the elevator at the end of the basement to return to her penthouse. The elevator goes directly up there."

Parker nodded and thanked Larry. Since Natasha was at the Art Institute Gala Friday night and had been seen by hundreds of people, a person looking like her was driving the Ford Falcon that night. Her sister, Denise, was that likely person. It had been a long but successful day investigating both cases, and Parker felt solutions to the crimes might be coming into focus.

Later that evening he started to read Mark Twain's novel about Joan of Arc. The book had small print, and Parker was amazed Chet had read it in only two nights. He found the novel interesting but not as exciting as Chet had experienced and expressed it. Of course, Joan had recommended the book to him, and that made all the difference in his level of excitement. Their desires for the various forms of love were active and working to make them a couple. Since Parker was the one who'd brought them together, he wondered how their relationship would eventually play out for them. The novel, *Joan of Arc*, was going to take him far longer than two nights to read, and after he finished the opening chapters, he put the book back into his sport jacket pocket.

"You've started reading religious books about saints, my darling?" asked Rosemary as he climbed into bed next to her.

"Not really, my love. It's a novel about Joan of Arc that Mark Twain wrote at the end of the 1800's before Joan was canonized a saint. Mark Twain was a skeptic but fascinated by her life. He found her story difficult to believe, but it was well documented, especially her trial, where everything was recorded under oath, and so he accepted it, and wrote about it accurately. The Church has documented many seemingly impossible things for those who are interested. As we discussed before, sequential time is part of physical or material reality, and the Church paradoxically realized a long time ago that God was not a material being and was outside of time even though Jesus became man and entered time and human history."

(32) A Conversation with Paula

The funeral home was crowded for the farewell to Miles Clayton. There were people standing outside, waiting to enter because there wasn't room enough inside; the entire Regular Solids Investments organization was present, including William Pillsbury in a wheelchair, looking surprisingly fit—but with a sad demeanor—next to Natasha, who sat next to him in a regular chair. Parker spotted Paula Dean with the two young female clerks who worked in the main office, sitting together with other women. On the other side of the room was Jeremy Wilson next to Benjamin Damon and people from their auditing firm, along with the other Regular Solids board of directors. Miles Clayton's immediate family, his sister, her husband, and their two children were in the front row. The policeman who watched the testimony with Parker using the one-way mirror was also present but in plain clothes.

Miles was a veteran of the Army, and an American flag was draped across his closed coffin. A minister led a prayer service, followed by eulogies. Miles's coworkers, Jeremy Wilson, and Natasha all spoke, and then she read a letter from William praising Miles, his dedication to the firm, and even mentioning the regular solids tattoos he had on his forearms. Finally,

Miles's sister talked about her brother and then thanked everyone for attending. Six veterans saluted Miles, folded the American flag, and handed it to his sister. William Pillsbury, a veteran himself, saluted Miles from his wheelchair, tears in his eyes as he said goodbye to his protégé. As the group left the funeral home to form a line of cars into a procession that would make its way to the cemetery, Parker noticed Paula Dean was with four other women, and they were getting into a small car. He called her over and offered a ride in his car to the cemetery saying, "I'd really like to talk to you in private about who may have murdered Miles." She looked at him with wide eyes, nodded yes, excused herself from the group of women, and took the front bucket seat on the passenger side of his Oldsmobile Cutlass. Paula remarked that she'd been cramped riding in the other car and was happy to have a full seat to herself. Parker smiled at this as his Oldsmobile Cutlass followed the rear of a long line of cars in the funeral profession.

As they drove, Parker started talking, "Last week when I was in your office, the thought occurred to me that, instead of listening to dictation on those earphones, you were eavesdropping on Natasha's conversations, and, if you'd done that in the past, then you knew about Natasha hiring me to spy on Miles. Further, if you conveyed my assignment to him, then he might have changed his behavior because he was being watched. I believe you did that to protect Miles from Natasha in their battle over who was going to eventually run the company." He paused and looked at Paula, giving her the opportunity to either confirm or deny what he'd just said.

She remained silent and looked straight ahead.

Parker thought, *she may be regretting getting into my car.*

He continued, "Anyway, once I had this insight, I immediately put a tail on Miles and learned he went to your apartment a week ago Tuesday. Now if I was able to figure out that you were eavesdropping by merely visiting your office twice, then, over time, Natasha likely deduced as much. Thus, my first question is, at some point in time, did you notice a drop in the useful information that was forthcoming by listening to Natasha?"

Once again, she didn't answer, and Parker thought Paula was going to resist all his questions, but finally she said, "Yes, you're correct. I wasn't hearing anything of value. Moreover, a couple of times Miles was blindsided at board meetings by financial questions from Natasha. This made him nervous, and then Jeremy Wilson started telling him he was losing points with the board. However, I never suspected Natasha knew I was eavesdropping."

"I understand you don't think much of Jeremy's judgment."

"That's correct. He's a womanizer, and any man who does that to women is not to be trusted. When I learned Miles was murdered, I immediately thought it had something to do with work because he told me on Tuesday he was going to get some evidence that would show Natasha was unfit to run Regular Solids. Miles didn't tell me he was going to a motel, but given he went there and had a movie camera, I think he expected to interview someone who could discredit Natasha. The motel setting for a meeting to me indicates Jeremy was involved because he used motels for his sexual adventures and fantasies."

"So, you think Jeremy got Miles to go to the motel to get evidence from someone who knew about Natasha's indiscretions?"

"I've been tossing this over and over in my mind, and I think Jeremy did set this meeting up because he worked closely with Miles and knew Miles was competent and could run the company, but he thought Natasha was gaining favor with the board of directors, and he started to convey this to Miles. I also believe Jeremy wanted to get back at Natasha because she'd caught on to him and his womanizing, and she was pushing him away.

Jeremy and his ego could never handle something like that, and therefore he was turning against her."

"What makes you think Natasha was upset with Jeremy in this way?"

"My eavesdropping. I heard Natasha talking to her friends saying she had to be careful with Jeremy, and that he was no good. That rang true and matched my own experience with him."

Parker didn't say anything to Paula about her speculations; however, if Natasha had caught on to the eavesdropping, then perhaps she was deliberately giving Paula disinformation. Parker's conversation with Paula ended with the exchange, "So on Tuesday when Miles left your apartment, did he see Jeremy as an ally in his battle with her for the top job?"

"Yes, I think so, and that's why he went to the motel to gather evidence against Natasha. Jeremy got him to go there. He's a very smooth guy, but when Jeremy gets rattled, he really falls apart."

"You've seen Jeremy become unglued?"

"Yes, the night I rejected his advances. He thought he had me. When it became clear he didn't and I was leaving, he was walking around the room, half naked, muttering incoherently. I think he was crying."

At this moment, they'd arrived at the cemetery, parked the car, and got out to hear the final prayer. After a brief thank you by the family, everyone was invited to a luncheon by the Pillsburys. With a sigh, Paula said goodbye to Parker and rejoined her lady friends to attend the luncheon, while Parker made his way home for a bite to eat.

Rosemary, Nana, and Anna were all happy to have him home for lunch. Afterwards, they were off to do some grocery shopping. "You're going to be a bachelor this weekend, and so I need to stock up some food for you to eat," said Rosemary to Parker. She couldn't know how eventful the weekend was going to be for them.

(33) Stirring the Pot

Later that afternoon, Sergeant Boyle called Parker on the telephone about his plan to expand the investigation of Dave's murder. He planned to "stir the pot" and confront George Elkhart about his actual whereabouts the time of the murder. "We know he was in his local pub, but he may have left early," said Boyle. The sergeant was sending the police officers who originally spoke to the Elkharts back to their home to talk further, but, before he sent them, he wanted Parker to talk to Nicole about her father and the defaced photographs and see if he could learn anything. Parker didn't know if this was a good idea or not, but his father-in-law was the sarge and the person in charge of the investigation, and, thus Parker agreed to ask Nicole about why she defaced the photos of her father.

Thus, that night, Parker called Nicole on the telephone around half past seven, and, when she answered, he eased into the conversation, "I have some information for you, but before I get to that, here's the interest problem I promised to you the last time we talked." Nicole went to get a pencil and a piece of paper, and, when she returned, Parker gave her the problem, "A $1,000 loan is being repaid by $100 at the end of each year for as long as necessary, plus a smaller final payment. If the effective rate of interest is 4%, find the amount of principal and interest in the fourth payment."

"Okay, that seems fairly straight-forward," said Nicole, surprised by the easy problem.

"Yes, it's an easy problem; however, after you solve it, we need to discuss your methodology—how you went about solving it. That's the important fact about this particular problem."

"Okay, thank you for the problem. Now what's the other information you called about?"

Parker took a deep breath. He knew the task he agreed to wasn't going to be easy, "The police have photos you used as bookmarks in your calculus textbook. Your father's face was blotted out with a black marker on many of those photos. Would you be able to talk about that with me?"

Nicole screamed, "No, no! I don't remember—it was a long time ago. I forgot why I did that. Why are you doing this to me? I thought you were my friend." She stopped talking, and all Parker heard over the phone was her crying. Just like that, he was losing her.

"You're my friend, Nicole, and I'm trying to help you and also solve Dave's murder. I hope you're able to talk to me or someone about this. If not now, then some other time. But soon."

"I can't talk now—goodbye!" She hung up. Parker had gone too far and too fast, but he thought she'd be back once she reflected about what he'd said.

(34) Second Nicole Insight

The next morning the kids were up early, ready for the school day and excited about driving up to Twin Lakes, Wisconsin, later in the day for a weekend with their mother and grandparents. Unfortunately, it was cloudy, and the forecast was for rain in the afternoon and evening. However, that didn't dampen their spirits; the anticipation of a weekend in a place they associated with vacation fun overrode inclement weather. Moreover, the forecast for the weekend was good, as the rain would be gone, and clear weather and comfortably warm temperatures were expected. That Friday morning, Parker drove the kids to school while Rosemary started putting the house in order, with Anna following her and watching.

In the early afternoon, a light rain began to fall as Parker and Rosemary packed the station wagon with suitcases and vacation playthings for the family trip to Wisconsin. Anna helped by carrying small items. Later, Parker used his car to bring the older kids home from school, and, within minutes, they were out of their school uniforms and dressed for their weekend trip. There was much excitement as they got into the station wagon, each wearing a raincoat and carrying their final items—whether books, games, or toys—to bring on their trip. Parker, holding an umbrella, waved to them as Rosemary drove away with the family.

With the family on their way, Parker called Sergeant Boyle and told him the results of his telephone call to Nicole; namely, she screamed and hung up on him when he questioned her about the photos. Not at all discouraged by Nicole's response, the sergeant responded, "I'm still going to send a couple of my men to the Elkhart house tomorrow to question them further about their whereabouts the night of the murder. When we first talked to them, we verified he was at a local pub that night, but we will revisit the exact timing of events. We will tell them Dave Curtis was murdered that Friday night and our investigation has been expanded. We'll say their daughter, Nicole, has already been interviewed and is cooperating with us. We will then ask the Elkharts where they were on the night of the murder and pin down their timing.

"OK, that should get them worried if they are guilty of anything," responded Parker.

"Yes, and I will then have Detective Brendan watching the Elkhart house. He will follow George this weekend to see if he does anything. He has your phone number, and you have his number and address in case something arises over the weekend. I'm off to Twin Lakes, even though it's still raining. My guess is Rosemary and the kids left some time ago, and you're about to raid the refrigerator for some food she made for your supper," concluded the father-in-law with a laugh.

"Yes, Rosemary and the kids are on the highway and should be halfway there by now," replied Parker. "She did make her macaroni and cheese special, and all I need to do is warm it; however, I decided to eat it tomorrow night. Tonight, I'm going to the nearby diner for their Friday fish special."

"Well, that sounds good. I'll eat later after I drive up to Twin Lakes."

"Have a safe trip. I hope you and Grandma enjoy the grandkids this weekend."

After Sergeant Boyle's call, Parker mulled over various possibilities of how George Elkhart might react to the police visit if he was in anyway involved with Dave's death. He suspected George might visit his daughter to find out what she told the police even though the two didn't get along. He thought *a visit from George wouldn't be good for Nicole.*

In attempt to clear his head, Parker went back to reading Mark Twain's novel. By seven p.m., Parker was ready for supper. He closed the Joan of

Arc book, returned it to his sports jacket pocket where it was a perfect fit, and decided to visit the local diner for their Friday fish special, It was raining and dark, and through the window, he saw that a fog-like mist blurred the streetlights.

Once outside Parker opened his umbrella and started walking from his house toward the diner, but, after two blocks, he became aware he was being followed. The person wore a large raincoat with a hood, making it impossible—especially with the drizzle and darkness—to discern who it was. Parker quickened his pace, turning a corner and then running to and turning again into a side alley, hiding behind a dumpster. A streetlight dimly illuminated the sidewalk he'd just vacated, and the stalker walked quickly past the alley entrance, trying to catch up to him. The raincoat and hood covered everything except for a great pair of legs.

Parker made a quick decision and ran out of the alley calling Nicole Elkhart by name. She didn't look back and started to run. He yelled, "Nicole, why are you following me? Please stop!" It worked, and she stopped and turned around to face him. "Did you want to talk to me?" he asked, smiling as he approached her, closing his umbrella so she could see his face in the streetlight.

"Yes," she replied, "I was going to your house when I saw you come out and decided to follow you." Parker noticed her raincoat was completely drenched. Looking at her, he knew she'd been standing outside his house for some time, debating whether to ring the bell. Nicole fidgeted and looked away as Parker stood there. Inside her mind, she was simultaneously happy and afraid that they'd met this way and were now talking. She had stood in the rain a long time debating and unsure whether it was wise to ring his doorbell, and then he came out, and the decision to follow him was easy. Now here they were, and she remained both happy and afraid at what might now happen.

"Look, Nicole, I'm going to get a bite to eat at the diner over here—please join me. Let's get out of the rain."

Inside the restaurant, which was nearly empty, they took a side booth, avoiding the counter. Nicole took off her raincoat and hung it on a rack. She was wearing her loosely fitted white blouse and yellow hot pants and asked, "How did you know I was following you? Are you psychic or something?"

"I sensed I was being followed. I didn't know it was you before I hid in the alley, and you passed me."

"You *sensed* you were being followed, yet I was behind you? You didn't see, hear, touch, smell, or taste me, yet you knew someone was behind you? So you *are* psychic." She laughed and gave him a skeptical look.

Somehow Parker had sensed a presence behind him, but he didn't know it was Nicole. He didn't understand how he knew he was being followed, but he *felt* it. When he saw her pass as he hid in the alley, he knew it was her because he recognized her legs. Parker didn't want to talk or even think about Nicole's long and beautiful legs and quickly changed the topic by asking her, "Why did you come to my house tonight in the rain?"

Nicole stroked her hair as she thought. She bit her lower lip and then leaned forward, "I wanted to apologize to you in person for hanging up the phone last night. I shouldn't have done that. You've been a big help to me, and I'm close to completely figuring out what's been bothering me, and, when I do, I think I'll have the courage to talk to you about it, but I couldn't do it last night, nor do I want to talk about it now. But soon." She lowered her eyes. She had to control herself. She liked Parker—he was smart and kind, but, as she kept reminding herself, he was married and had kids. She promised herself she wouldn't flirt with him, but she couldn't help it. She liked Parker and was excited he was there talking to her.

"Apology accepted, and I'll be happy to talk to you about anything you want when you're ready," replied Parker.

Hearing this, Nicole's face lit up with a beautiful smile that continued as the waitress handed them menus. The waitress then stepped away and watched them behind her cash register. She'd seen many middle-aged men with younger women at her diner, especially on weekend nights, and wondered why so many older men made fools of themselves in front of younger women. Of course, this woman was flirting with him and wearing those hot pants, exposing her long, beautiful legs, which was like an open invitation to him, but what was wrong with the man that he was there and even wearing his wedding ring!? The waitress shook her head sadly and thought the 1960s were a terrible decade for basic decency. This certainly never happened when she was growing up.

As they looked at the diner's menu, Parker mentioned the Friday fish platter was a good bet if she liked fish. Nicole replied she preferred hamburger and would stay with that and then said, "Wait, I just remembered I brought you something to look at." Reaching into her purse Nicole took out a sheet of yellow legal-size paper that had been folded in half, "I found this sheet in a box of Hummel figurines Denise brought home with her. They were all wrapped individually in yellow paper from a legal pad. This sheet was at the bottom of the box, and it shows a mathematical diagram. I'm not certain what it represents, but I found it interesting and thought you might have some ideas."

Parker opened the yellow sheet of paper and was completely surprised because there was no mistaking the diagram. It was the same one Thomas Lawson had shown the night of his lecture, but more significantly, this *yellow sheet was the diagram Jeremy Wilson had drawn that night* and then held it above his head to compare it to what was showing on the screen. How did Jeremy's diagram make it into a box of Hummel figurines? Jeremy had the yellow pad in his hand when Parker saw him kissing Natasha as they sat in her limousine after the lecture. Somehow, the yellow sheet with its drawn diagram went from Natasha's limousine on Tuesday night into a box that Denise carried to her apartment the following Saturday afternoon, the day after Miles's murder. Parker now understood the insight he'd had that Nicole was the conduit to solving not only Dave's murder but also Miles's. The murder of Miles and how it went down suddenly came to Parker. He now *knew*.

(35) Breakthrough

Nicole looked at Parker with a puzzled face because he kept staring at Jeremy's diagram. "Wait," she said, "What's wrong? You look like something serious or important has happened," and she instinctively reached out to touch him with her hand.

Ignoring her hand, Parker looked up at her and responded with excitement, "You remember when we talked on the phone last Monday, and I asked you about a Ford Falcon being involved in another murder? This diagram you've just handed me gives me the insight that you can help me with the details to solve my other case. So now I need to talk to you about that crime and how Denise came to have this piece of paper."

"Wait, that's crazy. I don't know anything about that piece of paper or how Denise came to have it while she was away," said a completely amazed and somewhat confused Nicole.

Parker looked at her with an intensity that started to frighten her. "Let's talk, Nicole, and see what happens—you may know things that are important, but you don't realize them as important. I might bring them to light if I ask the correct questions. Is it okay, please, if I just ask you questions, and you honestly answer them for me?"

"Wait," Nicole said again, "I just heard you say the paper I handed you gave you an *insight*. Is this part of your psychic abilities? Like you somehow magically sensed you were being followed? You should know I don't believe in that nonsense. Duke University did studies over many years, and they were all negative or inconclusive about ESP being real." Nicole's pragmatic and modern education was showing again, and Parker relaxed. He had to make her understand he hadn't gone crazy.

"My questions and your answers will establish certain facts, which in conjunction with other facts may shed some light on the crime. If that happens, then it's a straight reasoning process, and no ESP or magic is involved. My insights or sudden thoughts are unexpected and simply happen. I believe, with a high degree of certainty, you can help me verify my thoughts on my second murder case if you cooperate."

Nicole wasn't convinced. "I don't know anything about your other case, and yet somehow I can help you if I answer your questions because of this insight you had? Are these sudden thoughts you have correct every time?"

"No, but even when they're wrong, they're always close to being correct; sometimes I don't understand them properly and need to be careful."

"Give me one concrete example of this from your experience," she demanded with pursed lips.

"I'll have the Friday fish platter and a cup of black coffee," said Parker to the waitress, who he noticed was hovering close to their table, almost afraid to approach, given the conversation she was hearing.

Nicole then added, "I'll have a hamburger with a big dill pickle and a cup of coffee. Oh, wait, make the order two dill pickles. I think I'm going need them."

The waitress grabbed their menus and scurried off, looking over her shoulder and shaking her head at them. Parker decided to provide the evidence Nicole requested, "Here's an example for you from April 4, 1968. I was driving west across the Fox River in St. Charles, Illinois, on my way to dinner. It was a mild spring day, and I had the car windows open, enjoying the beautiful weather. Suddenly a thought popped into my mind—Chicago Mayor Richard J. Daley had been assassinated. What a crazy thought! Where did that come from? I parked the car, entered the restaurant, and sat at a table. There was a TV above the bar. The program was interrupted by fast-paced music and a special bulletin announcement. My mind said the announcement was going to be about Mayor Daley's death. The announcer instead said Dr. Martin Luther King Jr. had been assassinated in Memphis. I was stunned—it was an assassination, but I had the wrong victim!"

Nicole Elkhart sat there, and her clear blue eyes were innocent and wide open. She looked at him with an expression of disbelief on her face that was evaporating into acceptance because every ounce of his demeanor, and the way he had expressed this experience, conveyed its truth. She'd asked for one concrete example, and Parker had just given her one.

"I believe you," she said. "You're telling me the truth. Something like that past experience just happened to you when I showed you that mathematical diagram." Now, similar to her reaction in the funeral parlor, Nicole was frightened by Parker. She didn't want him to know her terrible secret, but, remarkably, at this moment, Parker wasn't interested in her or Dave's murder but a different murder.

Parker nodded yes and acknowledged that seeing the mathematical diagram was similar to his assassination insight and then learning about the death of Dr. King from television. When Nicole handed him Jeremy's drawing, it hit him like lightning, illuminating events and showing him Miles's murder. Now Parker needed the backup story and the evidence to make the case in a reasoned manner that would convince Detective Sergeant Kevin Garber and others.

The waitress returned with their orders, and, in silence, they started to eat—Parker, his Friday fish, and Nicole, her hamburger. She mulled over their conversation while they ate. By recognizing his sincerity and the fact this wasn't about her, she was able to control her emotions. "Okay," she finally replied, stroking her hair and leaning in toward him, "You want to ask questions and have me answer them, and that process might reveal something important, even though I can't imagine what it could be; and that information might enable you to figure out your other murder. Do I understand you correctly?"

"Yes, you understand perfectly, but please say more rather than less—just let your words flow," Parker responded. He leaned in toward her. They were whispering, and their faces were now close to each other. She thought this might be a man she could really love. He forced himself to think about the case he'd just mentally solved and not Nicole's beauty.

The waitress, viewing the couple from a distance thought, *she's been flirting with him the entire evening, and now he's responding, making his move.*

"Okay, I'm ready. Ask your questions, Mr. Private Detective." Nicole lay her hands on the table, palm open, and she locked eyes with Parker. Subconsciously, she wet her lips with her tongue.

Parker momentarily hesitated, wondering, and decided to start with Natasha's firm, "My other case involves Regular Solids Investments. Have you ever heard of them or know anything about them?"

"Yes, they use the cube and a pyramid as advertising symbols in magazines, and they also have those figures on their checks when they pay you money."

"You've received checks from Regular Solids?"

"No, not me, but Denise, my roommate, would get checks from them when they paid her for the acting she did for them." Nicole was now enjoying Parker's questions.

"Denise worked for Second City—why was she receiving checks from Regular Solids?"

"Second City was her main employer, but Regular Solids would hire Denise to do a one-night performance or literary readings at some of their parties. Last winter and well into the spring, there would be a party or event almost every weekend. Denise would stay up late on Thursday nights, learning her lines for the Friday or Saturday night party, and then she'd come home with a check." Nicole paused and started stroking her hair, "I did her banking on Mondays if she was rehearsing at Second City, and, while standing in line at the bank, I got to be familiar with the geometry on their checks, which attracted my attention because of my background in math. I found the Platonic solids interesting."

Parker finished his fish and took a sip of coffee. Nicole finished her hamburger, ate her first pickle, and then started sucking on her second pickle, looking directly at him the entire time with a wry smile on her face. Parker retained eye contact, ignoring her body language.

"Do you think this acting performance Denise had last Friday, which caused her to go into seclusion, had anything to do with the Regular Solids firm hiring her?"

"I don't know—Denise doesn't talk very much about her work; however, I think that's possible."

"You have no idea where she was rehearsing and where she spent her nights during the two weeks when she wasn't with you?"

"No—the theater was her life; however, I know sometimes Second City would house their actors in a nearby hotel. If it were another theatrical company, I believe they'd do the same, so it's likely that's what happened."

"Did you and Denise ever talk about the future—boyfriends, and so on—and what you thought you'd be doing in five years?"

Their faces were still close to each other, and the waitress kept staring at them, expecting them to kiss at any moment.

"Not really. She was a quiet person—who only came alive on the stage. Besides, she was a generation ahead of me, and unlike me she wasn't interested in men; acting was her passion." Nicole, still stroking her hair, continued, "Once she told me, if she ever came into money, she'd retire to Santa Fe. She didn't care for cold weather and would find a warmer literary city where she could still be an actor but act at her leisure, not because she had to put food on the table."

"And that's apparently what happened with this one big performance she had last Friday night because she took off immediately," Parker said. "And wherever she was staying and rehearsing for her performance, she brought stuff back to your apartment, which included this folded piece of paper with the geometric diagram drawn on it."

Nicole nodded yes. For Parker, the case had come together and was coherent, but there was a further area that he had to explore with her.

"Who at Regular Solids was hiring Denise to do these literary readings and performances?"

"She told me it was Natasha Pillsbury, the president of the company. Natasha's signature was all the checks that I cashed for Denise."

"Did Denise talk about Natasha? Were they friends or was it merely a business relationship?"

"Denise didn't talk about her. I don't think they were friends. Denise would do a performance, and she received money. As far as I could tell Denise didn't have any friends other than actors and then it was all about the role they had."

With that, Parker pulled back from her, "Thank you, Nicole. The information you gave me is more than helpful. It's invaluable, and I think I have enough to construct with some confidence a consistent explanation as to how the murder happened."

Nicole looked amazed and then became excited, "Wait, we didn't say anything about the murder at all, and you think you've solved your case just based on the piece of paper I showed you with the mathematical diagram and this conversation? I don't even know who got murdered! And what about Denise? Is she in some sort of trouble?"

"I believe your ex-roommate is going to be fine. However, the police will have to talk to her, and the quicker the better. Thus, I need her contact information in Santa Fe."

Nicole wrote Denise's new address and phone number on the back of a paper napkin while Parker motioned to the waitress for the check and then paid for dinner. He gave the waitress a generous tip, but she felt disappointed because he and the young woman never kissed.

Nicole put on her raincoat, and once outside Parker asked, "How did you get to my house? Did you drive the Ford?"

"Yes, I'm driving up to the Fox Lake cottage tonight and studying there this weekend. I find it's a good place to study. And, by the way, that problem you gave me? Finding the principal and interest in the fourth payment is easy. The interest turned out to be $32.51 and then the principal was $67.49. That problem was too easy for a question to be on the actuarial examination."

Parker started walking Nicole to her car. The rain had stopped. "That's the correct solution; however, the question mentioned the loan was being repaid by one hundred dollar annual payments at the end of the year as long as necessary, plus a smaller final payment. What did you do with that information?"

"Originally, I started calculating the duration and the smaller payment, but then I realized I didn't have to do that work. I could get the required answer directly."

"That's the purpose of this problem. You can waste valuable time making unnecessary calculations. If you do that often on the actuarial examinations, you won't pass them because you wasted time and didn't solve enough problems. Prepared students will go to the heart of the problem quickly and not waste time with unnecessary work. As a matter of fact, going to the core of any problem quickly, whether it involves math or a personal life problem that an individual may have is the key to solving that problem, otherwise it may continue.

Nicole thought about that and then offered, "If you're trying to solve a murder, it's the same sort of thing, isn't it? You have to get to the heart of the matter and figure it out quickly; otherwise, time may make it difficult to solve later.

"That's correct," Parker replied. "Additionally, you have to deal with people – some of them innocent bystanders, some of them victims, and some of them guilty of a crime."

"Well, I'm happy I helped you with your other case. If you need something else from me, just ask." She looked at him wistfully— simultaneously hoping he'd ask her for something that showed he recognized her as a woman, and at the same time hoping he wouldn't. What would happen if he discovered her secret? Would he be horrified and dismiss her? She didn't want that to happen. Why was she attracted to this older married man with kids?

They arrived at where she'd parked the Ford Falcon. Unlocking the car door, she turned to him and said, "Maybe the next time we talk I'll be ready to tell you a few things about me, about what happened to me in the past, and, with that information, you might somehow solve Dave's murder. I need to think about the words I'm going to use." She got into her car, started it, rolled down her window, and said, "I'd like to kiss you; however, I'm learning not to do things like that because, as Mrs. Meyer has told me, I send the wrong signals to men. I must stop flirting. I need to control my impulses and desires. Besides, you're a married man with children. I shouldn't tempt you. I'm just going to say good night and sweet dreams to you."

And with that, Nicole pulled away in her car, leaving Parker standing on the street corner, alone.

(36) Parker's Second Dream

That night Parker had a dream. Nicole was standing before him, smiling and dressed in her usual white blouse and yellow miniskirt. Not the yellow hot pants she wore at the diner, but nonetheless showing her beautiful long legs. Parker couldn't contain himself and grabbed her. She squealed in delight, wrapping her long legs around his back, and pulling him toward her. Her face came close to his, and their lips touched. Fully aroused, Parker woke up. Rosemary wasn't there. She and his family were away for the weekend. He was alone in the house and alone in his bed—and he was dreaming of Nicole. As a woman, Nicole had gotten into his mind. Her natural beauty, intelligence, and personality had affected him as they had done to other men. For the first time, he correctly understood his father-in-law's apprehension about her when she was around him. As a detective Michael had seen much in fallen human nature and intuitively understood his son-in-law's weaknesses. The sergeant wasn't worried about Nicole stabbing Parker with a knife, but that Parker would become involved with Nicole, ruining his marriage to Rosemary, and hurting her and his family.

Parker got out of bed, went to the bathroom, and walked around the house, thinking and looking at photographs of Rosemary and his children. He thought about his life. What was happening to him? What was this unexpected physical attraction and desire for Nicole? He'd always been attracted to intelligent, caring redheads. Nicole was beautiful and intelligent but emotionally mixed-up, with dark hair. This physical desire for Nicole caught him unexpectedly, and now that he'd started thinking and dreaming about her, what was his response in real life going to be?

He went back to the time when he first realized he had a soul. That experience also happened unexpectedly. It was early one morning when he woke up, and the sun was streaming into his bedroom. He was in bed, alone on his back, looking up, and facing the ceiling. He wasn't thinking about God, nor was he praying, and yet suddenly he felt serenely happy and thought he was being embraced.

Parker always had trouble with the concept of a human soul. He knew the Church defined the soul as the immaterial, immortal, directly created principle that made a particular individual human; however, that definition, along with the writings of philosophers, whether they were Christian or Greek or other, left him cold because, when he was young, he didn't have any understanding of how there could be something that was "Parker"—and yet wasn't made of matter.

In contrast, the resurrection of the body was something he could understand. Someday, in God's Providence, Parker's body, albeit changed, would be reconstituted. As a Christian, he accepted this teaching as a necessary article of faith and had no trouble saying it, for example, at Sunday mass as part of the Nicene Creed. The Gospels, the letters of St. Paul, the empty tomb, and the testimony of Christians showed the historicity of the resurrection of Jesus from the dead. If a resurrection had happened once, then resurrection was possible, and it could occur again. The immortality of the soul was much harder for Parker to accept because the concept of a soul remained fuzzy to him. For years he didn't think about the soul, content with the idea of a bodily resurrection. Moreover, he didn't speculate about life after death. He knew that what God had started, death could not end.

Then came that early sunny morning, quite unexpectedly, when he was resting in bed on his back, eyes wide open, looking at the ceiling, sunlight pouring through the window. He was about to get up to begin a new day when he realized he was incredibly happy and serenely peaceful, and with that realization he became aware he was being embraced—not physically, because his five senses told him that wasn't happening. He didn't see, hear, smell, taste, or touch anything unusual, yet his mind recognized that feeling of being embraced—like a big, loving hug, not with arms around his body but by Someone enwrapping his soul. Parker didn't move. The encounter lasted several minutes. He'd never experienced anything like that before—and never had again—but, since that morning, Parker no longer had any problems with the idea he was a soul. He knew it and thought perhaps his soul was the source of his insights.

The fact that Parker knew he had a soul helped him that night when he dreamed of Nicole because he understood his love and desires for Rosemary and his family were stronger than any outside natural desires, and that, with God's grace, he'd be faithful to Rosemary and their family. He loved Rosemary, and she loved him, and their mutual love had produced four children who they loved and who in turn loved their parents. Parker even recognized, albeit dimly and imperfectly, that this family interpersonal love mirrors the Christian God, where the Father loves the beloved Son, who returns the love, and this loving relationship gives rise to another beloved, the Spirit, who receives their love and returns it to them. Thus, indeed, the interplay of love in a family could lead to a reflection and understanding of the love found in the Trinity.

But what about Nicole? He didn't understand what happened to her in the past but prayed she could resolve her issues. He thought he was going to be part of that resolution, at least in solving the murder of Dave Curtis, and he hoped there would be some other man in her life to take the place of Dave. In the morning, he'd contact Sergeant Garber and lay out the solution to the Miles Clayton murder. Then he'd keep a close watch on Nicole because he thought her case was about to conclude, and she'd need help. Having this plan and resolving to be faithful to Rosemary and his family, Parker was able to go back to sleep, no longer dreaming of Nicole but of light photons, which were not experiencing time.

(37) A Conversation with Sergeant Garber

The next morning, Parker telephoned Garber at the sergeant's home. "Sorry to bother you at home and on a Saturday morning, Kevin, but I think I have enough facts and in theory I've solved the Miles Clayton murder. If I'm correct, your officers should act this weekend. If possible, I think we should meet this afternoon, and I'll lay out everything and show you what I have."

"I'm almost speechless, Parker. Give me the thirty second version of what you have."

"I told you before that Natasha has a sister who is an actress by the name of Denise Walters. She's just moved to Santa Fe, New Mexico, and you need her to testify that she took Natasha's place at the Art Institute Gala. This allowed Natasha to murder Miles directly."

"Stop," shouted Garber, "the last time we spoke, Denise, wearing a red wig and driving her car, was the likely person who shot and murdered Miles. Natasha has an ironclad alibi because hundreds of people saw her at the Gala that night, and therefore, your operative did not see Natasha. He saw her sister, Denise, with a wig. My police are building a case against

Denise as we speak. We think she was jealous of her successful sister Natasha."

Parker ignored what the sergeant said and continued, "Jeremy Wilson was involved in getting Miles to the motel; however, without Denise's testimony, you may not have a case. You have to get Denise back to Chicago or have her deposed in Santa Fe as quickly as possible for you to press charges against Natasha before she gets wind of your investigation of Denise."

"My police through their investigation know that Denise moved and have found her Santa Fe address, but we are not going down there before getting enough evidence to arrest her."

Parker looked at the napkin where Nicole had written Denise's address and read it to Kevin.

"How the hell did you get her address? Is this part of your psychic insights?"

"Not really, I got her new address from her roommate. At first, I thought the killer might be Denise wearing a red wig and driving her Ford Focus the night of the murder, but when you lay everything out in a grid, you'll see that it can't be her. The evidence clearly points to Natasha as the murderer while Denise substituted for her at the Gala. Moreover, Natasha was helped by Jeremy who got Miles to go to the hotel that night."

The Sergeant was momentarily flummoxed, but the certainty in Parker's voice convinced him, "Okay, Parker, get down here with your grid and show me."

"I'm on my way!"

Kevin leaned back in his chair and thought *Wow, he's on top of this investigation but that's not surprising knowing Parker's training. He's an actuary and works through massive amounts of data to develop life insurance products. He's done the same thing here to solve a murder investigation!*

That afternoon, Parker sat with Sergeant Garber to make the case that Natasha murdered Miles. He started by showing separate photos of Natasha and Denise. "I think you can easily see that, if a red wig covers Denise's brown hair, and if eye-changing contact lenses, such as those deployed in Hollywood, are used, then Denise Walters with these two changes becomes a physical copy of Natasha Pillsbury. Moreover, Paula, the secretary, has heard over the telephone the voice of a woman who sounds like Natasha talking to Natasha. Thus, it's not a leap to say the actress Denise is that woman, and we have located Natasha's double. This also explains why Natasha publicized her double, in the newspapers and with me. She knew she might be seen at the crime scene and wanted the doppelganger story known. If someone saw her, then it was her double that was seen because she was at the Art Institute."

"Why would Denise, an accomplished actress at Second City, go along with this and get involved with a murder by pretending to be Natasha at the Gala?" asked Sergeant Garber.

"I don't think Denise knew anything about Miles or Natasha's plan to murder him—or knows he's been murdered. She was just offered big money to do this impersonation and took it because it provided her with the financial means to leave Chicago for Santa Fe. Moving there has been Denise's goal for some time, according to Denise's roommate, Nicole Elkhart."

"Nicole Elkhart and Denise Walters have never been interviewed by us, and their names normally would have never come to our attention with respect to this case," remarked Sergeant Garber.

"Yes, that's correct. I only know about them because Nicole is involved with another murder that I've been investigating, and Denise was her roommate. The two cases came together because Denise's Ford Falcon was used the night of the murder of Miles by Natasha, and then a mathematical diagram that Jeremy Wilson drew on a piece of paper came into Nicole's possession, and she showed it to me because we both love mathematics."

"My head is spinning," said Garber. "Can you start that last part from the beginning?"

"According to Nicole, who doesn't know anything about Miles but knows Denise as her roommate, the beginning was more than a year ago, when Natasha first hired Denise to do literary readings and perform soliloquies at her parties. Natasha, I believe, noticed that, even though she and Denise didn't look alike at first because of stark differences in hair and eye color, they were the same height and weight and had similar facial features. Moreover, both Natasha and Denise realized they also had similar voices and speech patterns, probably because they had the same father. Then, a few months ago, with a little bit of encouragement, Natasha convinced Denise to alter her appearance slightly and pretend to be Natasha. Denise successfully tricked several of Natasha's acquaintances into believing she was the real Natasha. This was just a test run, showing Denise was a good enough actress to fool people, and Natasha had established the existence of a doppelganger with the press, who follow her."

"And Natasha did this, and Denise went along with it because . . . .?" Garber questioned.

"Natasha did this because my investigation to find some dirt on Miles had failed, and she was convinced Miles was going to take over the company in the future. She wanted the top job enough and/or hated Miles enough to begin the plot to eliminate him. I think she also used the force of her personality on Denise, perhaps tempting her by originally suggesting this would be a good test of Denise's acting skills. Could Denise pretending to be Natasha get people to believe she was Natasha? Denise took up the challenge successfully and earned some acting money from Natasha besides."

"All of this isn't unreasonable and could be true, but I need more. Please continue."

"Somewhere in the relationship Natasha learned Denise wanted to move to Santa Fe but lacked the money to do so. She offered Denise the needed funds if she would take the role as Natasha and double in place of her at the Art Institute Gala. That would be a demanding role, and Denise would have to prepare for it and then be silent about it. She accepted the offer

and the promised money that would send her to Santa Fe. Natasha

instructed Denise about the people who would be at the gala and gave her

a script for each one. I think she got Denise to go into hiding in Natasha's

penthouse while she practiced the script, memorizing what to say to each

person at the Art Institute. The penthouse is large enough, and the

husband, William, and his aides are confined to his bedroom on one side

of the place. There would be plenty of room and time for Denise to

rehearse her part and memorize photographs of the people coming to the

gala. In the evenings, Denise likely practiced her lines in front of

Natasha."

"I'm with you," said Garber. "What happens on Friday night, the night of

the murder?"

"Denise in costume as Natasha leaves the penthouse and takes a cab to the

Art Institute, where she gives an award-winning performance. At the end

of the night, she takes a cab home and returns to being Denise in the

apartment around midnight. Natasha, on the other hand, takes the elevator

down to the basement and gets into Denise's car, the Ford Falcon, and

drives to the Open Doors Motel, murders Miles in room sixty-one, and then returns home around half past ten. Larry, who works twelve hour shifts, 6:00 p.m. to 6:00 a.m., on different nights isn't aware the other Natasha has taken a cab from the front of the condominium and returned that way. He only worries about the cars in the garage and will tell you, as he told me, that Natasha was gone two hours in the Ford that Friday night. Both he and Natasha are unaware that my operative, Jim Rowdy, had spotted her returning the car. Jim thinks he's seeing Natasha and is then confused because he learns from the press that Natasha was at the Art Institute. Of course, he did see Natasha! Denise, an actress, managed to fool everyone who saw her at the Gala that night"

"Why would Natasha go out to murder Miles as Natasha and not wear a disguise herself? She took a risk at the motel that she'd be recognized."

"Yes, she took a risk; however, to drive out of the garage and return, a disguise wouldn't have worked with the parking attendant. Larry wouldn't have allowed someone he did not recognize to remove the Ford Falcon from the garage. She could have tried to change her appearance once she got the car out of the garage and then ditched the costume after the murder before returning the car, but all of that would have slowed her down and introduced additional risks. If Jim Rowdy hadn't seen her driving the Ford when she returned, I wouldn't have questioned Nicole about the car and linked Denise to Natasha. Natasha's biggest risk was being caught with the gun in her hand at the motel. Once she successfully escaped from the motel, she was free. As it was someone did see Natasha in the parking lot, but that report was being dismissed because hundreds saw Natasha at the Art Institute. We'd still be searching for the identity of the double if it weren't for Jim's observation."

"Okay, you've given a possible explanation for Natasha's and Denise's movements. And it makes more sense than the case we were attempting to build here that Denise was jealous of her successful sister, Natasha, and killed Miles thinking that everyone would blame Natasha. However, what about Miles and Jeremy? How are they involved with the events that night?"

"This is a touch speculative, but we know Jeremy has used the one-way mirror room in the past, and likely boasted to Miles about his amorous adventures. Miles is looking to get something on Natasha, and Jeremy suggests Miles can film him in bed with Natasha by renting room sixty-one on Friday night because he'll be in room sixty-three with her. Miles is rightly suspicious because the film would also implicate Jeremy in adultery, but Jeremy brushes it off. If Benjamin Q. Damon found out he was having consensual sex with Natasha, it wouldn't hurt Jeremy at all in the eyes of Benjamin. He'd hired Jeremy for his financial and auditing skills and wouldn't judge his private life—Benjamin told me as much when I spoke to him. Benjamin, on the other hand, would be angry Natasha cheated on William, her bed-ridden husband and Benjamin's friend, and she'd never get his approval to run Regular Solids."

Garber observed, "Yet Miles certainly knew about the Art Institute Gala that night. Thus, to believe Natasha is going to be in room sixty-three, he has to know about the double taking Natasha's place at the gala."

"Yes, and that's why I think Jeremy is fully implicated in this crime. Jeremy had to tell Miles that Natasha was using a double at the Art Institute Gala. Miles went to the motel, thinking the real Natasha was going to be there, having sex, and he'd get it on film. Paula, through her eavesdropping, confirmed the existence of a double but made light of it, not realizing the real purpose of the doppelganger was to provide an alibi for Natasha. Natasha certainly needed an airtight alibi, recognizing that, without one, she'd be the chief suspect in a murder investigation since she had a motive to kill Miles."

Garber nodded agreement that Natasha's alibi was important to the case but added, "Miles didn't have to do anything, and he was going to be the Regular Solids leader. Thus, I wonder why Miles would go along with a caper like this, especially with Paula telling him she didn't trust Jeremy's judgment."

"Unfortunately, Paula, with her eavesdropping, was receiving misinformation from Natasha once Natasha realized what Paula was doing. Natasha was telling friends on the phone she had to be careful with Jeremy, and that he was no good. This resonated with Paula, but she incorrectly interpreted this to mean Natasha and Jeremy weren't allies. She conveyed that to Miles, who thought Jeremy was helping him in his battle with Natasha."

"And what was Jeremy's motive for going along with all of this and Natasha's plan to murder Miles?"

"He has a restless heart, to use an expression from St. Augustine. Jeremy is a womanizer and moves from woman to woman. Currently, he's having an affair with Natasha and recognized that, if she took control of Regular Solids, he'd in essence replace Miles because Natasha wouldn't be able to handle the finances of the firm by herself. As it is, that seems to be happening as Jeremy's one of the candidates to replace Miles."

Garber inquired, "Is there any hard evidence that links him to Natasha as a murderer? He has already stated his relationship to her was strictly business, nothing personal."

"He was kissing Natasha in her limousine after a lecture at which I saw him draw the diagram on this sheet," Parker responded, handing Sergeant Garber the yellow sheet he'd received from Nicole. "This sheet was brought back into Nicole and Denise's apartment last Saturday by Denise when she returned from her rehearsal stay with Natasha. It's evidence Jeremy lost or left it behind at Natasha's, and Denise picked it up when she was wrapping gifts, clearing out of Natasha's penthouse and returning to her own apartment."

Garber looked at the mathematical diagram, "It doesn't have his name on it that he drew it."

"That's true, and he'd probably deny drawing the diagram. Then it would be my word against his. However, this could lead to gathering evidence to arrest Natasha for murdering Miles. Denise is the key witness in upending Natasha. Denise must give testimony that she was Natasha at the Art

Institute Gala. Once that's established, then everything else will fall into place. Namely, you have the parking garage attendants who saw Joe Johnson, Denise, and Natasha driving the Ford Falcon on Friday and Saturday. Also, Joe Johnson, the part-time gofer for Natasha, is on vacation, but, once he returns, he can verify he picked up the Ford and drove it to the garage Friday afternoon because Natasha asked him to do so. The attendants will say the car was used Friday night by Natasha during the hours of the murder, and by Denise to drive home Saturday afternoon. I also suspect Joe Johnson may be the clean-shaven adult black man, Joe Hall, who earlier in the week made the motel reservation for room sixty-three. Natasha's chauffer would be able to verify Jeremy was in Natasha's limousine in the evening after business hours, kissing Natasha. You'll have my testimony, the testimony of my operatives, and Nicole's, all supporting the facts and inferences I've outlined here."

"What about the murder weapon? Where did Natasha get a revolver, and where did she ditch it after the murder?"

"My guess is the revolver belongs to William, an Army veteran, and Natasha returned it to the penthouse."

"That would clinch your narrative if we get a search warrant and find it in her house and match the bullets to the gun."

"The key here seems to be to act quickly, interview Denise, and not raise any suspicions with either Natasha or Jeremy. Right now, Natasha is relaxed because Denise left Chicago for Santa Fe and likely knows nothing of the murder. Joe Johnson, who delivered the Ford Falcon to the penthouse garage Friday afternoon, will return from vacation on Monday, and if he talks to the parking attendants, they may tell him I've been asking about the car, and that could get back to Natasha."

"Yes," said Sergeant Garber, "I see the need to talk to Denise as soon as possible."

Parker then handed Kevin the napkin from the diner, "Here's Denise's phone number along with her address in Santa Fe. Hopefully you can impress on her that she has to be careful of her position and not give anything away if she talks to Natasha."

Garber, during his verbal musings, observed there had been no mention in the press that Natasha was a suspect in the murder, and thus even if Denise had heard about the crime, she wouldn't have realized Natasha's involvement in it. Moreover, Denise had been in Santa Fe since last

Sunday, and it's unlikely there had been any coverage of a Chicago murder in New Mexico. Garber told Parker he'd talk to his detectives, contact Denise, and fly to Santa Fe tomorrow, a Sunday, to interview her.

(38) Saturday Night At Jimmy's

It was early Saturday evening, and Parker drove to Mrs. Meyer's house. He wasn't there to see her since he knew she'd be visiting her son and his family, but he wanted to talk to Richard Blackburn. Parker knocked on his door, and Richard greeted him with, "What do you want? It's been two weeks since the murder, and I don't wanna discuss the case anymore."

Parker surprised him with his reply, "Actually, Richard, I'd like you to take me to Jimmy's if you have the time and introduce me to the owner. If the place has some food, I'll buy you something to eat since it's supper time." Blackburn gave him a quizzical look, and Parker continued, "I have a photograph I'd like Jimmy to look at. This is a long shot on my part. It's almost like finding that needle in a haystack, but if he can identify the guy in the photo, then I have a suspect who may have committed Dave's murder. This doesn't involve you directly, but indirectly it may turn attention away from you and Nicole as suspects. Thus, I'm hoping you'll help me and take me to Jimmy's"

"I don't understand why Jimmy is supposed to know the person in your photo, but if it helps take the heat off my ass, let's go." The tavern was only two short blocks away from Mrs. Meyer's three family house, and

Parker and Richard made it there in a few minutes. It was early evening, and the bar was already full of guys who'd stopped in for early drink and would be leaving soon for late Saturday night events. Then the bar would really fill up with regulars that would stay the night. Richard and Parker asked the waitress for a menu and took an empty table that was away from the bar.

"What do you recommend?" Parker asked Richard as they each looked at their menus.

"The house's chili special. It's mild, not the spicy version, and they give you plenty in a large bowl. It goes down easy with any beer you like," answered Richard with some enthusiasm.

There was a thin man with gray hair wearing a tie and apron behind the bar, running back and forth, talking to the bar patrons and filling drinks. Parker guessed this man was Jimmy, the owner, and Richard confirmed it. The waitress came over. Parker told her one check, and the two men each ordered the chili special and a Miller.

Two large televisions, one on each side of the bar, were on. The TV closest to Parker's table was turned to WGN, and Jack Brickhouse, the sports announcer, was summarizing the recently concluded Chicago Cubs season. They'd finished second in the National League East, five games behind the Pittsburgh Pirates, and the Pirates were now off to play the Cincinnati Reds, who'd won the National League West. For Cub fans, it was the familiar "wait till next year" routine. It certainly was another disappointing season, but not as heartbreaking as the prior 1969 season when the New York Mets passed the Cubs in September and went on to win the World Series. "Sixty-two years without a World Series win," groaned Richard. "How many years can they go without a title? When I was growing up in the 1930s they won the National League pennant every three years; now they can't even do that—it's been twenty-five years since a Series game at Wrigley." Parker commiserated with Richard's feelings. They finished their chili, and Richard had a second beer. The early night bar crowd started to dwindle and the late night group hadn't yet arrived. Richard waved to Jimmy to come over.

He did and took a chair at their table, "Hi, Rich, what brings you out early this Saturday night?"

"Jimmy, I'd like you to meet Parker. Parker is a private dick and has a photo he wants you to look at."

"I'd be happy to," said Jimmy, smiling and immediately understanding. "I get this from time to time. It's usually, 'was this guy in your tavern on such and such date?'" He had a big smile on his face, knowing this could be important and that at this moment he was the center of attention.

"You got it, Jimmy," Parker said to him. "In this case, you must go back two weeks ago Saturday night, and this person would be a stranger to you. I believe this was his first visit to your bar. You probably never saw him before and are likely never to see him again, but you might remember if he was here two weeks ago. Here's a photo of him." Parker handed him the defaced photo of George Elkhart that Sergeant Boyle had given him earlier in the week. "Just ignore the black X across the photo. You can still see his face clearly."

Jimmy took the photo and gave it a close look. His head started nodding up and down. "Yes, he was here. A stranger absolutely but that makes it easier for me to remember if I see the face again in a reasonable amount of time. This guy came in around ten and had already been drinking. He took that chair over there in the corner. It was the only seat available. Spent most of the time brooding; didn't talk to anyone around him. At first, I thought he might be trouble for us, but he just sat there, went to the john once, and walked out around midnight. You'd already left, Rich."

"Really," said Blackburn, "let me look at his mug." He took the photo and stared at it, "I don't know him at all, and I don't remember him being here. Of course, I was at the bar, and he was in the corner behind me the entire time. I never saw him, but who the hell is he?"

"The man who likely committed the crime, Richard," Parker responded. "I don't want to get Jimmy directly involved, but I do thank you, Jimmy, for verifying that the photo of this man was here in your tavern two weeks ago Saturday."

With that, Jimmy started shaking his head. "I hope you're not going to ask me to testify in court. I probably wouldn't do that. The last time I identified in court a customer I didn't know by using his face from a photo, his lawyers came back with photos of other guys who looked like their client. I had to admit maybe their client wasn't the one I identified. It was very embarrassing."

"No, don't worry, Jimmy. I don't think there will be any involvement on your part in this case. The police will have to get evidence, but now they'll know where to go. It's good news, Richard, the needle in the haystack has been identified." With that Parker paid the bill, and he and Richard walked out of Jimmy's as the rear TV's coverage went from sports to the stock market, with the report that the Dow continued to hover around 760 while the TV closest to the exit had a news show on the continuing US involvement in Vietnam and Indochina.

"Never should have gotten in that damn war," said Richard.

Back home, Parker took a shower and got ready for bed. The phone rang. It was Sergeant Brendan. "George Elkhart went to Nicole's Berwyn apartment. She wasn't home, and then he went to a local pub. After a couple of hours, he tried again at the apartment. She wasn't there, and he finally went to his house. George really wants to see his daughter and is likely to try again tomorrow."

"He won't find her because Nicole is up at Fox Lake for the weekend. George may figure that out and head up there tomorrow. If that happens, please try to get in touch with the Fox Lake police. Explain the situation to them and ask for the police to get an officer over to the cottage as soon as possible." Parker then gave Detective Brendan the address of the cottage and concluded the conversation with an explanation, "The cottage isn't isolated, as there are other houses all around the lake, but I don't think it would be good for Nicole to be alone with her father right now." After

Parker hung up, he decided to go to Fox Lake Sunday afternoon. Nicole

had indicated she might be ready to talk more about what had been

troubling her from the past, and, if Parker could pin that down, then the

reason for Dave's murder might become clear.

(39) Nicole's Confession

The next morning, Parker went to a Sunday mass before driving to Fox Lake. He had packed a lunch consisting of a sandwich, an apple, and a soft drink to eat as he drove. It was a beautiful early autumn day with some clouds, a gentle breeze, and a mid-60-degree temperature. He thought his family was probably enjoying the weather at Twin Lakes, and he could envision his father-in-law and John at the horseshoe pit. Traffic was light heading north, and he made good time. He pulled into the Elkharts' driveway, parking his Cutlass behind Nicole's Falcon. She was on the porch, seated at a table with her study notes and pencil in hand, similar to the way Parker had found her before. This time, however, with the arrival of cooler weather, she'd switched to wearing long slacks instead of her miniskirt. Additionally, Parker noticed she had a silver headband in her hair. Her dark hair had always fallen straight down to her shoulders, but the new headband, shining in the sun, pulled her hair back slightly. "What brings you here?" she shouted as Parker got out of the car and started walking toward the house. "Why are you all dressed up?" Parker was wearing a good pair of black shoes, dark blue slacks, and his sports jacket over a white, short-sleeved shirt, and no tie. This was one of his Sunday church outfits, and he hadn't gone home to change, instead wanting to get to Fox Lake as quickly as possible.

"I'm coming directly from church with the hope of talking to you during one of your study breaks," Parker responded.

"Now's as good a time as any since I'm tired and have hit a wall with my studying," she responded. "How's that other case of yours—the one involving Denise—coming along?"

"I gave all the information I had to the police yesterday, and they're following up on it. I think it will yield results, especially after your input, so I want to thank you again." He paused and then shifted to the case that directly impacted Nicole, "With respect to Dave's murder, have your parents talked to you in the past couple of days?"

"No, I haven't had any contact with them in weeks."

"Last night, I found out your father went to your Berwyn apartment. It wouldn't surprise me if he did it again today since, apparently, he really wants to talk to you. I wonder if he knows you've been using the summer house. Has he tried to reach you here on the telephone?"

"My parents disconnected the Fox Lake phone a long time ago. I don't think they come out here very much. I often wonder what I'd do if they showed up unexpectedly while I was here. They used to always come together, and as long as my mother was with him, I think I could handle it; but if it were just George, it would be unbearable for me." She stopped and then turned to Parker, "Wait, George is looking for me, and that's why you're here—right? You're thinking he might be coming here!"

"That's a possibility. You also gave me hope last Friday that you might be ready to talk about what's been bothering you, and I thought a beautiful autumn day like today might be the time. What do you think, are you ready to discuss what's been troubling you?"

She didn't answer his question but changed the subject by asking her own question, "Do you know who showed up here yesterday to see me?" Before Parker could guess, she said, "Frank Lawson!" Parker thought Frank was bothering her again but was pleasantly surprised by what Nicole then related. "Yes, Frank came to see me yesterday afternoon. He brought me this silver headband I'm wearing and a dozen yellow roses and apologized several times for being a jerk and a pest in the past. He said he'd never do that again. He knows yellow is my favorite color because I often wear it. He was a gentleman. I almost felt sorry for the times I made fun of him or deliberately teased him with my miniskirt or hot pants." She shook her head back and forth, as if she were remembering some of her past put-downs of Frank. "But given his age, he's rather immature when it comes to women."

"Yet he keeps coming back to you, and certainly the last time we talked, you wanted him to go and stay away," Parker remarked.

"Yes, but this time it was different," she quickly added. "He knew I'd be taking an actuarial examination in a month and promised he wouldn't bother me in any way during the next few weeks. He said, after the exam, he wanted to take me out to celebrate the end of a grueling exam schedule. He hoped, at that time, I would consider him again. If not, he'd just go away and find someone else. I could hardly believe it, but that's what he said. He also said he'd devised this great piece of mathematics regarding entropy he wanted me to look at the next time he called. He said it showed the arrow of time pointed only to the future and demonstrated it wasn't possible to return to the past, but the future was open. He seemed excited about his math and got me intellectually excited. He was a completely changed person, and I was so taken aback by his visit and demeanor that I started to like him again!" With that she touched the silver headband that Frank had given her. "After he went, I couldn't study for at least a couple of hours. I kept thinking of him. I had to stay up late to get caught up with my studies, and now I'm very tired."

"Does that mean we're not going to discuss what's been bothering you?" asked Parker, a touch of sadness in his voice.

"I really need to take a nap to think clearly to talk about my past. Can you please stay here on the porch while I take a quick nap inside, and then we can talk?"

Of course, Parker said yes and stood by the front door as she went inside. He saw the yellow roses in a vase on the kitchen table, and he heard the bedroom door close and lock as Nicole disappeared for her nap.

With extra time on his hands, Parker reached into his sport jacket's left inside pocket and brought out Mark Twain's, *Personal Reflections of Joan of Arc*. He continued reading the novel as he sat outside next to the study table. He noticed Mrs. Novak, the neighbor, working in her front yard, kept looking across the bushes in his direction. He didn't wave to her and continued reading about Joan of Arc defeating the English at the Battle of

Orleans. He thought Mrs. Novak must have had a field day yesterday when Frank arrived with the yellow roses and the silver headband.

About one hour later, Nicole came out on the porch. "Did you manage to get some sleep?" Parker inquired.

"Yes, and I feel much better, thank you. What are you reading?" Parker showed her the cover of the book with its shield and sword and its title and author. "Wait, Mark Twain? The Mark Twain who wrote Tom Sawyer and Huckleberry Finn? That Mark Twain also wrote a book about Joan of Arc?" asked Nicole with some astonishment in her voice.

"Yes, the great American novelist wrote about St. Joan. It was his last novel, and he spent years researching her life to write it. In his autobiography, he stated, 'I wrote this book for love, not money.'"

"I learn something new every day," said Nicole sitting down next to Parker. Then, shifting her thoughts from the St. Joan novel, she came right to the point of his visit to the Fox Lake cottage. "You came here today because you're worried my father, who's been to my apartment, may come here to look for me. Why do you think he's looking for me? Have you talked to him about me or been in contact with him?"

"I haven't talked to him recently, but the police are investigating Dave's murder and spoke to him and your mother for a second time yesterday. I think he's now nervous and wants to find out what you told them about him and the murder."

"I haven't talked to George in months. What do you think I could tell the police about him or the murder that I haven't already said to them?"

"You haven't told the police why you're estranged from your parents, or at least from your father, or the reason why you had a fight with Dave and broke up with him right before the murder."

"These are all private matters and have no bearing on the crime."

"That's difficult to believe—once again I think you know something that would quickly solve this case if you opened up about it. Just by answering certain questions truthfully, as you did about Denise's case, you could help solve Dave's murder." Nicole didn't answer, and Parker continued, "Of course, there's a difference between Dave's murder and the murder in my other case. In the other case, you were completely ignorant of the facts surrounding it. With Dave, you're not ignorant of certain facts because they involve you and Dave. It's true it may involve a private matter between the two of you; however, to get to his murderer, you may have to make them known."

She sat back in her chair, stroking her hair, touching her new silver headband, and saying nothing.

Parker persisted, "Perhaps if I asked the questions, as I did the other night at the diner, you could decide whether you wanted to answer them or not?" He looked at her encouragingly.

That worked. Nicole's eyes flashed and she said, "Go ahead, Mr. Private Detective. Fire away."

Parker went directly to the issue, "Later that Saturday night, after you and Dave got back to his apartment from your dinner, did he try to sleep with you?" When Sergeant Boyle asked her this question, she said no, and that she broke up with Dave that night because she'd grown tired of him. This time, there was a pause from Nicole, and she was ready for the truth, "Yes, he tried."

"Why did you tell him 'No'?"

"We were just dating and making out. I didn't want intercourse, and I told him that," she said as her eyes started to tear up.

338

"What did Dave say or do at that point?"

"He said he'd been patient, and he loved me; didn't I love him? Why would I refuse him?" Nicole was starting to sob now. "I told him it was difficult for me. He said he had a condom; that I wouldn't get pregnant. He'd be careful. He kept asking me about whether I loved him or not. I told him honestly I wasn't completely certain about my feelings; I was confused about sexual intercourse. He didn't understand that and kept after me. I was crying, like I'm crying now." She used her handkerchief to dry her eyes and attempted to compose herself. Parker remained silent. Then Nicole blurted out the truth, "Dave demanded an answer, and so I told him what happened to me—my father sexually abused me as a young teenager, and since then I couldn't really love him or any guy the right way. I was too afraid." She then looked at Parker and continued, "I used to say I didn't know what was bothering me. Really, I've always known but never thought about it because I kept pushing it away. George told me I liked it, and that it was natural. For a brief time, I almost believed him, but I knew it was wrong. I was confused, but I got out of his house. I've finally figured it out, and I told Dave that night, and now I've told you. I finally understand myself better, and I'll be all right."

She didn't sound confident and ran back into the house. Parker heard the bedroom door slam. *There it was*, he thought, *both simple and ugly at the same time—teenage sexual abuse had left a wound in the young Nikki.* Sex and romantic love were all mixed up in her, and the result was a Nicole who, up till now, could only tease men who showed an interest in her as a woman. And, even worse, she didn't know how to handle her genuine feelings when she found a guy attractive, and thus she backed away after flirting with him.

(40) Conflict

Parker sat there a long time, outside on the porch, waiting. Inside, Nicole's sobs faded away. She'd either fallen asleep again or was just resting in the bedroom. Parker got up, returned the Mark Twain book to the inside left pocket of his sports jacket, kept the jacket hanging on the chair, and went inside the house. It was getting close to supper, and the sun was heading west. Parker looked in the refrigerator and saw eggs, cheese, and apples. Bread was on the counter, along with tea bags. He knocked on the bedroom door. "Nicole, I'm going to make us cheese omelets for supper— how many do you want?"

"Oh, wait—I'll get up and do it." She came out of the bedroom, asked Parker to sit down, and went to work cooking the omelets. She continued talking, "I tried to tell my mother about what George was doing to me, but she brushed me off. I think my mother may have suspected, but she never acknowledged anything. There was no communication among the three of us, and I could never say to them what I just said to you. I started dating guys early in high school. Both my mother and George tried to stop me from having boyfriends, but I enjoyed bringing dates into the house and annoying them. I went off to college on a scholarship and at eighteen moved in with Denise, a woman twice my age, but it got me away from George."

"Given the age difference, how did you and Denise manage to find each other?"

"A lady friend of my mother helped at that time. Her daughter, Denise, was looking for a roommate because, being an actress, she was always traveling somewhere and thought it would be good to have someone else living in the apartment."

Nicole finished making the cheese omelets, washed a couple of apples, boiled the water, and poured the tea. Parker moved the vase of yellow roses from the kitchen table to the countertop, and they ate their supper at the kitchen table. "Are you driving back to your apartment tonight?" Parker asked.

"No, I'm staying another day. I still have study time from the company to take." She caught his frown. "If my father shows up, I'll just yell next door for the Novak's—they know George, and everything will be okay." Parker wasn't certain about that; however, George Elkhart had the entire day to come up to Fox Lake if he thought Nicole was here. They finished eating. Parker turned on the front porch light and went out on the deck, preparing to leave.

A waxing crescent moon hung in the western horizon, giving faint light. A sudden cool breeze sent a chill through his body, and Parker put on his sports jacket. The lake was quiet, just the breeze glancing gently over the water. Somewhere in the distance a dog barked. Twilight had arrived. Apprehension that he was leaving her alone in potential danger troubled Parker as he brought Nicole's study materials into the house and placed them on the kitchen table, now cleared of dirty dishes.

Outside, he heard a car door slam. He told Nicole to turn off the kitchen light and quickly moved to the front door, locking it, turning off the front porch light. The cottage went dark. Through the front window, he saw George Elkhart standing next to his car and looking puzzled at Parker's car. On seeing her father, Nicole placed a hand over her mouth and stifled an "Oh, no" as she slumped onto the living room couch. The recent police interview of George Elkhart moved him to search for his daughter tonight at the cottage, just as he'd searched for her at Dave's apartment the night of the murder after Frank Lawson had visited the Elkhart house and inadvertently angered him by mentioning Nicole and Dave may have run away together.

George banged on the front door and turned the knob. Parker had locked the door, but George had his key, and, a few seconds later, the front door opened. George Elkhart entered the house. The remaining twilight shone across the room on Nicole's face. In a trance, she blinked and looked at her father, "Daddy?" Her childlike voice frightened Parker. "Daddy, it's Nikki. You haven't come to hurt me again?"

Parker moved out of the shadows so George could see him. Startled and surprised, George took a step back. Unlike Dave Curtis, who'd accused him of sexual abuse and been killed in a drunken rage, Parker remained silent. But Elkhart recognized him, and he knew by the look on Parker's face and Nicole's plea that Parker knew of his crimes. He turned and ran out of the cottage. Parker ran after him and caught up to him as he reached his car. George spun around. Silver glittered in his hand. He lunged upward and plunged his switchblade into the left side of Parker's chest, just as Parker pushed George's face hard with his right hand, forcing the back of his head to crash against the roof of the car. George groaned and fell unconscious to the ground. The switchblade protruded straight out of the left side of Parker's sports coat—held firmly in place by Mark Twain's book.

Suddenly two cars pulled into the driveway, illuminating the scene with their headlights. Detective Brendan jumped out of the first car, a pistol in his right hand, "Oh, God! No, Parker! You have a knife in your heart!"

"It's okay, Detective. It's a switchblade, and it's stuck in a book behind my sport coat. It never reached my skin, let alone my heart." The second car was the Fox Lake police, and two officers looked at Parker, with the switchblade protruding from his chest, and George Elkhart unconscious on the ground, "What's going on here?" asked the officer in charge.

"This man, George Elkhart, attempted to kill me with his switchblade. I'm a private investigator, and I plan to file a complaint against him. There's a murder investigation going on in Chicago. It's likely George is the killer, and this switchblade is the murder weapon." Parker took out a handkerchief and carefully removed the switchblade, placing it as evidence into a large envelope that one of the policemen had. The second policeman handcuffed George and helped him to his feet as he came out of his stupor, taking him over to the police car, arresting him for attempted murder, and reading him his rights. Parker asked Detective Brendan to call

Rosemary using the police radio and tell her to prepare the guest bedroom because he was bringing "the missing woman" home tonight. By this time, a good-sized crowd from the neighboring houses had gathered near the police cars. All the neighbors were holding flashlights, including Mrs. Novak and husband. She was moving from person to person, spreading the word that George Elkhart, someone they hadn't seen in months, was being arrested. Parker walked back to the house because Nicole had come out of her daze and was standing in the doorway.

"What happened—I must have fainted, and when I came to there were police, and George was in handcuffs."

Parker told her she hadn't fainted. Rather, she'd gone into a trance, and she couldn't stay in the cottage alone, where she'd been abused. Parker said his wife was preparing the guest room for her, and that she was going to spend the night with them. Nicole was still shaken by her father's appearance. She quickly packed her clothes and books. After stopping at the police station, where Parker signed the complaint of attempted murder against George, they were in his car on the road. He turned on the radio, and they drove without talking, listening to music.

The song, "Bridge over Troubled Water," came on. With lyrics by Paul Simon and sung by Art Garfunkel, the music filled the car, "*When you're weary, feeling small; When tears are in your eyes, I will dry them all; I'm on your side, oh, when times get rough; And friends just can't be found; Like a bridge over troubled water; I will lay me down; Like a bridge over troubled water; I will lay me down.*"

Very softly Nicole began to sob, "That song is beautiful and so appropriate for me right now. Thank you, Parker, for being at my side. I'm so grateful."

"*When you're down and out; When you're on the street; When evening falls so hard; I will comfort you; I'll take your part, oh, when darkness comes; And pain is all around; Like a bridge over troubled water; I will lay me down; Like a bridge over troubled water; I will lay me down.*"

Many times, the song was interpreted as referencing the troubles the United States was having in the 1960s, which included President Kennedy's assassination, the struggles for civil rights, the Vietnam War, the growing drug culture, Dr. King's assassination, the decay of many American neighborhoods, the cultural change from the 1950s to the 1960s, and Senator Robert Kennedy's assassination, followed by the Grant Park riot at the 1968 Democratic National Convention. In short, for many in the United States, the troubled water in the song was associated with images of riots, Vietnam, and war. That was not the way Nicole was hearing the song on this night. It was personal and directed to her. Moreover, Parker sensed the "I" in the lyrics was, in Nicole's mind, Parker himself. Hearing the first verse of the song, she'd just thanked him for being by her side. Parker was grateful for the upcoming third verse of the song, as the lights of the passing cars reflected off the silver headband in Nicole's hair. He wanted and then prayed the opening words of the third stanza of the song would redirect her thoughts from him to Frank, who had given her the yellow roses and then the silver headband, now shining in the reflected lights of the passing cars.

"Sail on silver girl; Sail on by; Your time has come to shine; All your dreams are on their way; See how they shine; Oh, if you need a friend; I'm sailing right behind; Like a bridge over troubled water; I will ease your mind; Like a bridge over troubled water; I will ease your mind."

The song was over. Nicole didn't say anything; she was thinking and lost in her thoughts and inner world. They drove the rest of the way, listening to the music on the car radio.

Rosemary, having received Detective Brendan's message, was expecting

Parker and Nicole. When they arrived. She showed Nicole to the guest

room. The two women started talking, and it became clear they needed to

talk. Since the kids had been asleep for some time, and Parker was

exhausted, he excused himself and went to bed. He quickly said his

evening prayers—for Rosemary and his children; for his mother, sister,

and her family and his deceased father; for Michael Boyle and his clan,

which included Rosemary's brothers and sisters and their children; for all

his friends, the actuaries, the police officers, government workers, and

church leaders; and now newly added to his prayer list, Nicole and Frank.

He drifted off to sleep quickly but was aware Rosemary and Nicole

continued their conversation in the guest room, and that he likely would be

mentioned in their talk. It would be good for the two women to discuss

him, a private investigator, who was a married father of four. He had

confidence Rosemary would be a positive influence on Nicole and would

be able to help her after Nicole's trauma of being confronted by George

and finally verbally acknowledging his abuse.

(41) Resolution

Nicole sat on the bed in the guest room, crying softly, "It's over—it's finally done. I can finally talk about it, but I still don't understand why this happened to me."

Rosemary sat next to her and reached out with her hand.

Nicole took her hand and held it, "You have a wonderful husband, Mrs. Spooner. He always spoke the truth to me. Thank you for taking me into your home."

"You're welcome, Nicole, and whatever has happened in the past can be turned into something good if you recognize not only your strengths but also your own weaknesses. Tell me, do you pray?"

"Not really."

"Prayer helps people understand life better. Events become clearer to those who pray."

"Then please say a prayer for me now."

Rosemary continued to hold Nicole's hand and bowed her head, "Heavenly Father, help Nicole discern the truth, according to your will, and guide her to your love so she may know it and avoid evil. I ask it in the name of Jesus, your beloved Son." She then made the sign of the cross.

Nicole hugged her and confessed, "I am attracted to your husband. He has these insights that are enticing and frightening at the same time. I want him to acknowledge . . . to . . . to *like* me, but I'm afraid of what might then happen."

"He does like you, Nicole, very much. I know that, but you see he has the gift of Faith, and Faith is an insight into reality. It leads to discernment and then certitude," replied Rosemary, returning the hug. "Tonight, and every day, say your prayers and then don't worry. All will be well."

The two women retired for the night. Rosemary went to her bed next to Parker, where she said a special prayer for her husband, who had to deal with murder along with beautiful, intelligent women like Nicole. At the same time, Nicole, in the guest room, reflected on her religious beliefs. She'd been brought up without any religion, and this bothered her as she grew older. She knew Christians thought Jesus was a divine person who had a divine nature and, because of Mary, His mother, also a human nature. His humanity made it possible for Him to directly communicate with—and to instruct—the people around Him, and His teachings continued to the present day. Moreover, there were many like Rosemary and Parker, who thought they encountered Jesus at mass under the appearances of bread and wine. This encounter made a positive difference in the way they lived—in what they did and what they would not do. Nicole promised herself she'd investigate this way of life. A television was on in the guest room, and the movie *Casablanca* came to its end as Ilsa walked away from Rick and stayed with her husband. Nicole turned the TV off and said a prayer for herself as she drifted into sleep. In that moment, she was poor in spirit and knew she needed God and His grace.

The next morning, they were all up early. The kids had been alerted by Rosemary that there would be an extra person at the breakfast table, and they acted normally in front of Nicole by being friendly to her while at the same telling their father all about their great weekend—all of this as they ate their cereal and fruit and drank milk. Nicole looked attentively as she listened to the breakfast conversation. Her talk with Rosemary had shown Rosemary to be a genuine and concerned person, and Nicole admired her.

John described how he and Grandpa played horseshoes, and how he was getting better with his throws, starting to make ringers, and giving Grandpa good games. "I think I'll beat him next year," said John with confidence. Grace and Grandma played croquet against some neighbors with equally exciting results, while Rosemary took Peter and Anna out on the water, all of them in life jackets with Rosemary driving the motorboat. The kids then described the rest of their weekend activities while finishing breakfast, brushing their teeth, gathering their schoolbooks, and running outside to get into the car to be driven to school by Rosemary. This was all very routine, nothing dramatic, and yet Nicole recognized a certain order and beauty in what was happening. Nana then arrived to take care of Anna, allowing Parker to discuss the upcoming day with Nicole, "Sergeant Boyle will want to interview you again, based on what happened yesterday, and I'm confident he'll arrange to get your car returned to your apartment. In the meantime, you're welcome to stay here and study if you want."

"I'd like to talk to my mother, face to face," said Nicole. "Do you think it would be possible for you to drive me to her house today?"

Parker was surprised by Nicole's unexpected request and said he needed to make phone calls to plan his day before he could answer her. While she waited, he showed her his desk, and she took her study materials and started working on interest problems. Parker got through on the phone to

Sergeant Boyle, who immediately asked, "While I was enjoying my weekend, you were out chasing George Elkhart and nearly got killed? What happened?"

"I didn't see the 5-inch switchblade in his right hand. Fortunately, I had a book in my sports coat that stopped the blade, and I was able to bang his head hard against the car. Has he said anything to the police regarding his arrest?"

"Not a word to the police. But he has a lawyer, who's trying to get him released on bail by claiming George didn't know what he was doing. He's also claimed you were chasing him, and he was afraid and only defending himself. However, possessing and using a switchblade in an attempted murder, and being the chief suspect in the murder of Dave Curtis, there's no chance any judge is going to release this guy on bail. We'll examine his switchblade, and Dave's wounds are likely to match that blade. Now we need George's motive for the murder."

Parker responded, "George sexually abused Nicole when she was a young teenager, and she told her boyfriend Dave about the abuse the night he was murdered. George went up to Dave's apartment, looking for Nicole. Dave accused him of sexually abusing Nicole, and George plunged his switchblade into Dave's back. That's the case we need to build against George."

Sergeant Boyle expressed surprise, "Nicole confessed sexual abuse by her own father? She never indicated anything like that when we interviewed her. Where are you getting this story?"

"With some difficulty, Nicole finally told me about how George abused her, and she also told Dave about the abuse the night of the murder. The remainder of my narrative is inference, but it hangs together, given George was at Jimmy's that night. Nicole is at my house now and asked me to drive her to see her mother. She didn't give me a reason, but it may be a good idea. Martha Elkhart may have suspected the abuse but ignored Nicole's attempts to talk about it. I think Nicole wants to confront her, and that may be a good way to build more of a case against George. What do you think?"

"What's Nicole doing at your house?" the father-in-law's voice sounded troubled with apprehension at the idea Nicole was in his daughter's home.

"I drove her there last night. I couldn't leave her alone at the Fox Lake cottage after George's appearance sent her into a trance. Rosemary talked to her and put her up in our guest room. Oh, by the way, we need Nicole's

Ford Falcon to be driven down here. She may need a car, and that Ford Falcon played a role in the murder on my other case. I'd like the car to be with Nicole. Would you be able to get someone to drive it here today? I left the car door unlocked, and the keys are in the glove compartment."

Boyle gave a relieved laugh when Parker mentioned Rosemary showing Nicole the guest room, "Son-in-law, you're a man on fire and becoming a high-risk detective. You're leaving the staid actuary script in the dust. Okay, take Nicole to see her mother. I'll get her car back here. Bring Nicole into the station this afternoon so we can get another interview with her and have her abuse statement on the record."

With the Dave Curtis murder concluding, Parker got on the phone with Sergeant Kevin Garber to talk about the Miles Clayton murder, and Garber quickly filled him in, "We were in Santa Fe yesterday interviewing Denise Walters, and we confirmed what you said. She was Natasha's double the entire night at the Art Institute Gala. Thus, the woman driving the Ford Falcon the parking garage attendant and your operative saw that Friday night was the real Natasha Pillsbury. She was active exactly during the time when Miles was murdered, and she had a motive, but we now have to make a case that it was Natasha who pulled the trigger."

"How much did Denise, her half-sister, know about the murder plot?" Parker asked.

"Nothing at all," answered Garber, "and, in our interview, we didn't mention the murder to Denise. Even now she's not aware her half-sister is a likely murderer. In our interview with Denise, we said we were investigating a crime, and secrecy was important, so we couldn't reveal all the details to her, but we wanted to verify what she was doing that Friday night. She said she was acting at the Art Institute. She didn't mention at first that she was pretending to be Natasha, but this came out naturally during the conversation. She said, in the past, she'd done literary readings at the Art Institute at the request of Natasha and then had played roles in one act plays. When we asked her what role she played Friday night, Denise answered, without hesitation, that she was Natasha Pillsbury for three hours. It turns out the two sisters weren't close growing up. Denise's mother kept her distance from her ex-husband, and, when he remarried, Natasha was born, but there was virtually no contact between the two girls growing up. They only really connected when Natasha started hosting social events and needed an actress. In any case, our interview with Denise was a success, and we thanked her for the statement and told her to keep everything quiet, and that we would get back to her once the investigation was over."

"Good, you've demolished Natasha's alibi, and she certainly had a motive to kill Miles, given her desire to run Regular Solids."

"Yes," said Garber, "we'll now interview the parking garage attendants and Joe Johnson to establish that Natasha arranged for and drove the Ford Falcon the night of the murder. We think Jeremy was involved in enticing Miles to the motel that Friday night and must figure out how to get him to talk about his involvement in the crime. How do we get those details to close this case with certainty? If you have any bright ideas as to how to stir the pot, let me know."

Parker told him he'd think about it, and they ended the conversation with Parker wondering if "stir the pot" was an expression all homicide detectives used.

(42) Two More Surprises

Nicole was busy studying but was happy Parker would drive her to see Martha Elkhart and pleased the police were going to bring her car down from Fox Lake. Parker also informed her Sergeant Boyle asked them to stop by the station so Nicole could update her interview and add the charges of sexual abuse of a minor against George Elkhart to the record. Parker then placed her suitcase into his car. Rosemary had returned from taking the kids to school and shopping, and Nicole gave her a hug and thanked her for the hospitality she'd been shown, while Nana and Anna waved goodbye as the father and Nicole drove away.

In the car, Parker mentioned Denise and Natasha Pillsbury had the same father, thus making them half-sisters. Nicole didn't know who Natasha was other than she periodically saw Natasha's name in the newspaper about hosting some social event. Parker told her Natasha was the president of Regular Solids Investments. "So Denise was working for her half-sister when she did readings and acting for them," said Nicole. "She never told me that. I knew Denise's mother because she and my mother were friends, but I never got to meet or know her father because her parents divorced right after Denise was born." She then added, "That's one reason why I want to talk to my mother. I'm not sure I believe George is my real father."

Parker was surprised and looked at her, "What makes you say that?"

"I have four brothers and sisters, and they all look like they could be related. They all have light brown hair and eyes, and all of them are on the short side of height, as are George and Martha. I have dark hair, blue eyes, and am reasonably tall for a woman. How did that happen?"

"I think genetics can get tricky because recessive genes pop up unexpectedly. Have you ever seen photographs of your grandparents or some of your cousins?"

"Unfortunately, no. Family history was never strong with us. The photographs on the wall are all I know, and they're mainly for show. I think my mother tried but could never quite put it all together, given George's temperament. Seeing your family around the breakfast table this morning and talking to Rosemary last night has been an eye opener for me. She's a wonderful person, and I wonder if I could ever be anything like her if I ever married and had children."

"You're an intelligent woman, You'll find the right man. If you and your husband have children, you'll raise them properly," said Parker, looking directly at Nicole.

She smiled. "I believe you, Parker, and I want to change my life. I want to stop flirting and teasing and acting aimlessly around men. I'll get that part of my life under control. I'll understand myself better. I know what happened to me, how I reacted, and I now understand what I have to change, going forward. I'll be okay." This was the second time Nicole had said something like this to Parker. The first time was right after her confession about being sexually abused, and she ran off crying into her bedroom. Parker didn't believe her then when she said she was going to be okay, but he believed her now. Not only had she confessed what happened to her, but George had appeared one last time to frighten her, and he was now in custody. Moreover, Nicole had talked to Rosemary, observed their family, acknowledged what had happened to her, and had now made a firm commitment to change her ways.

When they arrived on the Elkharts' block, Parker asked Nicole if she wanted him to come in with her or not. She said, yes, she wanted him with her when she met her mother, and after he found a parking space on the next block, they walked over to the house. Martha Elkhart answered the door, and Nicole said, "Mr. Spooner and I want to talk to you about George." Martha let them in, and they sat on the living room couch. Parker took another look at the photographs of her family, verifying what Nicole had mentioned to him; namely, she didn't look anything like her brothers and sisters. A photograph of the five siblings standing together showed Nicole, the only one with blue eyes and dark hair, the same height as her two brothers and several inches taller than her two sisters.

Martha said to them, "A lawyer called last night, saying George had been arrested for attempted murder and was being held in a Fox Lake jail. The lawyer said the charge was bogus, and he'd be in court today to have George released. I haven't heard anything this morning."

"Mommy, I don't think the charge against George is bogus. They also suspect he murdered my ex-boyfriend, Dave Curtis. I don't think George will be released anytime soon."

Mrs. Elkhart sat back in her chair and said nothing. She didn't cry. She almost looked relieved. "Is this why you came here this morning, to tell me this news?"

"Yes, but I also wanted to ask you a question that's been bothering me for a long time, and that I've been trying to figure out. It's very personal, and you may not want to answer it, but I hope you will. Mr. Spooner has been helping me, and, without him, the last two weeks would have been impossible for me to handle. I'll ask him to go outside if you don't want to talk in front of him, a stranger; however, I need you, my mother, to answer me truthfully."

Mrs. Elkhart looked at Parker, and, suspecting what was about to happen, said to her daughter, "Whisper your personal question into my ear."

Nicole got up off the couch, bent down, and whispered into her mother's ears.

The mother then said to Parker, "I have to talk to my daughter in private. Please wait outside."

Parker got off the couch, opened the door, went outside, and tried to make himself comfortable sitting on one of the concrete steps. He noted Martha had called Nicole, "my daughter." That was surprising progress for her, given his first visit when she announced Nicole was no longer her daughter. After fifteen minutes on the steps, Parker's backside began to hurt, and he got up and started to pace in front of the house. When that got tiresome, he returned to sitting on the concrete steps but in a different position. After another fifteen minutes, he returned to pacing and then sat again for a third round, repeating the exercise for a fourth time. Finally, after what seemed like an eternity, the front door opened, and Nicole and Martha came out, teary eyed and hugging one another. It appeared the mother and daughter had reconciled whatever problems they had in the past.

"I was correct. George isn't my real father," announced Nicole in the car as they drove away from the Elkhart house. "My mother had an affair with a young man twenty-three years ago when George was on a hunting trip. She was bored with George and flattered that some young stud found her attractive. It was just a couple of nights, and she stopped it after George returned. When my mother discovered she was pregnant, she thought it was the stranger's child and not George's, but that only became clear as I grew because I didn't look like any of my siblings. She knew I looked like her lover, with dark hair, blue eyes, and long legs. George was suspicious, and despite my mother's denials to him, she believed he knew. He started to drink more and began slapping my mother when he became angry. Now, in some strange way, it's clearer to me why he went after me. He appalls me, and he ruined my teen years, but he couldn't handle my mother's unspoken infidelity, and my presence grated on him. I think in his sick mind, he went after me to get back at my mother who had been unfaithful to him. Anyway, it was a blessing to get out of his house when I did." She stopped talking, dabbing at her eyes with a hanky, and they drove in silence for a few minutes before she started talking again.

"All my siblings married and left the house, and that's when George started touching me. He said this was normal, and I should like it. I knew what he was doing wasn't right, and, at the same time, boys excited me. I started accepting their interest in me. I felt I couldn't tell anybody about George, and both my parents were adamantly against my dating. I think my mother was seeing her lover in me, worrying about what might happen to me with my boyfriends and not realizing George's abuse. According to her, when I started trying to talk about George's abusive behavior, she thought I was referring to his slapping me, which he also did to her, and she believed his harsh discipline might be good for me. I could never have used the words 'sexual abuse' with her before today, and she finally apologized to me for his sordid behavior, and her indifference. Then we both started crying. It feels so good to finally confirm George isn't my father."

"Did she tell you the name of your biological father?"

"No, she wouldn't do that because, even though she hasn't seen him in all these years since the affair, she knows from newspapers he still lives in Chicago. She said he doesn't know about me, and she wouldn't want me looking him up. One of these days, I'll get it out of her."

Parker stopped the car, and they went to lunch at the Wimpy's close to the Area Six station. They ate their hamburgers quickly, and Nicole reached into her purse and took out some money, saying "Let me pay for my hamburger," and with that a small photograph also came out of her purse and fell on the counter. Nicole picked it up and looked at it. "This is a photograph of my mother and her lover. They stopped at one of those subway photo booths and took four photos of themselves. Two went to the lover, and my mother kept two, and she decided to give me one today. I now have a picture of my mother with my real father." She was happy to have that photograph and handed it to Parker so he could view it. To Parker's great surprise, he recognized both individuals. A much younger Martha Elkhart looked like the photograph he'd observed earlier, hanging on her living room wall, even though the photo booth snapshot wasn't in color. Meanwhile the identity of her lover was a shock for Parker. It was a young Jeremy Wilson!

Parker sat there in the diner and thought Nicole's good looks, her height, along with her long legs and her dark hair and even her love of financial problems—it all made more sense now that Jeremy was identified as her biological father. He returned the photo to Nicole and thought how strange life was, and how events can come together in inexplicable ways, connecting people. He said nothing to Nicole about her two fathers—one who raised and then abused her and the other who was her biological father and who was unknown to her—and that both men had been involved in separate murders. She'd learn her real father's name sometime in the future if her mother decided to give her Jeremy's name. For now Parker thought silence about her biological father's name and crime would be the best for Nicole. Parker processed how he and Nicole were the people who brought resolution to two murders. They were the connections that actualized reality in the macro-world.

Parker and Nicole left the diner and went to file a police report on the events at Fox Lake. The updated police interview with Nicole went well, and Sergeant Boyle concluded it by telling them the switchblade George used against Parker matched the knife wounds on Dave's body. This, along with George Elkhart's initials and fingerprints on the switch blade, were enough to charge him with Dave Curtis's murder. Nicole looked relieved that the case had been resolved, and George's deeds finally revealed and acknowledged, not only by the police but also by her. The Ford Falcon had been driven to the Area Six station by Fox Lake police, and Nicole left the station to find it while Parker went out with her to get his own car.

(43) A Conversation with Joan and Chet

As Nicole and Parker were walking out of the Area Six headquarters, they met Chet Wojcik, not in uniform, and Joan Jobin, who were entering the building. They greeted Parker with such enthusiasm that Nicole looked not only surprised but almost frightened. Joan was hugging Parker tightly, "What a surprise, Monsieur Spooner, merci, thank you for telling Chester about me!"

"Yes," said Chet, "We really don't know how to thank you enough for introducing us and wish we could do something for you."

"Not a problem," Parker responded. "What brings the two of you here on what apparently is a day off for Chet?"

"Yes, I'm not working today. I got a vacation day, so Joan, who is off on Mondays, and I could roam around the city. I was just going to show Joan the building here where I work, and later we're going to a French film she's been wanting to see," responded Chet.

"It's an Eric Rohmer film called *My Night at Maud's.* It was nominated for Best Foreign Language Film and Best Story and Screenplay. It's advertised as a romantic comedy, and this version has English subtitles, which convinced Chet to accompany me," said Joan, gently taking his arm and slipping it around her waist.

"I've read a couple of reviews of this movie, and I'm anxious to see it." added Chet. "Roger Ebert writes the movie is about love, being a Roman Catholic, body language, and the games people play. Then he states it's just about the best movie he's seen on all four subjects. That's high praise from a great movie critic. He particularly likes a long scene where a man and a woman talk about love, sex, marriage, and divorce, with things said and unsaid and body language conveying hidden tensions and thoughts."

"Described that way, I should probably see the film myself!" said Parker. "I have to deal with people who have committed crimes and should turn themselves in, but who are resisting. Things said and unsaid, and body language, can make all the difference in those situations. Anyway, enjoy the film, and, by the way, Chet, that book about Joan of Arc I borrowed has been ruined. I apologize, but you'll have to tell your library it's beyond repair, with a deep cut in every page. I'll reimburse you for whatever they fine you."

"What happened?" asked Chet.

"A guy attempted to stab me, but your book in my coat pocket stopped the blade. Thus, you see, by loaning me the book, you've already done something for me!"

Joan put her hand up to her mouth, "Oh my, how horrible! And yet how wonderful that the book stopped the knife. Is that the book with a drawing of St. Joan's protective shield on the front cover?" Parker nodded yes and smiled, catching Joan's meaning of the incident. She was a natural theologian, with a love for her saint and an understanding that divine providence is the plan by which God orders all things to their true end, and since God is the universal cause of all causes, nothing escapes His providence. Parker wished he could grasp that truth better, but he knew he was only alive today because he'd told Chet to look for Joan at a dance, and after they found each other, Chet read a novel recommended by Joan, which Parker subsequently borrowed from Chet, and the thickness of that book stopped a switchblade.

It was time for Joan and Chet to go. They said their goodbyes and disappeared into the police station. Nicole and Parker watched them and then turned to each other.

"Thank you, Parker, for everything. I feel like I've been set free, and I'll seek professional help if I need it in the future. I'm beginning to believe again, and I'll never forget you, Rosemary, and your family. I'll always remember what you've done for me. God bless you."

"Good luck with your exam, Nicole. I'm happy for you," he said, giving her a hug.

As Nicole walked away, she thought to herself that, if Parker wasn't a married man with children, and perhaps a touch younger, then she wouldn't be walking away from him. But the reality was that he was happily married with his family, and she had more actuarial exams to pass and needed to reconnect with her mother and half-siblings. She knew she was young and believed her future was open. In the past, she'd liked Frank as a teacher and a person, and now his recent approach to her had raised her hopes that perhaps something good might yet happen for them. She also promised herself she was going to investigate the coherence of faith she'd sensed in both Parker and Rosemary, and which she longed for and hoped was true.

As Parker watched Nicole walk away, he thought to himself that, if he wasn't already married and happy with Rosemary and his family, and perhaps a touch younger, then he wouldn't have allowed Nicole to walk away from him. He knew being was the fifth philosophical transcendental, and many people had difficulty with reality and had a sense of alienation or emptiness and were uncomfortable with being at home in this world. By the grace of God, that wasn't true for him and his family. He and Rosemary had accomplished much together, and he was grateful. He said a prayer that Nicole's terrible experience of abuse would help her develop a heart of love toward others, especially to those who never knew and needed love. Once her mind and heart connected, he believed she'd be on her way to living a good life. Moreover, she had a mathematical mind, which meant she could easily accept the universe was ordered by a mind and had a purpose.

(44) Closing the Net

Back home, Parker called Detective Sergeant Garber and learned the police would be talking to Joe Johnson later in the afternoon. They had also secured a search warrant of the Pillsbury penthouse for tomorrow morning to hopefully retrieve a .357 caliber revolver. Garber expected that, if the bullets taken from Miles's chest matched bullets fired from that gun, he would have enough, along with the statements from the parking garage attendants and Joe Johnson, to book Natasha on a murder charge. He'd be coordinating the interviews of those witnesses with the search for the gun. All of this should be enough to bring Natasha to justice, but Sergeant Garber was uncertain as to how to bring Jeremy Wilson into his net. Parker then told him Jeremy Wilson had been involved in an affair twenty-three years ago and was the father of Nicole, Denise's roommate. Parker thought the affair and the daughter might be used to bring Jeremy into the police net, and that he could help the police in accomplishing that goal.

What the police had on Jeremy was that, in the past, he had used the motel room where Miles was murdered. He almost certainly set Miles up that night to be in the room so Natasha could kill him—and Jeremy could thus advance his own career. The evidence that linked Jeremy to Natasha was their romance, and a yellow piece of paper with a mathematical diagram on it that went from Jeremy to Natasha's penthouse to Denise, who took it back to her apartment, where Nicole found it and showed it to Parker. Linking Natasha to Denise, her doppelganger, in this manner would certainly cause Jeremy anxious moments, but would it be enough to convict him? Kevin and Parker discussed a plan to "stir the pot" with Jeremy.

Parker said, "I saw Jeremy was in bad shape when he learned of Miles's death. I heard him groaning in his office and expressing sorrow."

"The two had worked closely together, and now Miles was dead," remarked Kevin.

"Paula said she saw Jeremy crying when she refused his advances."

"What does that tell you about Jeremy?"

"He's not an evil person. He didn't harass Paula for sex even though he was in tears."

"The tears could have been an act to get Paula to change her mind."

"Perhaps, but I think if you come down hard and only confront him, you won't get anywhere. You have to arouse his conscience. As mentioned, I think it's even possible that Nicole being Jeremy's daughter—if he knew it—might be an additional factor that would surprise Jeremy and eventually allow him to display his humanity."

I doubt it, but if you want to try your approach, it will have to be quick because tomorrow morning I expect to arrest Natasha based on the evidence we discussed and then in the afternoon have Jeremy arrested as an accessory based on his relationships with Natasha.

With that Parker immediately called Jeremy's office and asked his secretary for an appointment tomorrow afternoon regarding a confidential matter and got on Jeremy's calendar for a one o'clock meeting.

The next morning, Sergeant Garber confirmed to Parker his police had found a .357 revolver used by William during his Army days in the Pillsbury penthouse. Natasha was at work, and William was home, cooperating with the police but shocked they had a search warrant for his penthouse. It would take time to determine whether this revolver was the murder weapon but Garber was confident because the interview with Joe Johnson went very well. Joe confirmed the parking garage attendant's

376

story that he was one who drove the Ford Falcon into Natasha's driving space Friday afternoon. He did that because Natasha requested he pick up the car from Denise's apartment, and then went on to say Natasha also asked him to book room sixty-three for Friday night at the Open Doors Motel using a pseudonym. Joe casually offered these two gofer requests Natasha made that week. Joe apparently didn't know Miles had been murdered because he went on vacation before the story broke, and the police didn't ask or tell him about the murder. Garber was ecstatic, and he was off to arrest Natasha based on the evidence given by the motel witness who had seen her at the motel, the parking attendant, and Jim Rowdy, all of whom saw the real Natasha that night, given Denise's testimony that she was Natasha at the Art Institute Gala.

Sergeant Garber wished Parker good luck in softening Jeremy at their one o'clock meeting because Garber was coming in with police at half past one to arrest him as an accessory to the murder of Miles.

(45) A Conversation with Jeremy

That afternoon, when Parker arrived at Damon Accounting, he was ushered into Jeremy's office by a secretary, who then closed the door behind her. Jeremy, impeccably dressed in his blue suit and a matching tie, sat at his desk. Parker wore a good pair of slacks and a sport coat, different from the one that had a hole in it. Based on what he was about to do, Parker hoped this sport coat would last longer than the prior one. He now had less than thirty minutes before the police barged through the door to arrest Jeremy. After introductions, Jeremy immediately asked, "Mr. Spooner, you asked to see me regarding a confidential matter, and I know you're a private investigator and did some work in the past for Natasha Pillsbury, and thus I agreed to meet with you; however, I can't think of any reason why you'd want to talk to me."

"Bear with me a few minutes, Mr. Wilson. I have a number of items to bring to your attention, all of which are connected. Some of them may surprise you, but collectively they're important and should be of definite interest to you." Jeremy nodded, and Parker continued, "First, as you mentioned, I was hired several months ago by Natasha to investigate Miles Clayton because Natasha didn't trust him; however, the investigation didn't find anything and was stopped. Second, a few days ago, Natasha asked me to return to her office to discuss a double who was posing as her. Natasha hoped to alert all her friends and drive the imposter away; however, if she wasn't able to do this, then she asked me if I'd be willing to find this double and stop her. I told her I'd help if she asked. It turns out, she never asked me, but I located the double anyway." Here Parker paused and smiled inwardly when Jeremy's eyes reacted to the news about the double being found. "Third, I have a photograph of a young woman I helped in another one of my recent cases. I'm going to show you her photograph." With that he handed Jeremy the photograph of Nicole that Frank had given to him when he first hired Parker.

"She's a beautiful woman," Jeremy said, after a few seconds of studying the picture, "Why are you showing me her photo?"

"She doesn't know your name, but her mother, one of your former lovers, said you're the father. She said it was a two-day affair that happened twenty-three years ago. I'm not interested in asking you to do anything for your daughter or to shake you down for money. The fact you have this daughter is something I want you to be aware of as I continue." Parker looked at him directly in the eyes during this exchange.

"I don't believe this is my daughter," said Jeremy, surprised at Parker's words, and with that he threw the photograph back at Parker. It landed on the floor at Parker's feet.

Parker picked the picture off the floor and returned it to his jacket pocket, saying "She's a beautiful young lady," and continued without acknowledging Jeremy's denial. He thought Jeremy would continue to listen and not throw him out because Parker had caught Jeremy's attention when he mentioned he'd found Natasha's double. "A couple of weeks ago, I saw you at a talk given by Thomas Lawson, where he discussed a model of eternity, as defined by Boethius. I wonder what you thought about the idea that everything that has ever happened in physical time could be conceptualized as happening simultaneously."

Jeremy looked surprised at the shift of topic and tried to collect his thoughts because his mind was thinking about the picture of his daughter who had his black hair and blue eyes. "I didn't think that idea made much sense. My recollection is the location of that simultaneous moment was off the grid, at negative infinity. Where is that?"

"It's outside of time. It's timeless. You may have heard stories of people who briefly died and were revived. Many of those folks experienced their entire life all at once. They returned to life at the last split-second and told researchers what happened when they died and were free of time. It's difficult but possible, using imagination, to think about your entire life from the earliest memories to death, all at once."

"My life isn't over, so I can't do that," responded Jeremy.

"Exactly, you have a future because we do live in sequential time," Parker said smiling, leaning forward in his chair. "There are many potentials now, but, going forward, only one is going to be actualized in time as your future. You have the opportunity to make up for things that happened in your past."

"Is that your point in all of this? I have a daughter through a past mistake, but now I can start living correctly?"

"Yes, that's absolutely the case. You're free and can begin living a different life in the future." With that point established, Parker turned to desires to get Jeremy's mind on Natasha and continued, "My point is also about human desires, including sexual pleasures or a desire for wealth or an egocentric desire that may come from running a company like Regular Solids. Desire is a gift from God, but it must be ordered properly; that is, a desire may be ordered toward a particular end and constitutive of a person's identity and fulfillment. I hope every person gets their desires ordered correctly, including the desire to do good for others. Many desires, if not ordered to doing good, can spin out of control and end up harming people and then the person who has the desire." Jeremy looked at Parker. He didn't know how to respond and said nothing. He looked very uncomfortable now, seated in his chair. Parker's words had made an impact.

Parker continued, "My final point is that I have a copy of the diagram Thomas Lawson displayed at the Big Bang presentation." He handed Jeremy a Xerox copy of the diagram Jeremy had drawn on his yellow legal pad. Jeremy looked at it and became confused because he recognized he'd drawn it and wondered how Parker had come to have a copy. He looked at Parker and then back at the drawing a couple of times before asking, "This is an exact copy of my diagram from the lecture. I recognize it. How did you get this copy?"

"Denise Walters, when she left Natasha's penthouse on Saturday morning, had a box of Hummel's, each one wrapped in yellow legal-size paper to protect it, and at the bottom of the box was the yellow sheet with your diagram. I recognized it because you raised it above your head at the lecture, which enabled everyone behind you to see it, including me. Denise's roommate is your daughter, the beautiful woman in that photograph, and she gave me the drawing you made that night. It went from you into Natasha's limousine and then into Natasha's penthouse, where Denise used the paper from your legal pad to wrap and protect her Hummel gifts—and then to Denise's roommate, Nicole, your daughter, who gave it me. I made a copy of the diagram before I gave your original to the police. They know Denise, an actress, is Natasha's half-sister and *was her double at the Art Institute, allowing Natasha to murder Miles.*"

Jeremy went ashen that the police knew the details of the murder. Parker felt that a troubled Jeremy had a conscience and might acknowledge it with a little bit of firmness.

"The police will be here shortly to arrest you as an accessory to murder." Parker paused and then asked slowly, "Jeremy, why did you help Natasha kill Miles, the man you worked with at Regular Solids?"

"I'm going to call my lawyer. Get out of my office." Jeremy reached for his telephone.

"Jeremy, please, take a moment to think!. Did you really want Miles dead? You set him up in room sixty-one and would have been very happy to have Miles filming you and Natasha having sex and enjoying yourself. But that's not what happened. You didn't show up at the motel. Natasha did and murdered Miles."

Jeremy froze with his hand on the phone and looked directly at Parker. His inner self told him in a no uncertain way that he done wrong. He moved his hand off the phone and sat back in his chair, "I didn't think she would actually go through with it."

"You're a lover Jeremy and have fathered at least one beautiful child. Natasha apparently is a hater and has now given the world one dead person." Jeremy groaned and put his hands on his head. That was the way Parker saw him last week on his way out of the Damon building.

The two men sat there. There was a commotion outside Jeremy's door. Sergeant Garber and two policemen came in announcing Jeremy's arrest as an accessory to the murder of Miles Clayton. They were surprised to see Parker calmly seated in a chair and Jeremy in tears at his desk.

(46) A Walk in Grant Park

Several months later, as winter was ending, Parker and Rosemary were walking in Grant Park with their four children on a Sunday afternoon. They wore overcoats, but there was no snow on the ground, and the sun was shining brightly in a cloudless sky. The family looked at the different sights, including the beautiful Chicago skyline. As they walked, the kids were running around, laughing, and having a good time playing word games.

"So, my darling husband, would you summarize what's happening in Natasha's murder case for me?" Rosemary inquired.

"After Jeremy's arrest, all the remaining facts in the Miles Clayton murder fell into place. William Pillsbury's revolver from his Army days was identified as the murder weapon. Since William was bedridden, and only he and Natasha had access to the gun, and it was Natasha who had a motive to kill Miles, and it was Natasha who asked Denise to double for her, and it was Natasha who was out Friday night driving Denise's Ford Falcon, all the evidence pointed to her as the murderer. When Jeremy Wilson confessed he'd aided Natasha by setting up Miles in room sixty-one of the motel, it was over. Jeremy didn't think she'd go through with the murder and was horrified when she did. According to Jeremy's testimony, Natasha was known to set up plans and then at the last moment change her mind and never implement them. In this instance, Natasha told Jeremy she directly asked her husband the Friday morning of the Art Institute Gala whether he'd support her as the next chairman of Regular Solids. When William told her Miles would be the next chairman, and she would remain as president, Natasha was devastated, and his decision and her jealous anger of Miles sealed his fate."

"Did she confess to the murder?"

"Her lawyer continues to plead temporary insanity. Many are surprised Natasha, although she disliked and even hated Miles, went through with the murder. They believe, given her position and money, a normal mind would never consider murder."

Rosemary shook her head sadly, "Anger is a terrible emotion when it gets out of control. You recall, darling, that in the Sermon on the Mount, Jesus spoke about the commandment against murder and warned anger toward another is wrong and must be controlled. Natasha, for whatever reason, wasn't able to control her anger at Miles, and it led her to commit murder.

It's terrible what uncontrolled passions can do. And what about your other case? What's happened to Nicole?"

Parker smiled, "Nicole passed her November examination and is now studying for the next exam. She's given up her apartment and has reconciled with her mother enough to have returned living with her. She's been dating Frank Lawson. George Elkhart pleaded guilty to the murder of Dave Curtis, remains in jail, and is waiting to be sentenced."

Parker stopped and decided not to say anything more about Nicole. He also thought there was no need to mention to Rosemary that, in the Sermon on the Mount, Jesus also spoke about the commandment against adultery, recognizing that lust is wrong and must be controlled. Parker knew this, and, as such, he remained a friend to Nicole, but at a distance, grateful for Rosemary, his four children, and their interconnected love.

"So, my darling husband, as a private investigator who gets involved in murder cases, how do you see these cases in relation to the big issues in life, issues involving God and happiness?"

Parker responded, "I think religious and metaphysical questions are important and need to be discussed within a healthy society. Thus, I think about the reality in the world we observe and wonder about our relationship to the world we cannot observe. There's much we don't understand about reality. In particular, the micro-world, which is hidden to our senses, remains a mystery. I wonder if changes of matter and energy reflect changes in substance. I think about entanglement in the micro-world and the way events become connected in the observable world, and the hidden God who reveals and clarifies through evidence all of reality in physical time. But time itself remains a mystery to philosophy and science. Yet most people believe in free will, the ability to make choices, and in cause and effect. Physical time does make free will possible, and sequential time is required for events to occur one after another and for effect to follow cause. Nevertheless, I ponder the nature of human desires and how to order them properly for God's will and the greater good. I wonder about the ongoing struggle all individuals have between good and evil and between love and sin. I ponder *agape* and what you call unwavering love and what others call unconditional love. Perhaps one of these days someone will come up with a way to make these concepts clearer to everyone."

Rosemary stands on her toes, looking up to her husband and hugging him. "The doctor confirms I'm pregnant. The surprise is two heartbeats. How do you feel about twins?"

"Two of everything is wonderful," says Parker, giving her a lingering kiss.

Anna runs over and stretches her arms out around the legs of her parents.

The three older children watch and then rush to join the family hug. In

these present moments of unwavering love, time stops.

The End.